Hi g

This is the first book in my brand new series *Agent 21*.
In it, the main character, Zak, loses his family in a
tragic accident and is then recruited by a government
agency to become Agent 21.

On his first mission Zak is sent out to Mexico. I've
worked in and travelled throughout Mexico many
times, and believe me when I say it's one of the most
dangerous places on Earth. It's run by notorious drug
cartels, who not only fight between themselves but
also fight the security services.

This is fast-paced and action-packed as always.

I hope you enjoy it.

CHRIS RYAN
SAS HERO

- Joined the SAS in 1984, serving in military hot zones across the world.

- Expert in overt and covert operations in war zones, including Northern Ireland, Africa, the Middle East and other classified territories.

- Commander of the Sniper squad within the anti-terrorist team.

- Part of an 8 man patrol on the Bravo Two Zero Gulf War mission in Iraq.

- The mission was compromised. 3 fellow soldiers died, and 4 more were captured as POWs. Ryan was the only person to defy the enemy, evading capture and escaping to Syria on foot over a distance of 300 kilometres.

- His ordeal made history as the longest escape and evasion by an SAS trooper, for which he was awarded the Military Medal.

- His books are dedicated to the men and women who risk their lives fighting for the armed forces.

AGENT
21

Also available by Chris Ryan, and published by
Random House Children's Books:

The One That Got Away

CODE RED
Flash Flood
Wildfire
Outbreak
Vortex
Twister
Battleground

ALPHA FORCE
Survival
Rat-Catcher
Desert Pursuit
Hostage
Red Centre
Hunted
Blood Money
Fault Line
Black Gold
Untouchable

Published by the Random House Group for adult readers:

NON-FICTION
The One That Got Away
Chris Ryan's SAS Fitness Book
Chris Ryan's Ultimate Survival Guide
Fight to Win: Deadly Skills of the Elite Forces

FICTION
Stand By, Stand By
Zero Option
The Kremlin Device
Tenth Man Down
Hit List
The Watchman
Land of Fire
Greed
The Increment
Blackout
Ultimate Weapon
Strike Back
Firefight
Who Dares Wins
One Good Turn *(Adult Quick Read for World Book Day 2008)*

CHRIS RYAN

RED FOX

The right of Chris Ryan to be identified as the author of this work has been asserted in accordance with the Copyright, Designs and Patents Act 1988.

The Random House Group Limited supports the Forest Stewardship Council (FSC), the leading international forest certification organization. All our titles that are printed on Greenpeace-approved FSC-certified paper carry the FSC logo. Our paper procurement policy can be found at www.rbooks.co.uk/environment.

Mixed Sources
Product group from well-managed forests and other controlled sources
www.fsc.org Cert no. TT-COC-2139
© 1996 Forest Stewardship Council

FSC

Set in Adobe Garamond 13.5 / 17.5 pt

Red Fox Books are published by Random House Children's Books, 61–63 Uxbridge Road, London W5 5SA

www.kidsatrandomhouse.co.uk
www.rbooks.co.uk

Addresses for companies within The Random House Group Limited can be found at: www.randomhouse.co.uk/offices.htm

THE RANDOM HOUSE GROUP Limited Reg. No. 954009

A CIP catalogue record for this book is available from the British Library.

Printed and bound in Great Britain by CPI Bookmarque, Croydon, CR0 4TD

CONTENTS

PROLOGUE

It didn't take them long to die. It never does. Not if you do it right.

Al and Janet Darke had been looking forward to their trip. Lagos in Nigeria might not have been their first choice, but as the university where they worked had paid for them to come here for an international climate-change conference, they didn't want to miss the opportunity of travelling around a bit once it was over.

They were a quiet couple. They kept themselves to themselves. They had both felt a bit scared when their taxi drove them from the airport into the busy, noisy, dirty city of Lagos. Cars sat in traffic jams, bumper to bumper. Their fumes made it difficult to breathe. Some of the buildings they passed looked quite grand; others were just shacks made out of metal sheets. And there were thousands upon thousands of people, everywhere. It made Oxford Street at Christmas look like a desert island.

So when they arrived at their hotel – a posh one called the Intercontinental, bang in the middle of the city – they holed up in their room for a bit. Getting used to the heat and to being in a strange place. A shower. Some food.

'Zak would like it here,' Janet said as they stood on their balcony and looked out over the chaos.

'If Zak was here,' Al replied, 'he'd be out there nosing around already. You know what he's like.'

Janet smiled. Yeah, she knew.

It felt weird coming away without their son, but it was 22 April and the summer term had just started so they didn't have much choice. Not that a couple of weeks out of school would have harmed him. Zak was a smart kid. Good with his hands. Good with his brain. The kind of boy who knew how to take care of himself. He had seemed perfectly happy to be staying with Janet's sister and her family. Vivian and Godfrey were a bit severe, but Zak got on well with his cousin Ellie. His parents were sure they'd be having a good time.

The sun set about 7 p.m. – a blood-red ball that drenched Lagos with its glow before it plunged into darkness. Al and Janet dressed for dinner and prepared to meet the other conference delegates who'd come from all over the world. They wouldn't know anyone – not even any of the eleven other British guests – and they were glad to have each other.

PROLOGUE

The dining hall was splendidly set. To look at it, you wouldn't know that barely a mile from this hotel there existed one of the seediest slums in the world, so poor that the people who lived there had to use the streets as a toilet. Here were crisp, white tablecloths, fizzy water in bottles and appetizing baskets of freshly baked bread rolls. There were five large round tables, each with ten place settings, and a table plan pinned to a board by the entrance. When Janet and Al checked it they saw, to their relief, that they were sitting next to each other. To Janet's right there was a professor from Helsinki in Finland; to Al's left an American journalist. The couple accepted a glass of wine from a smartly dressed waiter with a tray of drinks, then went to find their seats.

The Finnish professor was an eccentric-looking man with a bald head but a bushy white beard. He was already sitting down when they approached, but stood up when he saw Janet. 'Allow me,' he said, and he pulled out her seat for her. 'My name is Jenssen. It is very nice to meet you . . .' He glanced at the name tag on Janet's place setting. 'Dr Darke.'

Janet smiled. 'And you, Professor Jenssen.'

The American journalist didn't arrive until everyone else was sitting and the waiters were serving the starter. He was hugely fat, and had sweat pouring down his face. 'Africa,' he said with a huff as he plonked himself

3

down on his seat. 'Every time I come here, I promise myself I'll never come back. Perhaps I should listen to myself a bit more.'

Perhaps you should, thought Al Darke, but he didn't say it out loud. Instead, he thanked the waiter who had just placed a plate of food in front of him. Slices of colourful fruit were laid out on the plate like a fan, with some kind of dressing drizzled over the top.

'This looks delicious,' Al said.

'Give it three days,' the journalist replied. 'You'll be begging for a cheeseburger.' Al saw, though, that he tucked into his food with gusto.

Al was halfway through his starter when he noticed that his nose was running. Embarrassed, he grabbed his napkin and held it to his face. By the time he had covered his face, though, he felt moisture seeping from his eyes and his vision was blurred. He turned to look at Janet. Her eyes were wet too, the pupils as small as pinpricks.

'What's happening?' Al started to say. But as he spoke, his chest collapsed into a fit of coughing and he found himself struggling for breath.

'*Al . . .*' Janet was looking at him with fear on her face.

The pain came next – a horrible, sharp needling behind the eyes and in the throat. Al felt dizzy. He looked around the room. About half of the guests had stood up, and from the way they clutched their heads and throats, it was clear they were suffering the same symptoms. At the far end of the room, one man collapsed. Al was half aware of the waiters, buzzing around them like panicked bees. They didn't know what was happening any more than the diners.

Al felt himself slump in his seat. He couldn't help it – it was as though his muscles had turned to jelly and he had lost the power to control them, even in order to breathe. His eyes fell on the half-eaten fruit. The bright colours of the mango and papaya looked ten times brighter, and they burned into his retinas. He turned to his wife.

'The food,' he said.

Janet Darke didn't hear him. For her the room was spinning more violently. People were shouting around her, but all she could really concentrate on was the nausea. She wanted to be sick, but was too weak to do even that.

Al and Janet weren't the first to die. The professor from Helsinki was already slumped on the table, his face in his half-eaten plate of fruit; and the American journalist was twitching on the ground. They knew it was coming, though. With what little strength they had left, they reached out with their hands and clasped their fingers together.

AGENT 21

When the Nigerian police arrived half an hour later, they needed to prize Al and Janet Darke's hands away from each other before they could remove the bodies.

PART ONE

1

THE SHADOW

Six months later

'Darke!'

Giggling in the classroom.

'Darke!'

Zak looked up. He'd been staring out of the window, where the late afternoon sun was glowing over the school football pitch. He had a pencil in his hand, which he twirled through his fingers. On his table there was a circuit board. It was covered with transistors and diodes and connected to a small loudspeaker.

'Zachary Darke,' his physics teacher, Mr Peters, said in a nasal voice. Peters had bad skin, square glasses and a tragic dress sense. He'd only been teaching at the Camden High School in North London for six weeks, but in that time he'd managed to make himself unpopular with pretty much everyone. 'You've got ten minutes left to complete your assignment. I don't think staring out of the window is a very good way to—'

He was interrupted by a noise. Zak had flicked a switch and the sound of Lady Gaga singing 'Just Dance' filled the room. The physics teacher *had* told them to construct a transistor radio, after all.

Peters was a total nightmare. He loved to set his classes almost impossible tasks and watch them squirm as they failed to complete them. All of them except Zak. He was good at stuff like this, but even that didn't seem to impress Peters. The jokers at the back singing along to the music didn't impress him either. His pockmarked neck turned red. 'Turn it off, boy.'

'Yes, sir,' Zak replied. He stared back out of the window.

Mr Peters walked up to Zak's table. Zak had grown tall in the last year – taller than a few of the teachers, even. It meant that some of them, like Peters, puffed themselves up when talking to him. 'Showing off isn't a very attractive habit, Darke,' he said.

'I wasn't, sir. I was just—'

'Quiet. I don't want to hear another word from you.'

'No, sir,' Zak said, and went back to his daydreaming.

He had plenty to daydream about.

When the police had showed up six months ago on the doorstep of his uncle and aunt's house to tell him what had happened to his parents, they had said it was food poisoning. An acute case, a terrible accident. It had affected everyone in the hotel dining hall that night. Fifty of them. And for a while Zak had believed them. Why wouldn't he? The story had made it onto the news, and he was too shocked and upset anyway to think about it much.

But as time passed and the Nigerian police had refused to release his parents' bodies for burial, Zak had grown suspicious. If it had been just food poisoning, then why the delay? Why couldn't they just send his mum and dad back so they could have a proper funeral? And what was so virulent that it could kill fifty people at a single sitting? Zak had hit the Internet, done his research. There was botulism; *e. coli*, maybe. But Mum and Dad had been in good health. Those kind of bacteria might have made them feel very unwell, but kill them? And everyone else they were dining with? Not likely.

When school finished, he walked home with his cousin Ellie. She was in the year above, but they were good friends. This walking home together thing was a new one, though. Zak used to skateboard everywhere on the board his mum and dad had got him for his thirteenth birthday. However, he didn't have the heart to use it now, which was why he preferred to walk.

Ellie chattered away like she always did. Zak's cousin was a tall, pretty girl with long, honey-coloured hair and one of those friendly, open faces that people quickly take a shine to. Zak heard her, but didn't listen. Something else had caught his attention.

For two weeks now, maybe three, Zak had had the strangest feeling. More than once, he'd thought he was going mad. He knew that nobody could *really* be following him, but it happened almost every day – twice a day, sometimes – that he was walking down the street, or buying something in a shop, or doing whatever he was doing, and he'd get that familiar, unpleasant feeling. A hotness on the back of his neck. A tingling.

At first, he would turn and look around. But he never saw anybody. Or he saw lots of people, just walking past or milling about. After a bit, he didn't bother to turn. Instead, he would keep walking and try to look out of the corner of his eye. That was more successful. He'd sometimes be able to sense somebody walking along the opposite side of the road, or standing by the school gates. Whenever he turned to look, however, the person was gone. It was like they had a sixth sense – although Zak's sensible side told him that was impossible . . .

He had the feeling now. They were walking along Camden Road. It was busy with the early rush-hour traffic, and the pavements were full of school kids. But there was something else – like a dark shadow on the edge of his vision, walking in the same direction on the opposite pavement.

Zak looked firmly ahead and tuned his ears in to Ellie's conversation.

'. . . so *I* told her that there was no way I was going if—'

'Ellie, shh.'

She looked at him. 'Don't be so rude,' she said.

'Sorry. But listen, you see that turning up ahead to the right?'

Ellie looked ahead to see what he meant. It was a small turning about fifteen metres away that led into a little cobbled mews road. 'Jasmine Mews?'

'When we get there, turn into it, then run like hell to the end and hide.'

'Why?' Ellie asked. 'What's going on, Zak?'

'It's just a game,' Zak said. 'I want to play a trick on someone. You up for it?'

Ellie shrugged. 'Suppose so,' she said.

They continued to walk. Just as they reached the side street, Zak and Ellie turned sharply; and the moment they were out of sight of the main road, they ran down the cobbled mews.

There were only a few cars parked here, outside the small, cottage-like houses. At the end of the street was an alley running at right angles. They turned left into it, then stopped, out of breath. Zak pressed his back against the wall and peered round the corner.

He saw a man. From a distance it was difficult to make out his features, but he was quite tall, maybe in his sixties with a tanned face and scruffy, shoulder-length hair. The man stood at the end of the mews for just long enough to see that it was deserted. Then he quickly turned and walked away.

Zak felt Ellie tapping his shoulder. 'What's going on?' she whispered.

'I don't know,' said Zak, his voice a million miles away. 'I just don't know.'

The next day was Saturday. Zak woke early. He always did these days. Since his parents' death, sleep was hard to come by. He got dressed and went downstairs.

To his surprise, his aunt was already up. She was standing in the small kitchen, her hair in a net and a cigarette in her hand, boiling the kettle. She looked over her shoulder, saw Zak then turned her attention back to her tea-making. No 'good morning'. No nothing. He shrugged and headed back towards the stairs.

His uncle and aunt – Vivian and Godfrey Lewis –

didn't want him there, and they weren't afraid to show it. After Mum and Dad had died in Nigeria, they'd agreed to take him in. It had been a choice between them or moving up to Macclesfield where his other cousin, Ben, lived. But Zak hadn't really wanted to relocate north, and Ben had a habit of ending up in crazy situations. So Vivian and Godfrey it was, and they didn't let a day go by without reminding Zak in some small way that he wasn't really welcome in the small terraced house of 63 Acacia Drive.

'Zak!'

His aunt was at the bottom of the stairs. He turned round to look at her.

'We're taking Ellie out for the day. Lunch and then a movie. You'll be all right here, won't you?'

Zak tried not to look disappointed. 'Yeah,' he replied. 'I'll be fine, Aunt Vivian.'

He continued walking up the stairs.

Ellie was in the doorway of her bedroom, still in her pyjamas. She had obviously heard her mum, and as Zak walked past, she mouthed the words 'I'm sorry' at him. He gave her a smile – it wasn't her fault, after all – then continued towards his room.

A tap on his shoulder. Ellie had followed him and as he turned round she gave him a hug. 'I wish you could come with us,' she said.

Zak smiled. There was something about Ellie that

always made him feel better. 'I'll be fine,' he said. 'Have a nice day, yeah?'

Ellie and her parents left at half past nine. The house was quiet. Zak spent some time on the family computer – he'd installed some plug-ins that kept his browsing history private, just in case he got in trouble for using it. But it was sunny outside and he felt cooped up. He decided to go for a walk.

There was a garage at the end of the road. Zak stopped off there and bought himself a can of Coke with the last of his change. He'd inherited what little money his mum and dad had, but it was in trust and his uncle and aunt weren't exactly the generous types – at least, not when it came to Zak.

He walked to the park. It was busy – lots of younger kids out playing football or mucking about on the swings. A few people walking their dogs. Zak sat apart from them all on a wooden bench in the dappled shade of a tree. He sipped his Coke slowly and watched everybody enjoying their Saturday morning.

By the time Zak saw him, he didn't know how long the man had been standing there. He was about fifty metres away, alone by the park railings and looking directly at Zak. He had hair down to his shoulders and a tanned, lined face. There was no doubt about it – he was the same man who had followed him and Ellie yesterday.

Zak felt himself crushing the Coke can slightly. Half of him wanted to stand up and rush away; the other half wanted to sit here. To stare the guy out.

The other half won.

Zak felt his skin prickling as the man walked towards him. Even though it was hot, the man wore a heavy coat and had his hands plunged into the pockets. He didn't look directly at Zak, but kept his gaze elsewhere; and when he sat next to him on the bench, he barely seemed to know that Zak was there. He removed a silver cigarette case from his pocket and lit a thin, black cigarillo. The sickly smell of cherry tobacco filled the air.

Zak played it cool. He took a sip from his Coke before speaking. 'Feel like telling me why you've been playing follow-my-leader?' he asked.

'It's a beautiful day, Zak. A lovely day for a walk.'

Zak tried not to look surprised that the man knew his name.

'Tell me what you want, or I'm out of here.'

Only now did the man look at him. He had piercing green eyes that looked rather youthful despite his leathery tanned face and long, grey hair. He also looked mildly surprised. 'You're free to go, of course, Zak, at any time at all.'

A pause.

'So why have you?' Zak asked.

'Why have I what, Zak?'

'Been following me?'

The man smiled. 'Because I'm interested in you, Zak. I was very sorry, by the way, to hear about your parents.'

'You seem to know a lot about me,' Zak said.

'Oh,' the man replied, 'I do. More than you might imagine. Congratulations, incidentally, on your achievement in your physics lesson yesterday. I understand that you were the only one who succeeded in making a transistor radio. A sound knowledge of electronics could be a useful skill, in certain lines of work.'

As he said this, he raised an eyebrow. It made Zak feel distinctly uncomfortable. He downed the rest of his Coke, crushed the can completely and stood up. 'I'm out of here,' he said. 'Stop following me, all right, otherwise I'll call the police, tell them I've got my very own stalker.'

The old man inclined his head, as if to say, *It's your choice.* Zak started walking away.

'Just one thing, Zak.' The man's voice stopped him short, but he didn't turn round. 'If you want to know the real reason your mum and dad died, we might want to talk some more.'

Zak didn't look back. He didn't say anything. But he didn't move either.

'I'll be here tomorrow,' the man continued. 'Half past eleven. Think about it.'

Elsewhere in the park, children were shrieking with pleasure. A cloud briefly covered the sun, then drifted away again. Zak experienced it all in slow motion as the old man's words echoed in his head.

He turned.

The wooden bench was empty. And when he cast around trying to find where the stranger had gone, the old man was nowhere to be seen.

2

TWO LESSONS

Zak's bedroom was tiny, with just a bed and a bedside table, an alarm clock and a framed picture of his parents. There was no desk for him to do his homework, and as he wasn't allowed to do it at the kitchen table it meant he had to study lying on the floor. The wallpaper was old and flowery – the sort of thing an eighty-year-old lady might like.

He didn't sleep well that night. It was hard to say what spooked him more – that the old man had been following him, that he had known his name, or that his words had confirmed something that Zak had thought all along: that his parents' death wasn't what it seemed. More than once, as midnight crept into the small hours, he thought he might be going mad. He'd read about it, after all. When something bad happens to people, they start imagining things. Maybe the old man was just that – a figment of his imagination. An invention.

But deep down, Zak knew he wasn't going mad. He

knew what he'd seen, and what he'd heard. He also knew that nobody else would believe him except, perhaps, Ellie, and something warned him against getting her mixed up in all of this.

He nodded off just after dawn, and woke with a start when he heard a knock on his door. His alarm clock said 10 a.m.

'Yeah?'

The door opened and Ellie appeared. 'Can I come in?' she asked.

'Sure,' said Zak, and he sat up.

She had toast for him, and a cup of tea. Zak knew what she was doing – trying to make up for the fact that her parents hadn't included him yesterday. 'You didn't have to do this,' he told her.

'I know. I just thought today, maybe we could—'

'I've got to be somewhere,' Zak interrupted.

Ellie blushed. 'OK,' she said, before standing up.

'I'll be around this afternoon,' Zak said. 'Let's do something then.'

Ellie's eyes softened. 'Yesterday was *really boring*,' she whispered with a smile. 'Just thought you'd like to know.' She left the room.

Zak got dressed: jeans, trainers and a black hooded top. Normally he wore a hoodie because he liked the style. Today he was glad to be able to hide his face. He didn't know why.

On the driveway in front of the house, Uncle Godfrey had the bonnet of his Ford Mondeo up and was peering closely at the engine. 'Isn't it working?' Zak asked him.

His uncle glanced up at him. 'Don't you worry about it, Zachary. I can sort it out.' He climbed into the driver's seat and turned the ignition. The car coughed and spluttered, then fell silent. His uncle tried again. Same result.

Zak glanced into the engine. It didn't take him more than a couple of seconds to work out what was wrong – one of the spark plugs was loose, stopping the engine from firing. Hidden by the raised bonnet he put his hand in, found the plug and tightened it by a turn and a half. He just managed to get his hand out before his uncle tried the ignition again and the car purred into life.

'Told you I could sort it,' his uncle said as he got out again. 'Well, don't stand there gawping, Zachary. Haven't you got anything to do?'

Zak allowed himself a brief smile. 'Yeah,' he said, walking away from the house and wiping his oily hand on his jeans. 'Actually, I have.'

He arrived at the park early. He wasn't sure why – it just seemed like the right thing to do. It was even busier than yesterday – the weather was warm and it was

Sunday morning. He avoided the bench. Instead, he headed to a copse of trees about thirty metres away. It wasn't thick, but one of the trunks was sturdy enough to hide behind and it gave him a view of the bench.

He looked at his watch. 11.21. No sign of the man. The air was filled with the shouts of children playing on the swings and slides. In the trees, he heard a bird call and instantly recognized the trilling for what it was: a chaffinch, warbling in the gentle morning sun.

11.25. Nothing. Zak didn't know why he felt nervous. Obviously the guy wasn't coming. He'd been stupid even to turn up.

The kids continued to play.

11.30. Two women with prams sat on the bench and started gossiping.

'You're an idiot, Zak,' he murmured to himself, glad that he hadn't gone straight to the bench, because sitting there by himself would have made him feel even more stupid.

'I wouldn't say that.'

Zak felt a sinking feeling in the pit of his stomach just as the aroma of cherry tobacco hit his nose. He spun round and there he was, standing about five metres behind him: the man, wearing the same clothes as yesterday.

'How did you get there?' Zak demanded. 'I didn't hear you.'

The man looked unsurprised. 'You weren't supposed to hear me,' he said.

Zak was feeling angry now. 'Why didn't you just go to the bench, like we said?'

The stranger raised an eyebrow. 'Why didn't *you?*' he asked. And when Zak didn't reply, the man said, 'You could think of that as your first test. Or maybe your first lesson. Trust nobody. After everything I've heard about you, Zak, I'd have been a little disappointed if you'd trusted me, of all people. Someone you'd never met before. Someone whose name you don't even know.'

'I'm going home,' Zak said, turning away. 'I've had enough of these riddles.'

The man inclined his head. 'You could,' he said. 'Only of course it isn't really home, is it? Not really.'

Zak stopped. The man's words had sent ice down his spine – not because he seemed yet again to know so much about Zak, but because they were true.

'Wouldn't you like to know my name?' the man said.

'I'd like to know what you're playing at.'

'I'm not playing, Zak,' the stranger said. 'Allow me to introduce myself. You can call me Michael.'

Zak looked at him. 'What do you mean, I can *call* you Michael? Is that your name or isn't it?'

Michael raised an eyebrow. 'Names, Zak, are like

clothes. Easily changed. And just because a person has more than one, it doesn't mean that any of them are any less real. Yes, Michael is my real name. One of them, anyway.'

'That doesn't make sense.'

'Not now perhaps. But if you come to work for me, it soon will.'

This crazy old man and his riddles were starting to get to Zak. 'Work for you?' he said. 'What are you talking about? I'm not in the market for a job. You know, being thirteen and everything.'

For the first time, Michael smiled. 'The market for a job?' he said. 'Very good. Very good, Zak.' He brushed a strand of hair off his forehead and his green eyes twinkled. It made him look, for a moment, much younger. 'I'll enjoy working with you. Mr Peters said I would.'

'What? Peters? What's he got to do with this?'

'A great deal, Zak. Mr Peters is one of our most accomplished people, and a very valued talent scout.' A weary look crossed his face. 'You aren't about to ask me about *his* name as well, are you?'

Zak thought of his physics teacher – the cross, pinched face, the bad skin, the awful clothes and zero personality. The only thing that man was accomplished at was being a bore and a bully.

'You look surprised, Zak. It's worth remembering

that people are not always what they seem. Call that lesson two, if you like.'

'I get enough lessons at school.'

'Of course,' said Michael. 'And by all accounts you are uncommonly good at them. But those sorts of lessons are a little limited in scope, are they not? That's why we sent Mr Peters in. To find out how you might cope if we were to school you in certain topics lads your age don't normally find on their curriculum. I'm happy to say that his reports have been extremely positive. Shall we walk? Or would you really prefer to leave without hearing what else I have to say?'

The chaffinch trilled again in the trees. 'We'll walk,' Zak said.

They walked together away from the playground and into the green, open common beyond.

'I'll be straight with you, Zak,' said Michael.

'That would make a nice change.' *Seeing as how so far you've been about as straight as a paperclip*, Zak thought.

'I work for a government agency. You don't need to know which one. In fact, it wouldn't make any difference if I told you because you won't have heard of it. Hardly anyone has. Even the Prime Minister is kept in the dark about us. So if you decide at the end of this conversation that you want nothing more to do with us, my advice is to keep quiet about everything

I've told you. You won't find us mentioned on the news, or on the Internet. Try to persuade people we exist, and they'll just think you're imagining things.'

'Sounds like you're the one who's imagining things.'

Michael appeared not to hear him – or if he did, he ignored Zak's comment and just carried on talking.

'People don't apply to work with us. They can't. It's not exactly as if we can just put an advertisement in the paper. We have to find them. That's why we have people like Mr Peters. All schools need temporary teaching staff now and then, and it's a very useful cover for us to insert our scouts. But the people we're looking for are of a very particular type. It's a crude way of putting it, but they fit a profile.'

Michael stopped, and so did Zak. They looked at each other.

'*You* fit a profile, Zak,' the old man said. 'A very precise one.'

He continued to walk. Zak had to jog a little bit to keep up with him. 'What do you mean?' he asked. 'What sort of profile?'

'Intelligent,' Michael replied. 'Oh, your school grades are very good, of course, but that's not quite what I mean. You have a particular aptitude for certain disciplines: science, languages. You're physically fit, and as you proved just a few minutes ago, you have exceptionally good intuition.' He smiled. 'You remind me a bit of myself as a young man, in fact.'

Zak felt himself blushing. 'You could be describing anyone,' he said.

'Not quite anyone, Zak. But you're right. These attributes in themselves aren't enough to set you apart from the crowd, so to speak.'

'Then why are we having this conversation?' Zak asked.

Zak sensed that Michael was choosing his words carefully.

'Forgive me, Zak, but would I be right in saying that, since your parents passed away, there are very few people in the world who would actually . . . *miss* you?'

Zak felt a sudden emptiness in his stomach. He walked on in silence. Deep down he knew it was true. Apart from Ellie and her parents there was no other family close by, no real friends. Zak had always been a bit of a loner. He knew people saw that in him, and they kept their distance.

Michael was speaking again. 'Your uncle and aunt are reluctant guardians, are they not?'

'Yeah,' said Zak. 'You could say that.'

'From the information at my disposal,' Michael continued, 'the arrangement is not a happy one.'

'You've got a lot of information at your disposal, haven't you?'

'Yes,' Michael said. 'I have, haven't I?'

Another silence as they carried on walking.

Zak was interested, despite himself. Interested enough, at least, to start asking some questions of his own. 'When you say "working for you", what do you mean?'

'The duties are varied,' said Michael, and Zak couldn't help thinking he was avoiding the question.

'Spying?' he asked. Better to get things out in the open.

Michael looked straight ahead as he walked. His expression didn't change. 'That's not a term we use,' he said. 'But yes, the gathering of intelligence comes into it. If you accept our offer, however, you'll be trained in many other skills.'

'Like what?'

'Skills,' Michael repeated. 'There are situations, you see, when having a youngster like yourself would be a great asset for us. These situations would not be without risk. It's important that you are equipped to deal with this risk. To cope in scenarios where you're by yourself, undercover, with only your training to help you.'

As Michael spoke, a cloud drifted in front of the bright morning sun, just as it had the previous day. Zak fought off a shiver, but he didn't know if it was the shade that caused it, or Michael's words. They had reached the edge of the park, where iron railings with spikes on the top ran into an open gate that led to the main road.

'If you decide to accept this offer, Zak, you need to understand what you're taking on. Your life will change. You'll never see the people you know again. Zak Darke will disappear.'

'I can't just disappear.'

'It's something we would deal with. It may be, Zak, that you like your life the way it is. That the future appears rosy. That number 63 Acacia Drive and its flowery wallpaper holds the key to your happiness. If that's the case, I urge you to forget about everything I've said today. If it isn't, well then, you should think about it carefully. Once you decide to go down this path, there's no turning back. None at all.'

Zak looked around. They'd walked a fair way – the playground was a few hundred metres in the distance and the noise of traffic had replaced the sound of playing children.

'I'm not interested,' he said. 'To be honest, I don't even believe you're who you say you are. So stop following me around unless you want me to go straight to the police.'

Michael acted as if he hadn't heard Zak. For the first time, the old man removed one hand from his coat pocket and held out a business card. It was entirely plain, with a telephone number printed in black on one side. No name. No nothing.

'Don't feel you have to make a decision now,' he said. 'Or even tomorrow, or next week. Just when, and if, you're ready.' He kept holding the card out until Zak eventually took it. As he shoved it in the back pocket of his jeans, Michael spoke again. His voice was light, as if this was just an afterthought. 'Of course,' he said, 'there are certain advantages to our line of work, Zak. We get to learn things about people. Information.' He looked directly at Zak, and his gaze seemed to pierce right through him. 'You might even find out, for example, the real reason your parents died.'

Zak stared at him.

The old man looked up at the sky just as the sun came out again. 'What a beautiful day,' he said, his voice suddenly breezy. 'I think I'll continue this delightful stroll. You won't see or hear from me again, Zak. Unless, of course, you decide to call that number.'

And without another word, Michael turned and walked back the way they had come. Zak stood and watched him, until the old man mingled with the crowd around the playground, and disappeared from sight.

3

FAMILY BUSINESS

For the rest of that day, Zak paced around North London. His mind was a jumble as he remembered snippets of the conversation with the man who called himself Michael:

I work for a government agency... Try to persuade people we exist and they'll just think you're imagining things... There are situations when having a youngster like you would be a great asset for us... You might even find out the real reason your parents died...

It was that last statement that rang in his head most clearly of all.

And when, later that afternoon, he made his way back to Acacia Drive, he noticed something. At no point since Michael had walked away had he sensed anybody following him. As he stood with his back to the door of number 63, everything was as it should be. Nobody was watching. He went straight up to his room, where he mulled over the events of the day until it was time to sleep.

The weather turned the following day. Grey clouds and drizzle. Ellie had flu, so she didn't leave the house with him like she normally did. Zak decided to skateboard into school. He was the proud owner of an Element board with Ricta wheels – the last present his mum and dad had ever bought him. His parents had never had much money, and Zak had been surprised when they'd given him such a cool board. He looked after it carefully now, keeping it under his bed – not least because every time Aunt Vivian saw it, her eyes nearly popped out of her head and she referred to it as 'that filthy thing'.

Outside the house, Zak slung his school bag over his shoulder and kicked off. At the end of Acacia Drive he turned right and a few minutes later he was steaming down Camden Road, expertly swerving out of the way of other pedestrians. He had just boarded past Jasmine Mews, however, when he braked. Two boys had clocked him and they were blocking the road. Zak felt his heart sink. Marcus Varley and Jason Ford were both in his class and had a habit of making a nuisance of themselves. Zak was one of the few people who had stood up to them, but it hadn't made them back off and he'd learned just to keep out of their way. They had big grins on their faces and that was always a bad sign.

Zak tapped one end of the board and it flicked up into his hands. He jutted his chin out. If these two bullies thought they were going to intimidate him, they had another think coming.

'Something wrong, lads?' he asked.

'Give us the skateboard, Darke,' said Varley.

Zak rolled his eyes. One thing was for sure – nobody would be asking *these* two to do anything dangerous or exacting. In a situation requiring brains and fitness, they'd be as much use as a chocolate teapot.

'Don't take it personally, guys, but actually I'd rather stick my head down the toilet.'

Jason Ford sneered. 'That could be arranged,' he said, and he pulled something from his pocket. It was a knife – about four inches long and gleaming sharp. 'Hand it over.'

'Don't be an idiot, Jason,' Zak breathed. 'That's not a toy.'

'What's wrong, Darke? Scared? Hand over the board.'

Warily, Zak laid the skateboard on the ground and stepped back. The two boys grinned at each other again and Jason stepped onto the board. You could tell he'd never used one before. He stretched out both arms to balance himself, waving his knife around in the air as he did so.

'Be careful,' Zak said.

'Shut up, Darke.'

It was Marcus's fault that it all happened. He clearly thought it would be funny to give Jason a little push. He didn't check the road, so he failed to notice the double-length bus that was speeding towards them.

'Marcus, no!' Zak shouted, but too late.

Jason rolled backwards. When the skateboard hit the kerb, he tumbled and fell onto his back.

The bus was only ten metres away and the sound of its horn cut through the air. Marcus froze and Jason, lying in the road, just stared in horror at the oncoming vehicle.

It was up to Zak to act. He jumped off the pavement and pulled Jason up by the scruff of his neck, before hurling him back off the road. The bus sounded its horn again and Zak leaped back onto the pavement – just in time to see the bus's wheels crush his skateboard to splinters.

'*NO!*' he shouted, and tears suddenly welled up in his eyes. 'My board!' *The board my parents gave me*, he shrieked silently. *Their last present ever . . .*

He spun round. Marcus looked like he was about to run away; Jason was lying on the ground, all the colour drained from his face. He had dropped the knife, which was lying on the pavement about a metre from him.

Zak picked it up and Jason started to gabble.

'Give us it back, mate . . . it's not mine, is it? It's my brother's . . . if he thinks I nicked it . . .'

Zak looked over at the remnants of his skateboard and fought back the tears. There was no point picking the bits up. It was ruined. Instead, he stepped back to the side of the road, bent down and held the knife over a drain grille.

'What's the matter, Jason?' he said through gritted teeth, trying not to let the emotion sound in his voice. 'Scared?'

He dropped the knife, waited to hear it splash and stood up again.

'See you in class,' he muttered at the two boys, and he continued making his way to school on foot.

He got there just as the bell was ringing and hurried down the busy corridors to his first lesson: physics. He was almost looking forward to seeing Mr Peters, to staring him down and working out from the reaction he got whether Michael's story about the teacher was true. Zak was good at reading people's faces. When he got into the classroom, however, he had a surprise. Peters wasn't there. Instead, standing in front of the whiteboard, was the deputy head, Mr Jobs – or Jobsworth, as everyone called him.

'All right, you lot – settle down,' Jobsworth called above the racket of the pupils taking their seats. 'Settle *down*!' He looked around the class. 'Has anyone seen Marcus Varley or Jason Ford?'

Zak said nothing.

'Where's Peters, sir?' called someone from the back of the class, and there were a few laughs.

'It's *Mr* Peters to you,' Jobsworth said. 'And I'm sorry to say that he's been called away on family business. We don't know when – or if – he'll be back.'

Nobody in the classroom appeared at all concerned by this news. Nobody, that is, except Zak. He sat down at his place, slightly stunned.

It made sense, of course. If Michael had been telling the truth about Peters, and he'd been at the school just to evaluate Zak, there was now no reason for him still to be here. Zak raised his hand.

'What is it, Darke?'

'What sort of family business, sir?'

Jobsworth looked offended by the question. 'Are you part of his family, Darke?'

'No, sir.'

'Then it's not your business, is it? Now then, what were you doing in your last lesson?'

A groan from the class. 'Transistor radios, sir.'

Jobsworth's eyes widened in astonishment. 'You

shouldn't be doing that for another two years,' he said, clearly a bit annoyed.

'Yeah, well we couldn't,' a voice piped up.

'Except *Darke*,' someone else added. And then in a whisper: '*Swot.*'

Laughter. Zak ignored it. 'Settle *down*!' Jobsworth shouted. 'Open your text books at page fifteen.'

And the lesson began.

The day passed slowly. Zak was glad when it was over, but he still dawdled back to 63 Acacia Drive. Michael's voice echoed in his mind. *It isn't really home, is it? Not really.*

No, thought Zak. *It isn't. It's just a place I live – if you can call it living*. He remembered the skateboard. It upset him and his thoughts drifted, as they so often did, to his mum and dad. *You might even find out the real reason your parents died . . .*

It was quiet back at his uncle and aunt's house. The grown-ups weren't yet back from work; Ellie was sleeping. Zak plonked himself in front of the family computer and launched a web browser, glad he had set things up so nobody would be able to track his searches. He Googled SECRET GOVERNMENT DEPARTMENTS. All he found were weird sites filled with absurd conspiracy theories. He tried to track down Mr Peters, even Michael. Of course, that was just a dead end. It wasn't like they had Facebook accounts. And so his Internet session finished like they all did, with him looking at the various news reports of the tragic food poisoning in Nigeria that had killed his parents.

Only it hadn't *been* food poisoning. If the strange old man was telling the truth, it had been something else.

Back in his tiny room, he sat on his bed and held the framed picture of his mum and dad. They looked very happy in it, and Zak felt anger rising up in him. They shouldn't be dead. There was more to this than anyone had told him. And he felt angry with Michael too, whoever he was. He should have just said then and there what had happened to them . . .

Zak fished the business card from his jeans pocket. It was a bit scuffed and crumpled now. He stared at the number for a full five minutes. Calling it couldn't do any harm, surely . . .

Once he'd made the decision, he moved quickly. His uncle and aunt were still out, so he hurried downstairs and found the cordless phone sitting on a coffee table in the front room. His brick of a mobile phone had given up the ghost weeks ago and his guardians hadn't thought it necessary to replace it. He took a deep breath, then dialled the number.

There was no ringing tone. Just a click and then silence.

'Er . . . hello?' Zak said.

No answer.

'Er . . . this is Zak. Zak Darke.' He felt a bit foolish.

'Have you come to a decision?'

The voice was low. It sounded weird, as if it had been distorted in some way. It certainly didn't sound like Michael.

Zak closed his eyes. 'Yes,' he said. 'I have.'

The voice continued. It was totally lacking in emotion.

'If you have anybody to say goodbye to, do it now. This is the last time you'll see them. It's better that way for them, and for you. Do not, repeat do not, suggest that you are going anywhere. We will come for you tonight.'

'What do you mean you'll come for me? When . . .?'

But the voice was gone.

A noise outside the room. It was somebody coming into the house. Zak guiltily dropped the phone back onto the coffee table just as Aunt Vivian walked in. 'Who were you talking to?' she demanded, her eyebrows furrowed in irritation.

'Nobody.'

'Don't lie to me, Zachary. I saw you put the phone down. Who were you talking to?'

'The speaking clock.' He raised his watch. 'It's running slow.'

His aunt narrowed her eyes. 'That's expensive,' she said. 'I'll deduct it from your allowance.'

Zak felt himself flaring up, but he mastered it. 'All right,' he said. 'Sorry.' He left the room and trudged up the stairs. On the landing he realized that his hands were shaking and it took several deep breaths to get control of himself.

Ellie's door, which had been closed, was slightly ajar. He knocked lightly.

'Come in,' his cousin called.

Ellie was sitting up in bed reading a book. 'Hi.'

Zak nodded in return. 'How you feeling?' he asked, and his voice cracked slightly.

'So so,' Ellie replied. She narrowed her eyes. 'How about you?'

'Er . . . fine,' he said. 'I think.'

'What's wrong? You look like you've seen a ghost.'

He gave her a weak smile, then sat on the edge of her bed and took one of her hands in his. 'Look, Ellie, I just wanted to say thanks. You know, for everything. For looking after me.'

She looked at him strangely, but didn't say anything.

'I just wanted to tell you, I'm going to be OK.'

'I know you are, Zak. Are you sure you're feeling all right?'

Zak frowned. He wasn't sure at all. He felt like he was in a fast-moving river and he couldn't do anything

41

except go with the current. Getting out of the water was impossible.

'Can I trust you?' he asked.

'Of course you can. Zak, you're scaring me. What's wrong?'

'Something's about to happen,' he heard himself saying. 'Don't ask me what. I want you to know I'll be safe.'

'What are you talking about?'

'I don't know,' Zak said. 'Not yet. But we never had this conversation, all right? Don't tell your parents, don't tell anyone. It's for your own safety, and theirs.'

He saw tears in Ellie's eyes. 'Zak, you're scaring me. What's happening?'

But he couldn't tell her. He bent down, put one hand on her shoulder then kissed her lightly on the cheek. Then he returned to his bedroom.

There was only one thing he could do now, and that was wait . . .

4

A THIEF IN THE NIGHT

The house was silent.

Zak had waited until he'd heard the sound of his uncle and aunt going to bed. They had checked on Ellie, but not him, switched off the landing light and retired to their room. He lay quietly for another ten minutes, before slipping out of bed and changing from his pyjamas into some warm clothes. Once he was dressed, he climbed back under his duvet and lay on his side, watching the glow of his bedside alarm clock.

Watching and waiting, with butterflies in his stomach.

Midnight came and went. The house creaked and groaned, just like it always did. Zak remembered the time when he was much smaller and used to be scared of those sounds in the house where he'd grown up, until his dad had explained that it was just the beams contracting as the temperature dropped.

One o'clock. He was so wide awake it might as well have been midday. His mouth was dry with anticipation.

But then two o'clock arrived. The night was ebbing away and nothing was happening. Zak began to feel slightly foolish. Perhaps he should go to sleep and forget all about it . . .

It was eight minutes to three when he heard it.

At first he assumed it was just the house creaking again and he went back to his clock-watching. But when he heard the sound for a second time he realized it had a different quality. He also realized it was getting closer to his bedroom.

Zak sat up and threw the duvet off. His breath was suddenly heavy and his pulse was racing. When he saw his door open, he shivered and couldn't tell whether it was fear or excitement. A bit of both, probably . . .

A figure entered and quietly closed the door behind him. The only light in the room came from the glow of the alarm clock, so Zak couldn't make the intruder out very well – all he could tell was that he was tall, wore dark clothing and had a balaclava over his head.

'Turn off the clock.' The man's voice was so quiet, it was little more than a breath.

'Why?' Zak asked.

'You need your night vision. The clock compromises it. Turn it off and don't ask any more questions.'

Zak flicked a switch on the alarm clock. Darkness filled the room.

He heard the man's voice again. 'Take your pyjamas.'

Zak wanted to ask why, but didn't dare. He removed the pyjamas from under his pillow and then, almost as an afterthought, groped in the darkness for the picture of his mum and dad. 'Leave it,' the man breathed.

'No way,' Zak said. 'I'm—'

He didn't finish the sentence. The man stepped forward, grabbed his hand and forced him to return the picture to the bedside table. 'Let's go,' he whispered. 'Don't make a sound.'

Zak's eyes were growing used to the darkness now, but as they trod lightly out of the bedroom, he saw that the bathroom door was open and a street lamp from outside gave them some light to work with. They crept downstairs. And at the bottom of the stairs, Zak stopped.

Even in the darkness he could see that the place was in chaos. The hallway was home to a chest of drawers that contained hats, scarves and other outdoor gear. Only now it didn't, because its contents were scattered over the floor, as if someone had been rummaging through them, looking for something.

'Come on,' breathed the man, and he headed down the hallway to the front door. As Zak followed him, he glanced into the front room. The coffee table was upside down; the TV was missing; the whole place had been ransacked.

The door was open and the man was gesturing at him. Zak, still clutching his pyjamas, followed him out into the early morning air. The intruder closed the door so quietly that Zak didn't even hear it click. Only now did he remove his balaclava. He was probably in his late twenties and had a square face with thick blond hair. His nose was flattened and his forehead was set in a permanent frown. He nodded at Zak without smiling, then swiftly turned and walked down the street.

Zak followed. They didn't have far to go. The man stopped by a vehicle parked about twenty metres away – a white van with misted rear windows and a sign on the side with a phone number and the words 'Emergency Plumbing Service – 24 hour call-out'.

'I thought people like you were supposed to drive Aston Martins,' Zak said. He tried to sound confident, but his voice trembled slightly.

'People like me,' replied the man, 'drive whatever makes them anonymous. Aston Martins don't do that.' He opened the rear doors and Zak saw the family TV lying on its back, along with the DVD player and various other items he couldn't quite make out.

'You did all that just now?'

'Get inside.'

'I didn't hear you break in.'

'I'm quiet. Get inside.'

Zak had a moment of doubt. He looked over his shoulder back at the house he had just left. The street lamp outside it flickered slightly; 63 Acacia Drive was bathed in its yellow glow. Zak had no fondness for that house, but now it was time to leave, a part of him wanted to run back inside to the familiar flowery wall-paper. Back to his ordinary life. To get into this van was to take a step into the unknown . . .

'Why have I brought my pyjamas?' he asked suddenly. Nervously.

The man didn't explain. He just put one hand on Zak's back and gently but firmly pushed him into the back of the van. The doors shut behind him and once more he was plunged into darkness. Moments later, the engine started and the vehicle pulled away. Zak had to stop himself shivering . . .

He didn't know how long they drove for. It was difficult to judge time in the darkness. He sat in the corner of the vehicle, clutching his knees, trying to make sense of what had just happened. When Ellie and her family woke up, the first thing they would see was that they'd been robbed. He could just imagine the reaction – Aunt Vivian screeching, Uncle Godfrey bellowing. He felt sorry for Ellie having to be part of it. Sorry and guilty. He didn't know how long it would be before they realized that he was gone, and he didn't know what they would think either. That he had stolen everything?

He narrowed his eyes in the darkness. No. They might think that at first, but when they discovered that his pyjamas weren't there, they'd change their mind. Because if he intended to rob the house and run away, he'd hardly do it in his nightclothes . . .

The van, which had been twisting and turning, suddenly increased its speed and Zak imagined they were on a motorway. They drove for perhaps half an hour before he felt the vehicle veering from the main road and slowing down again. More twisting and turning before they came to a halt. The noise of the engine died away, but outside the van there was another sound, loud and mechanical. It grew louder as the doors opened, and when Zak peered outside, he saw what it was.

A helicopter. He felt slightly sick.

'Get out,' the blond man said. 'Quickly.'

Zak did as he was told, and immediately his unruly hair started blowing around in the downdraught of the chopper. It was still dark, and they were in the middle of a big field with no sign of any houses nearby. In addition to his abductor, there was a second man – much shorter and wearing a black beanie hat.

'Where are we?' Zak yelled above the aircraft's engines.

'Just get on the chopper,' the man yelled. 'Now.'

'Are you coming with me?' he asked.

The man nodded and pointed to the helicopter. Its side door was open but there was no sign of anyone inside other than the pilot. Zak staggered towards it, keeping his head low and covering his ears with his hands. The man followed him and, once they were both safely inside, he closed the door. The short man stepped round to the front of the aircraft and gave the pilot a thumbs up, before running back to the plumber's van.

Inside the chopper, Zak sat in one of the empty seats in the main cabin. The pilot looked back at him and made a gesture telling him to strap himself in, which Zak did. The moment his seat belt clunked together, the helicopter rose into the air.

'Where are we going?' Zak screamed over the noise. He'd never been in a chopper before, and he felt vulnerable as the ground disappeared underneath them.

But neither the pilot nor his frowning, blond-haired companion answered. They just looked straight ahead, bathed in the light from the chopper's dashboard. If Zak had been feeling uneasy before, he felt doubly so now. But it was too late to do anything about it. With a turn of his steering lever, the pilot caused the aircraft to veer to the right. Then they straightened up and continued to fly through the night air.

Zak felt disorientated. Through the window of the chopper he could see lights of the towns over which they flew, but there was no way of knowing which towns they were or in what direction they were flying. It was only when dawn arrived after a couple of hours' flight time that Zak was able to work it out. The first glimpses of light came from the right-hand side of the chopper. He knew the sun rose in the east, so they must be heading north.

On the ground below he could just make out mountains and lakes. He consulted his mental map of the country. Were they passing over the Lake District? Or had they gone further north, into the highlands of Scotland? He realized it was Scotland when he saw a crinkly coastline up ahead. The chopper flew over the sea – it was grey and threatening in the almost-light of dawn, and it made Zak shiver, especially when he felt the chopper losing height and he could make out the foam of the choppy waters.

Then there was land: a sheer, craggy cliff with moorland on top of it. The chopper flew low – low enough for its downdraught to cause hedges to buffet in the wind – before it reduced speed and gradually rested on the ground once more. The hum of the engines grew fainter, and although the rotary blades continued to spin, Zak could tell they were slowing down.

The blond-haired man opened the side door and jumped down. He turned and held up one hand to help Zak out. Zak ignored it and dismounted from the chopper by himself. They ran away from the downdraught and he stopped to look around.

It was just about the bleakest place Zak had ever seen. The dawn light was still a faint, steely grey. It didn't do much for the featureless expanse around him. There were no trees; just moor as far as he could see, with only the occasional mound of crags erupting from the ground to break up the monotony. And in the distance, perhaps a mile away, a single house, lonely and imposing against the grey skyline.

The blond man pointed towards it just as it started to drizzle. 'That's where we're going.' He looked up at the sky. 'We'll run,' he said.

Without waiting for a word from Zak, he started jogging in the direction of the house.

The drizzle was becoming gradually more intense. The helicopter, which couldn't have been on the ground for more than thirty seconds, lifted up into the air again, leaving Zak on that featureless moor, getting wet. The blond man was already a hundred metres away and didn't look like he was prepared to wait. Zak pulled his hood up over his head, and ran after him.

It took a minute or so to catch him up. 'All right,' the blond man said when Zak was alongside him. 'Slow down, it's not a race. You need to learn how to conserve your energy when you're running. Anyone can sprint a couple of hundred metres, but for successful escape and evasion you need to know how to cover long distances.'

Zak looked over his shoulder. 'Who am I escaping from?' he asked.

'No one,' said the man. 'Not yet.'

They ran on in silence.

It took about ten minutes to reach the house, by which time Zak was totally soaked. He bent over to get his breath back. The blond man, although he was also wet, didn't seem remotely puffed. He strode up a flight of stone steps that led to an arched wooden door. On one side of the door, looking quite out of place on this big, old house, was an electronic keypad. The man typed in a number and Zak stood up just in time to see a red light shoot from the device and scan the man's retina.

A pause. And then a slow hissing sound as the big door swung open. A figure appeared in the doorway.

He was tall, with a deeply lined, tanned face and long grey hair spilling out onto his shoulders.

'Michael . . .' Zak muttered.

'Hello, Zak. Hello, Raf,' the man said. 'It's good to see you both here safely. All went well, I trust? I imagine you'd like some dry clothes, and something hot to drink.' He turned and disappeared into the house.

Raf looked at Zak. 'After you,' he said politely.

Zak trotted up the stone steps. 'You're too kind,' he replied. He walked up the steps, in out of the rain.

And then he spun round. The heavy door had hissed shut behind him. He couldn't help feeling as if someone had just locked him in.

5

GUARDIAN ANGELS

Zak found himself in a large, high-ceilinged hallway with a chequerboard floor and an immense stone fireplace in which there was a roaring wood fire. He and Raf headed straight for it, and it was only a few seconds before their wet clothes started to steam in the warmth.

'Where are we?' Zak asked.

Michael looked around fondly. 'St Peter's House,' he said. 'The island itself—'

'We're on an island?'

'Certainly,' Michael replied. He walked up to a table on the other side of the room and picked up two large, white mugs – one for Zak, the other for Raf. Zak took a sip. Boiled water, nothing more. He made a sour face, which Michael noticed. 'Drink it,' the old man said. 'Hydration is important. The island itself doesn't have an official name – not one you'll find on a map, anyway. Nobody lives here, but the locals on the

54

mainland call it St Peter's Crag. One name is as good as another. Or did I mention that to you before?' He brushed a strand of hair away from his forehead.

'You said something about dry clothes,' Zak reminded him. Even though the fire was warm, he was shivering.

Michael looked at Raf. 'Take him to his room,' he said.

Raf nodded. At the far end of the hallway there was an ornate wooden staircase ascending against the wall. Zak followed Raf up it, then down a long corridor with oak-panelled walls and thick, old-fashioned carpet. There were heavy wooden doors along the corridor at intervals of about ten metres, each with modern opaque white door knobs; and one at the very end. It was this door which Raf opened. He stepped aside to let Zak in.

It was a small room, though a lot bigger than the one he had at his uncle and aunt's house. In a far corner was a single bed with crisp, white sheets. Next to it was a clothes rail on which hung ten or twelve sets of Zak's trademark jeans and dark hooded tops, with several pairs of new trainers on the floor underneath. Hanging on one of the stark white walls was a huge flat-screen TV – fifty inches, Zak reckoned, maybe more – and beneath that a glass table with a PlayStation.

'It's been modified,' Raf said, when he saw Zak's

eyes linger on the console. 'Special strategy and reflex exercises.'

'No *Modern Warfare?*' Zak asked.

'You don't need a games console for that.' Raf walked up to the screen and put one finger to it. It immediately flickered into life, showing a plain web browser. 'You've got Internet access, but there's a firewall stopping you from sending emails or communicating with the outside world. Save yourself some time and don't try to hack it. You won't be able to.'

'What am I?' Zak asked. 'A prisoner?'

'Some walls,' Raf said, 'aren't there to stop people getting out. They're to stop people getting in.' Zak didn't think it was a very reassuring comment.

Opposite the flat screen there was another door, leading to a bright, modern bathroom. The lights flickered on automatically as soon as Zak walked in. 'Take a shower,' Raf told him. 'Put on some dry clothes. We'll come and get you in half an hour.' Without another word, he turned and left.

It felt good to get out of his damp clothes and feel the steaming hot water on his back, but it did nothing to stop Zak's uneasiness. Where was this place? *What* was it? He felt a million miles from anywhere, under the control of these strange people. He couldn't help thinking he'd made a very serious mistake . . .

Zak tried not to think about how they knew exactly

what size clothes he wore, but the clean jeans, top and trainers fitted perfectly. When he was dressed, he touched the flat screen just as Raf had done. It switched on and this time Zak checked the time on the top of the screen. 07.58. It had taken just under five hours for his world to change.

He thought of Ellie. She'd be awake now – they all would, and they'd have seen what had happened. They'd know he was missing. Zak felt a pang of guilt. But then he thought about why he was here. About his parents. A scowl crossed his face.

Zak reckoned he still had ten minutes before Raf came back to get him, and he wanted to know what was in the rooms along the corridor. He wasn't at all sure that if he left his own room the door wouldn't shut behind him, so he took one of the spare trainers and propped it against the door frame before stepping out into the corridor.

The closest two doors were directly opposite each other, about ten metres from Zak's room. He tried the right-hand one first, gripping the white door knob and trying to turn it. Nothing moved – the door was locked, but it puzzled Zak that there was no keyhole or keypad. As far as he could tell, the only way to unlock this door was from the inside. The same went for the door opposite. Zak pressed his ear up against the wood to listen to anything going on inside.

Nothing.

Then . . . footsteps.

They were coming up the stairs at the end of the corridor. Zak glanced guiltily towards them and hurried back to his room. He wasn't sure if he'd closed the door in time and he could feel his skin flushing. When Raf knocked and reappeared, though, he showed no sign of knowing that Zak had been snooping around.

Like Zak, Raf had changed, but was still dressed entirely in black – black jeans, black polo neck, black boots. 'Ready?' he asked.

'Yeah,' Zak said. 'I guess.' But ready for what, he didn't really know.

The room to which Raf led him was back on the ground floor. It was large, with a big oak desk in the middle and floor-to-ceiling windows, through which Zak could just make out the sea, grey and threatening in the distance – an impossible perimeter that he knew he could never cross. The air was thick with the aroma of cherry tobacco. Michael was here, smoking one of his thin cigarillos, but he wasn't alone. A woman stood in front of one of the windows. She was in her twenties with shoulder-length white-blonde hair and large, icy-blue eyes. Like Raf, she was dressed all in black, and she gave Zak a friendly, open smile as he walked in.

'Good to see Raphael picked you up OK, Zak,' she said. 'Wanted to do it myself – us girls are better at creeping around in the dead of night, you know.' She winked at him. 'Raf says it's because we're more sneaky, but that's such a horrid word. "Subtle" sounds much better, don't you think?'

Michael interrupted her. 'Zak, I'd like you to meet Gabriella. Gabriella, Zak.'

The woman walked forward. Her movements were like a cat's – elegant but silent. As she walked past Michael she brushed an affectionate hand against his arm and Zak noticed that her nails were painted in baby pink. 'Michael is *so* polite. He's like someone's grandfather, isn't he? Maybe he *is* someone's grandfather. I suppose we'll never know.' By now she was standing just in front of Zak, holding out her right hand. 'Call me Gabs, sweetie,' she said. 'Everybody does.'

Zak shook her hand a bit warily. 'Pleased to meet you, Gabs,' he said.

Gabs rolled her eyes. 'He's adorable,' she said to nobody in particular. 'You know, Zak, if Raf had a face like yours, he could fool anyone.' She winked at Raf. 'Of course, we wouldn't change him for the world, though.'

Raf's frown grew more pronounced, but he didn't say anything.

'That's enough, Gabriella,' Michael said. 'We don't have time to play. There are things Zak needs to know.' The old man walked to one side of the table and opened a drawer. He removed a piece of paper, then placed it on the table top. 'Have a look, Zak,' he said. 'Tell me what you think.'

Zak took the piece of paper. It was a printout of a newspaper article. The headline, in thick black lettering, was chilling enough, the rest even more so:

BOY KIDNAPPED IN BUNGLED ROBBERY, FEARED DEAD

A teenager, still missing following a robbery on Monday night at the Camden home of his uncle and aunt, is feared dead, according to police sources. It is thought that Zachary Darke, 13 – who was staying with relatives after the tragic death of his parents six months ago – disturbed burglars when they entered the house. Police believe he may have recognized one of the intruders and was abducted to stop him revealing their identity.

Zak felt himself shiver. It was like staring at his own tombstone.

He looked around at the others in the room. Michael's tanned face was expressionless. So was Raf's; he stood hulking nearby with his arms crossed. Only Gabs showed any concern, her big blue eyes full of sympathy and her lips parted.

'We'll plant it in the local newspaper in about a week,' Michael said. 'Are you comfortable with that?'

'Comfortable with being dead?' Zak asked. 'Not really. Do I get a funeral?'

'Alas, your body won't be found for some time. Which reminds me - I'll be needing a single hair from your head. You needn't look so perturbed, Zak, it's perfectly simple. We'll be on the lookout for a corpse of a similar size and shape as you. Suitably mutilated as to be unrecognizable, of course. We have ways of ensuring that your DNA is substituted for that of the deceased and for that I'll need a single hair from your head. In answer to your question, yes, I'm sure there will be a funeral of sorts. I wouldn't recommend investigating it, however. You never know what you might hear at such events. And in any case, your family and friends aren't the only people who need to say goodbye to Zak Darke. You do too.'

He took something else out of the drawer: a plain brown padded envelope, which he handed to Zak.

Zak emptied it out onto the desk. There were five documents: a red passport, slightly dog-eared; an old birth certificate; an out-of-date library card; a printout of some emails going back a couple of years; and a mobile phone contract. The passport and the library card both had photographs. Zak didn't know when the pictures had been taken, but he recognized the person well enough. It was him. A younger version, but definitely him.

He looked at the name on the documents. Zak Darke was nowhere to be seen. It was like he'd been scrubbed from the face of the planet and somebody else had parachuted in to take his place.

'Meet Harry Gold,' Michael said. 'The new you.'

Zak continued to stare at the documents. They made him feel incredibly uneasy and he was only half listening as Michael continued to talk.

'When I say "the new you", what I mean is *one of* them. Part of your training, Zak, will be to assimilate new identities, quickly and thoroughly. Harry Gold has not led a very interesting life, but even dull lives are full of facts. You need to know everything about him – not just the big things, like where he lives or what schools he's been to, but the little things too. His favourite food. What he likes to watch on TV. We have planted these little nuggets of information in the public domain, to make Harry seem like a real person. If somebody suspects you're not who you say you are, they'll test you by asking you about one of these inconsequential facts. And let's just say it'll be the kind of test where only ten out of ten will do. Do you understand?'

Zak nodded.

'Only four people in the whole world will know your real identity, Zak, and three of them are standing in the room right now.'

'Who's the fourth?' Zak demanded.

Michael carried on as if he hadn't spoken. 'It will be

necessary for other people to know of your existence, but not of your identity. They will know you only by the codename Agent 21.'

'Why 21?' Zak asked. 'What happened to Agents 1 to 20?'

A bland smile from Michael, and again he continued as though Zak hadn't even said anything. 'For the next few weeks, you will undergo a rigorous training schedule. Raf and Gabs will be your new teachers. Apart from them and myself, the only person you might see is an old man called Stan. He lives in a hut on the beach, and it's his job to make sure nobody arrives on this island without us knowing, and to take occasional deliveries of supplies – we don't want you starving, after all. If you see anyone else, it's time to worry. Is that clear?'

Zak blinked. This was all going so fast. *Too* fast. He didn't know who these people were. He didn't know if he could trust them. He was beginning to think he'd made a terrible mistake. 'I want to go home,' he said.

The other three exchanged a long look. 'People in your position always say that at first,' Michael said quietly. 'It's quite impossible, of course, but you knew that all along, didn't you?'

Zak didn't answer, so Michael continued as if nothing had happened.

'Good. Pay attention to Raf and Gabs, Zak.

Everything they teach you will have the potential to save your life.' He fixed Zak with a steely glare. 'I just hope you're as fast a learner as they say.'

Zak looked at the three of them in turn. They all looked deadly serious as they returned his gaze.

Me too, thought Zak. *Me too*. But he didn't say it.

He stuffed the documents back into their envelope. 'Isn't there something you've forgotten?' he asked.

Michael raised an eyebrow.

'When we met in the park, you said you'd tell me about my parents.'

A silence descended on the room. He was aware of Raf and Gabs glancing briefly at each other. Michael turned and walked over to the window, where he looked out towards the sea.

'As time goes on, Zak,' he said, 'you'll learn that too much information can be a dangerous thing.'

Zak felt himself flaring up. 'No way,' he said. 'You told me—'

Michael turned and held up one palm. 'Please, Zak, let me finish. Too much information can be a dangerous thing. So can too little. What is important is that you know what you *need* to know.'

'I *need* to know about my parents.'

'And you will,' said Michael, his voice calm, 'when the time is right.'

'*No!*' Zak shouted. 'We had a deal. You said you'd

tell me. You better had, otherwise I'm leaving. I don't care *what* you say.'

'Leaving?' Michael said. 'And how exactly do you propose to do that, Zak? I know you're a clever lad, but I'd be surprised if your skills extended to the flying of helicopters just yet. And the water really is rather choppy for swimming.'

Zak felt a twist in his stomach.

'And even if you do make it back,' Michael continued, 'what will you tell people? They certainly won't believe you about us, and if you can't come up with anything convincing, I'm afraid the only conclusion they're likely to come to is that you were in some way involved in the robbery of your uncle and aunt's house.'

Zak stared at him in disbelief; Michael avoided his gaze.

'Of course, I doubt your relatives would want to extend their hospitality to you if that were the case. You could always be fostered, and it's true that there are some excellent care homes, but I'm not sure that's a better option than 63 Acacia Drive, is it?'

Zak continued to stare. He couldn't believe what he was hearing. Michael had trapped him, and there was no way he could get away . . .

Michael continued talking as mildly as if he was discussing the weather. 'I have instructed Raphael and Gabriella to identify your weaknesses and build on your strengths. We have everything here that we need to do this. I might as well tell you now that you will only be able to gain access to those rooms in this house for which you have clearance.'

'Why?'

'Well,' said Michael, 'it's perhaps a little melodramatic to say that this house has secrets but . . . it does. Any rooms for which you have not been cleared will be impossible for you to enter, much like the two doors you just tried outside your own room.'

Zak shot him a quick look and Michael smiled. 'All the door knobs have fingerprint recognition technology,' he said. 'Only people with pre-approved fingerprints can gain access to certain rooms. In addition, the technology will check the temperature and pulse of anyone who tries to use the door knobs. Can you think why that might be?'

Zak shook his head.

'Well, Zak,' Michael explained, 'it would only be a moment's work to remove the hand of an authorized person from their arm and use it to gain access to restricted areas. Pulse recognition ensures that the hand is still . . . ah . . . *attached* to its owner.' The old man let that sink in before he continued. 'It might appear to you, Zak, that we are treating you unfairly. Nothing could be further from the truth. Our purpose is only to protect you until such time as you are fully able to protect yourself. There are a great many people out there who don't play by the same rules as ordinary folk. You are already their enemy. If they could get their hands on you right now, they would. No place is entirely safe.' He looked around. 'Even here. You would do well to remember that and work hard during your training period. It's for your benefit, after all.'

A stillness descended on the room as the adults stared at Zak. To break it, Michael addressed Gabs. 'Perhaps, Gabriella, you could take Zak back to his room,' he said. 'Our friend has a lot to think about, and I imagine he could do with some sleep.'

'Get some rest, sweetie,' Gabs had told him once she'd delivered him back to his room. 'You'll need it. And don't look so worried, Zak. Michael can be a little abrupt at times, but he's a sweetheart really. And we'll take care of you.' She put one hand on his shoulder, squeezed it slightly, then left.

Zak sat on the edge of his bed, trying to make sense of everything that had happened. He felt exhausted, physically and mentally. He also felt like he'd been conned. Michael hadn't forced him to come here, it was true; but he'd made it impossible to leave.

And then there was Raf and Gabs. Raphael and Gabriella . . .

Zak frowned. Something he only half remembered was nagging at him. He stood up and tapped the screen on the wall. The web browser instantly appeared. Another tap and a virtual keyboard covered the bottom half of the screen. Zak started typing. He concentrated on Raphael first, and soon had the information he wanted.

RAPHAEL — THE ANGEL OF HEALING

He stored that information away, then started searching not for Gabriella, but for . . .

GABRIEL — THE ANGELIC MESSENGER, BEARER OF TRUTH AND JUSTICE

Raf and Gabs weren't their real names. Somehow it didn't surprise him. And it didn't surprise him, either, when he continued searching and found . . .

MICHAEL — THE GREAT ARCHANGEL

Zak sneered. So Raf and Gabs were his guardian angels, and Michael was their leader. At least that was how they saw themselves.

To Zak they seemed more like his jailers.

6

CALACA

Six thousand miles away, in Central America

It was still early in the morning, but the sun was already fierce. All the cars around Mexico City had their windows firmly shut and the air conditioning on full blast – including the large black Range Rover that edged its way slowly out of the city. Whereas lots of vehicles were beeping their horns at each other in frustration, the Range Rover drove slowly and carefully. Its driver patiently waited at red lights; if another car cut across his path – and it happened often – he let them in. He did nothing to draw attention to himself. That would be stupid.

The further the Range Rover drove from the centre of Mexico City, the less heavy the traffic became. The driver was able to move faster, but he was still careful to stay within the speed limit as he headed south on the road to Cuernavaca. After forty-five minutes, however, he veered off to the right, following a small, windy road. The vehicle passed through tiny villages, where the inhabitants looked at it with interest. Big cars like his might be common in the capital city, but out here they were rare. The only cars these poor villagers were likely to drive were dust-covered and more than twenty years old.

'Stop.'

The instruction came from a man sitting in the back seat. It was a good job the windows of the Range Rover were blacked out, because if they weren't he would have attracted a lot of attention. He was, after all, a remarkable-looking man. He was incredibly skinny, and at some point in the past he had lost his right eye. He never spoke about how it happened, but most people who met him assumed it was as a result of violence.

Violence attracts violence, and this was a violent person.

The skin in front of the missing eye had grown over. There was only the faintest hint of a scar, which you wouldn't notice if you didn't know it was there. So to most people, the man in the back seat of the Range Rover looked as if he had been born with only one eye. His hair was shaved to hide the fact that it was balding, but he had a few days' stubble on his face. And even though the air conditioning in the

0542070 -
0800

CALACA

car was on, he was sweating profusely. He always did.

His name was Adan Ramirez. Behind his back, everyone called him *Calaca* – 'skeleton'. To his face, they called him 'Señor'.

The Range Rover stopped and the driver looked over his shoulder at Calaca. 'Here, Señor?'

Calaca looked out of the tinted window. The road was no longer winding, but straight. It stretched for a good two miles in either direction and there were no vehicles approaching. He nodded at the driver.

'Shall I do it, Señor?' the driver asked.

Calaca shook his head. 'No,' he replied. 'You will wait there.'

He opened the door and stepped outside into the brutal heat, where he instantly started sweating even more. Calaca walked round to the back of the Range Rover and opened up the boot. His lip curled when he saw what was inside.

It was a man. His mouth was gagged, his feet bound together and his hands tied behind his back. He scrunched his eyes shut because of the sudden influx of sunlight, before slowly opening them again. When he saw who was looking at him, he started to make squealing noises. He knew Calaca's reputation; he knew to be scared.

Calaca ignored the noises. He grabbed the man by his hair and pulled him out of the Range Rover. He

71

fell with a painful thud to the dusty road. Calaca kicked him. 'Get to the side,' he instructed. 'Now.'

The man couldn't get to his feet, so he shuffled like a worm to the edge of the road. Calaca bent down and removed the gag. 'What do you have to say for yourself?' he whispered.

'P . . . p . . . please,' the man stuttered. 'I will do whatever you want. *Please.*'

But Calaca shook his head. 'It is too late for that,' he said. 'You stole from my employer. You know what that means, don't you?'

The terrified man shook his head manically. 'It wasn't me. You've made a mistake.' Then he gave a low groan as Calaca pulled a gun from his pocket.

'You will tell me the truth,' he said.

'I swear, Señor, there is nothing to tell.'

'I will count to three. Tell me the truth and I might show you mercy. One . . .'

The man shivered on the ground. '*Please*, Señor . . .'

'Two . . .'

'It's not me you want.'

A horrible pause.

'Three.'

Calaca cocked his handgun.

'*Señor!*' the man squealed. 'I am sorry! Please, I beg your forgiveness. Spare me. *Please spare me . . .*'

The one-eyed man nodded and a calm smile

appeared on his thin lips. When he spoke again, he sounded almost pleased.

'This,' he announced, 'is from Cesar Martinez Toledo. It is what happens when you betray him. You can expect your family to receive the same treatment.'

And without another word, Calaca opened fire.

7

LOCKED AND LOADED

It was night, and Zak had awoken suddenly. For a few seconds he was confused and, not knowing where he was, started looking for the alarm clock he kept by his bed in Acacia Drive. Then he saw Raf standing in the doorway of his room, his flat-nosed, frowning face illuminated by the moon that shone through the window, and he felt a sinking feeling inside.

'Wake up,' Raf said.

Zak sat up in his bed. It was his first night on the island and it felt like he'd only fallen asleep two minutes ago.

'What time is it?' he asked. 'What's going on?'

'Midnight. Get dressed. We're going out.'

'Am I leaving?' Zak felt suddenly hopeful.

'Of course not.'

Gabs was waiting for them in the main hallway to the house. She smiled at him as he walked in behind Raf. 'You look tired, sweetie,' she said, running one hand unconsciously through her white-blonde hair.

'Funny that,' Zak replied. 'It being midnight and everything.' He looked around. 'Where's Michael?'

'Michael's left,' Gabs said. 'You won't be seeing him for a while.'

'So it's just me and my guardian angels, is it?'

Gabs and Raf exchanged a look. 'Didn't take you long to work that out,' Gabs said. She held something up. 'Put this on,' she said.

'What is it?'

'A blindfold, sweetie.'

Zak took a step backwards. 'No way,' he said. He looked at the two adults nervously.

Gabs just smiled at him again. 'What do you think we're going to do, Zak? Kidnap you?'

'You already did that.'

Raf walked up to Gabs, took the blindfold and approached Zak. 'Actually, Zak, we didn't. It was your decision to come here, and the sooner you start accepting that, the better. And if you think we're blindfolding you because we want to hurt you in some way, think again. This isn't the movies, you know. If somebody wants to kill you – and chances are that at some stage they will – they'll just do it. There won't be any of that James Bond stuff.' He handed over the blindfold. 'Put it on.'

Gabs was standing next to him now. 'You need to

start trusting us,' she said. 'Now's as good a time as any.'

Zak looked from one to the other. Both dressed in black, they had equally serious expressions as they stood there. Zak stared at the ground for a moment then, slowly, put on the blindfold.

Immediately he heard the main door open. Raf took his hand. 'Come with me,' he said, his voice as firm as his grip.

They exited the house, Zak treading carefully as he went. And then they started to walk. At first it was difficult – the ground felt treacherous underneath him and he tripped several times, although Raf was always there to pull him up. Soon, though, he got the hang of it and they started covering ground more quickly, even when the cold wind started to bite. After about an hour they stopped. 'You can take the blindfold off now,' Raf said.

Zak did so. He blinked and looked around. They were in the middle of a featureless stretch of moorland, and although the almost-full moon was bright enough to cast a shadow, he couldn't make out anything beyond about thirty metres. He shivered.

'Do you know where you are?' Raf asked him.

'The middle of nowhere,' Zak said.

'So how will you find your way home?'

'Follow my nose, I guess.'

Raf looked unimpressed. 'You can do better than that. Imagine you need to get to a rendezvous point, and you know that the RV is two miles to your north-west. How are you going to do it?'

Zak thought for a moment. 'Maybe I've got GPS on my phone.'

'OK,' Raf replied. 'GPS is good, but you can't rely on it. What if your battery's down? What if you've stumbled in a ditch and water's got into the mechanism? Let's say you've got no GPS.'

Zak chewed lightly on his lower lip. He was getting into this now. 'Map and compass?'

'You're in an area that has a lot of underground metallic ores. They're messing with the accuracy of your compass.'

'Does that happen?'

'Sure.'

'Then I don't know. Wait – hang on . . .'

He looked up.

The stars were astonishingly bright. There was no light pollution in this deserted place, so they glowed like the fires they were.

'Well done, Zak,' Raf said quietly. 'People have been using the stars to navigate since before there were even maps, let alone GPS. We might have all sorts of modern technology to help us, but that doesn't mean you should forget the old ways. The time will probably come when you need them.'

He put one hand around Zak's shoulder and pointed up. 'You see that constellation?' he asked. 'It looks like a saucepan with the handle bending upwards.'

'I see it,' Zak said.

'That's Ursa Minor. Some people call it the Little Dipper. The third star of the handle – the bright one – is Polaris. The North Star. Walk towards it and you'll always be heading north. You can work out your other bearings from that. Sometimes, though, you can't see Ursa Minor.'

'So how do you find the North Star?' Zak asked.

Raf's finger traced out another saucepan-shaped constellation. On this one, the third star of the handle bent crookedly down. 'That's Ursa Major,' he said. Then he moved his arm across the sky and traced out a W-shaped constellation. 'That's Cassiopeia. Polaris is about halfway between the two constellations. Have you got that?'

Zak nodded.

'Good. These stars need to become like friends. You never know when you might have to ask for their help. This technique works in the northern hemisphere. Do you know what that means?'

'North of the equator,' Zak said.

'Right. In the southern hemisphere you need to look for a constellation called the Southern Cross to show you which way is south. I'll show you that on a star chart another time.' He paused. 'Gabs was right, you know,' he said after a moment. 'You need to start trusting us.'

'Michael told me I shouldn't trust anyone.'

'Well, we're the exception that proves the rule. I know you're angry with Michael, but you can't let that get in the way. We're here to teach you and help you. We can't do that if you're fighting with us.'

And Zak knew Raf was right. He looked at his guardian angel. 'Just one thing,' he said.

'What's that?' Raf asked.

'Can we cut out these midnight alarm calls?'

Raf's permanent frown softened slightly. 'It's a deal,' he agreed. He held out his hand and Zak shook it.

'Now,' Raf continued, sounding suddenly brusque again, 'close your eyes and turn round three times. Keep your eyes closed.' Raf's voice grew more distant. 'The house is about three kilometres away to the south-east. I'll see you back there.'

When Zak opened his eyes, his teacher had disappeared.

'Raf!' he called. '*Raf!*'

There was no reply. Zak felt a little surge of panic. He was on his own.

It was incredibly bleak out here by himself. The wind ruffled his hair and in the distance he could just make out the sound of the waves crashing onto the beach. He shuddered. For the first time since being on the island he felt a desperate desire to be back within the walls of St Peter's House.

Stay calm, he told himself. *Remember what Raf just taught you . . .*

He looked up. It took a moment to orientate himself and locate Polaris again. South-east, Raf had said. He faced the North Star, then turned 180 degrees. That was south. He held out his arms at right angles, so his right was pointing forward to the south and the left was pointing east. South-east bisected the two. Zak started jogging in that direction. Every few minutes he stopped and checked his bearing against Polaris, and occasionally he found he had veered off course, so he readjusted his direction before continuing.

Zak had been running for about five minutes when he heard it – or thought he heard it. It wasn't much: just a vague rustling nearby. He found he was holding his breath as he stopped and looked around, his eyes straining to penetrate the dark.

'Raf? *Raf?* Is that you?'

No reply. Just silence. 'You're probably hearing things,' he muttered to himself, even as he felt a chill that was nothing to do with the cold night run down his spine. He quickly checked his bearings again and continued heading south-east. Only a little faster this time . . .

After about twenty minutes the house came into view. The yellow glow of the lights from inside almost looked welcoming.

Raf was waiting for him in a doorway; Gabs was nowhere to be seen. Raf looked at his watch. 'Twenty-two minutes,' he said. All traces of his former comradeship had disappeared and he seemed suddenly rather frosty. 'We really need to work on your fitness.'

'Did you come straight here?' Zak asked.

'Of course,' Raf said. 'Why?'

'Nothing.'

Raf shrugged. 'Go to bed,' he said. 'We've got an early start in the morning.'

When Raf said they would work on his fitness, he hadn't been joking. Both he and Gabs woke Zak at six the next morning. They gave him high-energy foods to eat – bananas and oatmeal – which they consumed in a gleaming kitchen at the back of the house, then handed him some running gear and told him to get changed.

It was a bright, crisp morning and the first couple of kilometres were almost fun as he tried to keep up with

Raf and Gabs. They maintained a punishing pace, however, and his muscles soon started to burn. 'Keep up!' Raf shouted as Zak lagged behind. He gritted his teeth, tried to forget about the pain and upped his speed.

'Ten miles,' Raf told him when they got back to the house. He and Gabs had barely broken into a sweat. 'We do that every day and increase it by three miles a week. Go and get changed. You've got tuition for the rest of the day.'

It started with Spanish lessons. Then Mandarin. Then Arabic. Both Raf and Gabs were fluent in them all. As Zak was struggling with the Arabic alphabet, Gabs smiled at him. 'We'll have you talking like a native in a few weeks, sweetie,' she said.

Zak wasn't so sure.

The days passed. They turned into weeks. The routine didn't change. Before long, Zak had almost forgotten why he was here, or the life he'd left behind. The training was everything, and it took up every second of his time. When he wasn't running, he was pushing weights; when he wasn't pushing weights, he was studying languages; when he wasn't studying languages, he was being tutored in the arts of navigation.

Every night before bedtime, Raf handed him a piece

of paper bearing facts about Harry Gold, Zak's alter ego. And every night he would learn them. Harry Gold's life was not so different to Zak's. He too had lost his parents to illness – his mother to a rare form of cancer, his father to the lung condition that had plagued him all his life; he too was an only child who had gone to live with relatives. When Zak mentioned this to Gabs, she just smiled. 'Of course, sweetie,' she said. 'The best disguises are the ones where you don't have to try too hard.'

He considered asking about his own parents again, but something told him Gabs wouldn't be any more forthcoming than Michael.

There was a lot to learn. After a week, Zak could recite Harry's personal details off by heart; after two he knew where Harry had gone on holiday for the past ten years; and after three he could name his imaginary extended family down to the obscurest cousins living in Eastbourne or the great-uncle who emigrated to Mexico fifteen years ago and hadn't returned to the UK since. Once a week, Gabs and Raf would test him with quickfire questions and Harry's past started to become second nature to him.

When Zak wasn't exercising his mind or his brain, he slept as soundly as the dead. He was four weeks in when he woke to the sound of the regular 6 a.m. knock on his door. 'Forget the running gear,' Raf's voice came from outside. 'We're doing something else today.' Zak changed into his jeans and hoodie then stepped outside.

'Come with me,' Raf told him.

'Where?'

'You'll see.'

He led Zak down into the basement. Zak had never been there before. At the bottom of the stairs there was a metal door with one of the opaque white door knobs. 'We've given you access to this room,' Raf told him. 'You can come down here to train any time you want.'

'Train in what?'

'Firearms,' Raf said, and the door clicked open.

Behind the door there was a firing range. It looked a bit like a bowling alley, but at the end of each lane there were no skittles: there were targets, shaped like human bodies with concentric circles printed on the chests. To the left-hand side was a glass table, and on the table lay a selection of weapons, with Gabs standing next to them in her trademark black clothes.

'OK, Zak,' Raf said. 'This is where it starts to get interesting.'

Gabs interrupted. 'You shouldn't say things like that to him, Raf.' Her face was very serious, her blue eyes intense. She ran one hand through her white-blonde hair. 'You need to listen to me carefully, Zak. Once you're activated, you'll find yourself in some dangerous situations. The whole reason Michael wants you as an agent is so that you can get access to places where adults would cause suspicion. Nothing's going to raise people's eyebrows more than kids with guns, so you'll find it pretty rare to be inserted anywhere with a firearm. You'll likely be surrounded by them, though, so you need to know how to recognize and operate the major types.'

Zak nodded.

'This isn't playground stuff, Zak. Each one of these weapons can kill you instantly if you don't use them properly.' She glanced at Raf. 'Interesting enough for you, Raf?' she asked.

Raf grunted and approached the table. He picked up the weapon on the far left-hand side. 'This is a handgun,' he said. 'We call it that because it's designed to be held in one hand. Your other hand supports the firing arm. Some people call them pistols – same difference. They're small, light and easy to carry. There are different types of handgun, but the ones you're most likely to come across are revolvers and semi-automatics. Revolvers have a rotating chamber that normally holds between five and eight rounds. Semi-automatics use the energy from firing one round to load the next into the chamber. You only need to cock the hammer once, and the gun will do the rest. Are you getting this?'

'I think so.'

'This is a Browning Hi-Power. It's one of the most common semi-automatic pistols in the world. There's a safety switch on the side, but some handguns have their safety in the handle, which means the gun will only fire when the user is holding it. If the weapon is loaded and the safety's on, we say it's locked and loaded. This gun fires nine-millimetre rounds – that's the size of the bullets – and has a thirteen-round magazine. All making sense?'

'Nine-millimetre, thirteen rounds,' Zak repeated. His brain ached from trying to take it all in.

Raf lay the handgun back on the table and picked up the next gun – a longer one this time. 'This is an assault rifle,' he continued. 'AK-47. Some people call it a Kalashnikov after the guy who designed it. This is the most popular gun in the world. Other common types of assault rifle are the M16, the Colt Commando and the C4 carbine. The AK fires 7.62 millimetre rounds – people refer to these as seven-six-twos or thirty calibres. The safety catch on an assault rifle typically has three settings: off, semi-automatic and fully automatic. When it's set to off, the weapon is safe; semi-automatic, each time you pull the trigger it will discharge one round; fully automatic and the weapon will continue firing until you take your finger off the trigger or it runs out of ammo.'

Raf moved on to a third weapon. 'This is a Heckler and Koch MP5. It's a sub-machine-gun. Machine guns are fully automatic; sub-machine-guns fire small-calibre rounds similar to pistols. MP5s typically fire seven to nine hundred rounds per minute. If you see somebody carrying one, duck.'

Zak nodded.

'We'll start with the handgun,' Raf said. 'Put these on.' He handed Zak a set of protective headphones, then he and Gabs both put some on themselves. Zak watched as Gabs picked up the Browning Hi-Power and inserted a magazine into the handle with a satisfying clunk. She approached one of the firing ranges, unlocked the safety catch and raised the handgun.

She fired three shots. One hit the target square in the forehead; the other two made holes in the centre of the chest. Gabs switched the safety back on and handed the gun to Zak.

He handled it gingerly at first. 'Don't be scared of it, sweetie,' Gabs said. 'You need to respect your firearm, but remember that you're in charge. Now, switch off the safety and raise your arm.'

Zak did as he was told.

'Steady yourself,' Gabs told him. 'When you fire

there'll be a recoil. You need to be ready for it. Take a shot in your own time.'

Zak lined the sights up with the target's chest – for some reason he couldn't bring himself to attempt a head shot. He took a breath and fired.

The recoil was worse than he was expecting, jarring his arm up and to the left. He looked hopefully at his target, but there wasn't even a single mark on it.

Raf and Gabs glanced at each other. 'We'll practise every day,' Raf said. 'We'll soon get you—'

But Zak was hardly listening to him. He had already lined up the sights with the target once more and this time he knew what was coming. He steeled himself, then fired again.

This time he didn't miss. A small hole appeared just above the heart area. Zak switched the safety back on, lowered the gun and removed his ear-protectors. He turned to his guardian angels. 'Every day, right?' he asked as Raf and Gabs shared an astonished look.

He returned to the table, and put the gun back in its place.

8

AGENT 17

As the weeks went by, Zak's training grew more intense. The runs grew longer, the weights heavier. His mind swam with new facts and techniques, his Spanish, Arabic and Mandarin became practically fluent and he learned to live with the constant bruising on both shoulders as he practised with the assault rifle. Raf taught him to drive, using an old Land Rover that bumped over the rough terrain around St Peter's Crag. 'Try not to break the vehicle,' he said without a hint of a smile. 'The RAC don't come out this far.' It was slow-going at first, but Raf was patient and in a couple of weeks Zak was driving like he'd been doing it all his life.

One day he ran with Gabs to the eastern edge of the island. Before they turned back, however, she stopped. 'Wait up, Zak,' she said. 'We're doing something different today.'

Zak nodded. He'd grown fond of Gabs. She was

straight-talking and no-nonsense. When your world had changed, you needed someone like that.

They were on top of a cliff and there was a stiff breeze. Gabs pointed out to sea. In the distance there was a tanker, grey against the horizon.

'See that ship?' she asked.

'Yeah.'

'Why?'

Zak gave her a puzzled look. 'What do you mean? Because I've got eyes and it's there. What are you talking about, Gabs?'

'All right then,' she smiled at him. 'When you're running about the island, do you ever see any animals apart from birds?'

Zak thought about it. 'No,' he admitted.

'Why not? After all, you've got eyes, and I can promise you they're there.'

'What are you getting at?'

'Concealment, sweetie. There'll be times when you need to hide. To camouflage yourself, either because someone's hunting you down or because you're observing them. You can't do that effectively unless you know why things are seen. Walk with me and I'll explain it to you.'

They started strolling away from the cliff edge. 'The first thing is shape,' Gabs explained. 'You knew that was a ship because you know what a ship looks like. I know what a human being looks like, so if I was observing you, I could easily recognize a full human shape. If you crouch down, though, or hide part of your body, my eyes would be less likely to pick you out.

'After shape, there's shadow. If you're hiding, you need to be aware of where your shadow is falling, otherwise it's a giveaway. Another giveaway is your silhouette. If you stand against a plain background, like the sky or a field, I'd be able to see you much more easily than if the background is uneven. Make sense?'

Zak smiled at her. 'All I want to know,' he said, 'is why you're trying to find me in the first place.'

'Pay attention to this, sweetie. It's important.'

'Sorry. Shape, shadow, silhouette. Got that.'

'Next thing is surface. If an object's surface is differ-ent to its surroundings, it'll stand out. Shiny things are the worst – if they catch the sunlight, they can be seen from miles. And spacing is really important.'

'What do you mean.'

Gabs pointed up ahead. 'See the boulders in that field?'

Zak looked. They were dotted all around. 'Yeah, I see them.'

'They're all randomly spaced. Nature's like that. Nothing is even. Remember that if you're trying to melt into the background. Last thing: movement. You might be so well camouflaged that I could be staring straight at you and not know you're there. But the second you move . . . it's bye-bye.'

Gabs's turn of phrase made him feel uneasy.

'I wish I'd known all this when Michael was following me back in London,' he said.

'I'm not sure it would have done much good,' Gabs replied. 'Michael can find just about anybody, even if they don't want to be seen.'

'Is he that good?' Zak asked.

'He's the best,' said Gabs, and there was no doubt in her voice.

They walked for a bit in silence.

'Gabs?' Zak said after a bit. Something had been bothering him and he didn't quite know how to say it.

'Yeah?'

'You know these operations I'm supposed to be training for? Nobody's told me what they are. You know, what to expect.'

'That's because we don't know yet. Me and Raf, anyway.'

'What about Michael? Does he know?'

'Maybe. He wouldn't tell us if he did.'

They walked some more.

'I'm scared,' Zak admitted.

'Good,' said Gabs. She didn't say it in a mean way; her voice was quite gentle.

'What do you mean, good?'

'Fear is an important emotion, Zak. You can't stop it, but if you can admit you're scared, that's the first step to controlling it. And if you can't control your fear, it can get in the way of you making the right decisions. A bit of fear is good. It keeps you alert. Trust me – in our line of work you don't want to get blasé.'

'I just wish I knew what our line of work was.'

'You will, Zak. When you're ready. There's still a lot for you to learn.'

Zak frowned. 'You know what scares me most of all?'

'What's that, sweetie?'

'Michael calls me Agent 21. But he wouldn't tell me what happened to Agents 1 to 20. I can't help thinking they must be . . . you know . . . *dead*.'

Gabs looked at him seriously for a moment. 'Would it help you to meet some of them?' she asked.

Zak nodded mutely.

'All right then.' She held out her hand. 'Agent 17, pleased to meet you.'

Zak blinked. 'You mean . . . *you're* . . .'

'Of course. And Raf is my predecessor, Agent 16. But to be honest, we prefer "Gabs" and "Raf". It's so much more personal, don't you think? Really, sweetie, you shouldn't look so surprised. What do you think they do with us when we've outgrown our usefulness?'

She winked. 'Find us a nice quiet little job in a garden centre somewhere? Come on, it's getting cold. Let's run back. Morse code this afternoon.' And without waiting for an answer, she started jogging.

It rained for the rest of the day. Zak was glad they were inside, even if the piece of paper Gabs and Raf gave him looked very complicated. 'Morse code is more than a hundred years old,' Raf explained, 'but you'd be surprised how useful it can be. You probably know how to send an SOS.'

'Dot dot dot, dash dash dash, dot dot dot?'

'Right. But once you're proficient, you can use it to transmit any message. Most pilots and air-traffic controllers are fluent, and so are special forces signallers. Morse code uses rhythm to transmit messages – sequences of short and long elements to represent different letters, using sound or light. That piece of paper shows you the Morse code alphabet.'

Zak studied it.

'Each dash is three times the length of a dot,' Raf explained. 'With practice, you should be able to deliver Morse code messages very quickly.'

'Let me guess,' Zak said. 'The practice starts now.'

Gabs smiled at Raf. 'He's getting the hang of it, isn't he?'

Morse Code Alphabet
The international morse code characters

A .-	N -.	0 -----
B -...	O ---	1 .----
C -.-.	P .--.	2 ..---
D -..	Q --.-	3 ...--
E .	R .-.	4 ....-
F ..-.	S ...	5 .....
G --.	T -	6 -....
H	U ..-	7 --...
I ..	V ...-	8 ---..
J .---	W .--	9 ----.
K -.-	X -..-	Fullstop .-.-.-
L .-..	Y -.--	Comma --..--
M --	Z --..	Query ..--..

They spent the remainder of the afternoon learning and practising Morse code. After two hours, Zak had memorized it. After another two, he could send and decipher simple messages. More than once he saw Gabs and Raf glancing at each other, clearly impressed by the speed with which he picked it up. By the time the lesson was over, though, his brain was exhausted. He excused himself and went straight up to bed.

Zak lay in his room for a little while, thinking. In his first couple of weeks here, he'd been angry. Angry with Michael and, by extension, with Gabs and Raf. Things had changed. Somehow the knowledge that his guardian angels understood what he was going through made him feel better. They'd been working him hard, sure, but he found he didn't mind that. He enjoyed it. The stuff he was learning on this craggy outpost of the British Isles was a load more interesting than being back at Camden High School, having to deal with idiots like Marcus Varley and Jason Ford. If it wasn't for the fact that he missed Ellie, and that every time he thought about what might happen to him in the future he wanted to be sick, things would be absolutely fine . . .

A knock on the door roused him from his thoughts. At least, he thought it was a knock at first, but soon realized it was more than that. A pattern.

--. --- --- -.. -. .. --. .... - ... .-- . . - .. .

Zak smiled. 'Goodnight, Agent 17,' he called, and he switched out his light. He might be uncertain about the future, but one thing was sure: tomorrow would be just as busy as today, and he needed a good night's sleep.

9

BREAK-IN

The funny thing about being busy, Zak began to realize, is that you don't notice how quickly time passes. Christmas came and went without any special celebration; then his birthday raced past – a day filled, as any other, with training.

But some days have more meaning than others. He had been on the island for six months when one morning he woke up at 5.30 a.m. – half an hour earlier than normal. He felt unusual as he climbed out of bed and into his bathroom. The lights – which were stark and white – flicked on automatically as he entered and he looked at himself in the mirror. The reflection that stared back at him looked different somehow. Older. The muscles in his arms were stronger, his face was lean and fit. His hair was still unruly, but his skin was a little more weathered from all the time he'd spent outside; there was a tightness around his eyes. Zak realized that he looked a bit like his dad – it was the first time he had ever noticed that.

His dad. The thought made him feel empty and he realized why he felt weird. He went back into the bedroom and tapped the computer terminal hanging on the wall. It switched on immediately and at the top right-hand corner he saw the date.

22 April.

A year to the day since his parents had died.

The months of training had been so intense that Zak had barely thought about them. Not properly, though they were always there in the back of his mind. Now he sat on the edge of his bed and stared into the middle distance, feeling empty.

The door opened. Zak looked over his shoulder to see Gabs standing there. She was wearing her usual black clothes and her large blue eyes were wide. 'I thought you might be up early today, sweetie.'

Zak looked away, embarrassed that he could feel tears in his eyes.

'Raf and I were talking,' she continued. 'We thought maybe you could take the day off.'

Zak looked through the window of his room. The early morning light was dreary and he could tell it would be a cold, unwelcoming day. But he also knew that sitting here in his room wasn't the best way to get his head in order. He stood up. 'No,' he said. 'I don't want a day off. Let's get to work.'

They spent the morning on emergency First Aid, practising cardiopulmonary resuscitation techniques, before moving on to modern languages and finishing up on the firing range in the basement. By evening he was exhausted. He ate a quick supper and went to bed early. The sooner this day was over, he decided, the better.

It was a noise that woke him. At least, he thought it was. Zak's eyes pinged open, and even though he stayed lying on his back, his senses were keen. He held his breath, eliminating the sound of his breathing from his senses. The moon shone through his window, casting long shadows inside the room.

Zak strained his ears. There was nothing. Just a thick blanket of silence.

The silence didn't last for long.

When they came, it was hard and fast. There was an icy shattering as the panes of the window burst inwards and a figure fast-roped in, followed by two others. For a moment, Zak was paralysed with terror; but then he moved quickly. He rolled from the opposite side of his bed and instantly made for the door – his only available exit point. They were too fast for him, though. All three men were dressed in black and had balaclavas over their heads. The frontrunner grabbed him and forced one arm behind his back.

Zak felt drained with panic. '*Raf!*' he yelled. '*Gabs! Help!*' All of a sudden the sound of roaring engines filled his ears; a bright spotlight shone in through the broken window. His attacker pulled out a gun – a matt-black Glock 17 – and pressed it to Zak's head.

Zak barely dared breathe.

'Say another word,' the man said, his voice muffled by the balaclava, 'and it'll be your last.'

That was enough for Zak. He felt his legs go weak, and it was all he could do to stand up.

Another of the masked men approached him. He was carrying some sort of harness which he pulled over Zak's head and secured around the back. The guy with the Glock pushed him towards the window and reached out, pulling in a long rope with a metal link at the end. He clipped this link to the harness and put the gun against Zak's head again.

'Jump,' he said.

Zak felt his stomach go. He peered out of the window. The noise was deafening here, the light blinding, but he could sense what was out there – a helicopter, hovering about twenty metres above the height of his window.

'I won't tell you again.' The man pushed Zak right up against the broken glass. He was rough, and he meant it.

Zak didn't have a choice. He climbed up onto the

edge of the window frame, took a deep breath and stepped out. He felt his stomach go as he fell three or four metres; but then there was a jolt that winded him and sent him spinning round in the air. Instinctively he grabbed the rope above him, but by this time he could feel himself being winched up. In less than twenty seconds somebody inside the chopper – masked and anonymous just like the others – was pulling him into the aircraft.

'*What's happening?*' Zak screamed in terror. '*Who are you?*'

No answer. One of the black figures unclipped his harness and pushed him towards the other side of the chopper. 'Put your hands behind your head and kneel down,' he shouted. Zak did as he was told.

He turned his head to look through the side window. The chopper's searchlight was spinning now, lighting up the ground below like a prison searchlight trying to find an escaped convict. '*Raf!*' Zak shouted. '*Gabs! Help me!*' It didn't take more than a few seconds to illuminate two figures on the ground. Raf and Gabs were both on one knee, weapons in each hand pointed up to the chopper. But it was obvious they couldn't fire on the aircraft – bring it down and Zak would go down with it . . .

He looked back to the other side of the helicopter. The three masked men who had abducted him had been winched back in. The aircraft made a sudden tilt, then veered off away from the house.

Zak's limbs were weak with fear. He counted the men in the aircraft – six in all, not counting the pilot up ahead, who was the only one without a balaclava, but the night vision goggles he wore obscured his features just as effectively. Three of the others had assault rifles pointed in Zak's direction. 'Where are you taking me?' Zak whispered.

No one spoke.

Zak tried to think clearly through the horror. What were his options? What were his escape routes? He remembered something Raf had told him. *If somebody wants to kill you – and chances are that at some stage they will – they'll just do it. There won't be any of that James Bond stuff.* He wasn't dead, which was something. It meant that whoever these people were, they wanted him alive. The guns pointing in his direction were just a threat, but even so, he wasn't going to risk anything stupid . . .

The side door of the chopper was still open. Through it, Zak could see moonlight on the sea. It meant they had left the island but his bearings were shot and he couldn't tell in which direction they were travelling. He raised his hands. 'You won't shoot me,' he shouted over the noise of the chopper, doing what he could to sound confident.

'So you might as well tell me where we're going.'

There was no hesitation. No warning. One of the armed men stepped towards him and for a sickening moment Zak thought the guy *was* going to shoot him. He raised his gun, though, and with a sudden, sharp crack brought it down on the back of Zak's shoulder.

Zak felt himself go dizzy. By the time he hit the floor, he was already unconscious.

The first thing Zak noticed when he awoke was the pain – a throbbing at the top of his back where the masked man had hit him, and a splitting headache.

The second thing he noticed was that he couldn't move.

The third thing was that he was cold.

Zak opened his eyes. He was tied to a chair with a thick rope, wearing nothing but his boxer shorts and T-shirt. He shuffled to see if he could move the chair, but he couldn't: it was fixed to the ground. The room he was in was big – about twenty metres by twenty. The floor and walls were made of concrete and it was empty except for a big searchlight mounted on a tripod, with a long flex leading to a power point in the wall. It was set up about five metres from where Zak was sitting; beyond that there was a single door. Closed.

He shivered.

The back of his mouth was dry. After sitting there for fifteen nervous minutes he called out: '*Hello?*' The word felt like it scraped his throat, and his hoarse voice echoed against the concrete walls.

Silence surrounded him once again.

Time passed. He didn't know how long. He heard Gabs's voice in his mind. *If you can admit you're scared, that's the first step to controlling it.* No worries there, then. He was terrified. He tried to work out why he was here; who had taken him. Michael had said there were plenty of people who wanted to get their hands on him, and that they didn't play by the same rules as 'ordinary folk'. But what could he tell these people? Gabs and Raf had spent the last six months training him, but he knew next to nothing about anything important . . .

The door opened. Zak jumped. Two men walked in – one tall, one short, but both dressed the same: black boots, black jeans, black tops, black gloves and black balaclavas. The taller man closed the door behind him just as Zak started to talk. 'Who are you? Where am I?'

They ignored him. The short man walked up to the searchlight and flicked a switch at the back. It burst into light, forcing Zak to clamp his eyes shut, and was close enough to give him a little warmth. He tried to open his eyes slightly, but the light was directed right at him. It hurt to look at it, so he kept them shut.

He heard a voice behind him. Low, muffled and serious. 'What's your name?'

Zak didn't know what made him say 'Harry Gold' instead of 'Zak Darke'. Instinct, probably – combined with six months of training. When he spoke, his voice was shaky and he worried that it sounded like he was lying. His inquisitor, however, just carried on with the questions.

'Where do you live?'

'Why are you asking me this?' He shivered again, despite the warmth of the lamp.

'Where do you live?'

'One-two-five Antrobus Drive, Muswell Hill, London.'

'What were you doing at St Peter's Crag?'

'Visiting relatives.'

'On a deserted island?'

Zak clamped his mouth shut.

Silence. He could hear footsteps around him and one of the men switched the light off. Zak opened his eyes, but he was still dazzled. By the time his vision returned to normal, the men had left the room and closed the door behind them. Zak was left alone with his fear.

They returned an hour later and switched the light on again. Zak clamped his eyes shut again.

'Nobody called Harry Gold has ever lived at one-two-four Antrobus Drive,' the man said.

Zak spotted the trick immediately. 'It's one-two-five,' he said. The information he'd spent so much time learning came easily into his mind.

His inquisitor didn't sound at all concerned that his trap had been sprung. 'There's no Harry Gold at one-two-five either.'

'Of course there is,' Zak said. 'It's my home. What's going on?'

But again there was no response. The men just turned the light off and left the room for a second time.

Zak was alone for longer this time round. Five hours, maybe six. The shivering grew worse as he became colder and more fearful. He grew tired too, and his head started to nod onto his chest. At that precise moment the door opened and one of the men entered with a bucket of water, which he threw at Zak's head. It was icy cold, and caused him to catch his breath sharply. By the time he had regained control of his breathing, the man had left again and Zak was wide awake.

After that he lost track of what was happening. The men came and went. They asked him the same questions over and over.

'Where have you been for the last six months?'

'At home . . .'

'Who is Agent 21?'

'I don't know what you're talking about . . .'

They asked him again and pretended that he'd given different answers – which he hadn't. He could tell what they were doing – trying to confuse him to the point where he really did start contradicting himself – but as time went on he found himself increasingly unable to keep track of what he'd said and what he hadn't. They came in at random intervals. Sometimes it was ten minutes between interrogations, other times it was an hour. And whenever tiredness threatened to overcome him, one of them was always there, bucket of water in hand, ready to wake him up. Before long he became truly desperate for sleep: not being allowed to rest had turned into the cruellest torture imaginable.

He was hungry too, and thirsty, but at no point did anybody mention food or drink. Zak tried to keep his mind off it by concentrating on his situation. How long had he been here? Twelve hours? Twenty-four? Longer? Maybe he should tell his captors the truth. After all, he hadn't done anything wrong. He didn't know anything about anyone. Maybe if he just admitted who he really was, they'd let him go free . . .

Or maybe they wouldn't.

His body was crying out for sleep now. He felt like

he'd do anything for it. When the two men entered and switched on the light, he heard himself begging them. 'Please . . . just let me go to sleep. I'll be able to answer your questions much better . . .'

The short man walked behind Zak's chair and bent over so his lips were just by Zak's ear. 'You can go to sleep, Harry,' he said, 'just as soon as you tell me the truth.'

'I *have* been telling the truth . . .' But Zak's energy wasn't really in the lie any more.

'We know you're *not*, Zak.' It was the first time they had used his real name, and he made a weak effort to look confused. 'You can't go to sleep until you do . . .'

And it was then that Zak knew it was over. He could try to resist, but the sleep deprivation was too acute. Sooner or later he'd have to give in. This was a battle he just couldn't win.

He closed his eyes.

'How did you know my name?'

As he spoke, he heard his own voice tremble. He remembered the Glock his abductor had pressed against his head. These men were serious. He didn't know what they wanted, but now they'd forced the truth out of him, Zak had a nasty feeling he was about to end up dead.

He breathed deeply as a feeling – as cold as ice – crept over his skin.

Silence.

The short man moved round to stand between Zak and the lamp, and the taller man joined him. Together they blocked the light and formed silhouettes. Zak blinked at them. His fear blunted every other sensation.

Except surprise . . .

It was the smaller man who peeled off the balaclava first, revealing a pockmarked face with a pinched expression and small piggy eyes that peered at Zak like a doctor assessing a patient.

It was a face that Zak recognized.

He blinked again and shook his head. 'Mr *Peters*?'

'A long way from Camden High, Zak,' Peters said, and he turned to look at the taller man, who was removing his balaclava to reveal a tanned, lined face and long, grey hair.

'*Michael*?'

Michael looked at his watch and then at Mr Peters. 'Twenty-seven hours. What do you think?'

Mr Peter's face remained stern. 'I think he needs to sleep,' he said, and without waiting for a reply he started to untie the rope that bound Zak.

It was like a dream. A nightmare. Zak's brain was exhausted and confused. A hundred questions buzzed around in his head; hot anger boiled in his veins. It had been a con – a long, dreadful, exhausting con.

But he was too tired to complain or even speak.

The men helped him to his feet and he staggered to the door. But that was the last thing he remembered. The rest was blackout.

10

A TROJAN HORSE

It was sunlight that woke him up. Bright sunlight, streaming through the window. He was back in his room at St Peter's House, covered by his crisp, white bedclothes. The window looked like new and there was no sign of the break-in. But something was different. On the right-hand side of his bed was a metal stand with a plastic bag suspended from the top. It was full of clear liquid. A tube coiled its way from the bag to a needle inserted into the back of Zak's hand.

'It's a saline drip. You needed rehydrating.'

Zak looked over in the direction of the voice. Michael was sitting in an armchair on the left-hand side of his bed.

'How are you feeling?'

'How do you think?' He lay back and looked at the ceiling. Everything started flooding back: the room, the lack of sleep, the questioning. And all for what?

One of Michael's little games? Not for the first time, Zak felt a deep anger with the old man. 'You've gone too far,' he muttered.

'Too far?' Michael looked surprised. 'I rather worry we didn't go far enough. Interrogations are never a walk in the park, you know.'

Zak thought about that for a moment. 'I failed, didn't I?' he said finally. 'It was all a test and I failed.'

'Some tests,' Michael said, 'are impossible to pass. You shouldn't be so hard on yourself. Interrogations are difficult, and we went out of our way to make sure you didn't suspect it was an exercise. All things considered, I think you did rather well. Raphael and Gabriella have done a good job on you.'

Zak frowned. Despite his anger, he was disappointed in himself and he couldn't help letting it show.

'Yeah, but I still cracked in the end.'

'Everyone cracks,' Michael said, 'in the end. Believe me, if you undergo a genuine interrogation, there's really nothing you can do to avoid the inevitable. We chose sleep deprivation as a tool. It's very effective, but most of the people you'll encounter won't be nearly so restrained. Trust me, you'll talk. *They'll* know that and *you'll* know that. The only question is how long you'll last.'

'If I'll talk in the end, what's the point in resisting?'

'There are lots of points. Maybe, given time, you'll find a way to escape; maybe, if we know you're in trouble, we'll be able to send in a rescue team; maybe it will be crucial for the operation in hand that you buy us a few hours before your captors . . .' He hesitated.

'Before they kill me?'

'One would hope it wouldn't come to that, of course. Whatever the case, there are two pieces of advice I can give you. The first is this: don't antagonize your captor. Be submissive, not confrontational. You don't want to push them.'

'And the second?'

'Don't forget the first time. You did well. You lasted twenty-seven hours. That's good by anyone's standards. You know you can do it. Remember that.'

Michael stood up and walked round to the other side of the bed. 'With your permission,' he said, 'I'll remove the drip now.' Zak nodded, and the old man pulled the needle from his hand.

'*Ow!*'

Michael ignored him. 'Come downstairs when you're ready. Raphael and Gabriella are waiting for you. We have things to discuss.'

He headed for the door.

'Wait,' Zak said.

Michael stopped.

'I thought nobody was supposed to know about all this. So who were the men who took me?'

'They were a unit from SAS headquarters in Hereford,' Michael replied. 'But they don't know who you are. They believed it was a genuine operation too.'

'In the habit of abducting kids, are they?'

Michael raised an eyebrow. 'They're in the habit of following orders. And they've done worse things than steal you from your bedroom, I can assure you.'

'What about Gabs and Raf? I saw them from the helicopter. Were they in on it?'

'Of course.'

Zak felt a little surge of resentment.

'And the room? Where was it?'

For the first time, Michael smiled. 'Here, of course,' he said. 'I told you this house had secrets. Do you think you'll be long? We have an awful lot to talk about, you know.'

Zak didn't hurry. He couldn't, even if he'd wanted to. His muscles were sore, his body weak. He got dressed slowly, like an invalid, and when he walked back down the stairs he gripped the banister to help him keep his balance.

Michael hadn't said he'd be in the office where they'd all met on the first day he'd arrived, but Zak guessed he would be. For the past six months it had been out of bounds – he'd tried the door knob a couple of times. But today the door responded to his touch. He walked in to see Michael sitting at his desk, Gabs and Raf behind him on either side, framed by the big windows and looking towards the door. Raf stayed where he was, his face expressionless; but Gabs rushed towards him, her big eyes full of concern. She gave him a tight hug and planted a kiss on his cheek. 'It's always the worst bit, sweetie,' she whispered. 'I'm sorry we couldn't warn you.'

Zak wriggled from her embrace. 'Whatever,' he said, and then felt a bit bad that Gabs looked hurt. 'You just did what you had to do.' He looked around the room. 'Mr Peters not joining us?'

'Unfortunately he has business elsewhere,' Michael said.

'I take it he's the fourth person who knows who I am.'

'Naturally. Take a seat, won't you, Zak?' Michael indicated a leather chair by the fireplace and Zak didn't need any encouragement to sit down. 'I'm pleased with your progress,' he said.

'You haven't been here to see it.'

'Raphael and Gabriella keep me well informed. Your fitness is good, your skills are excellent. I think the time has come to activate you.'

Zak swallowed nervously. 'What does that mean?' he asked.

'It means we're going to put you in the field.'

'Another test?'

A pause. 'No, Zak. Not another test. This will be for real.'

Gabs looked like she was about to say something, but Michael held up one hand to stop her. He opened one of the drawers of his desk, took out a slim, rectangular device, about twenty-five centimetres long, and tapped it. The lights in the room dimmed and a white panel descended from the ceiling against the wall opposite Zak. 'Sitting comfortably?' Michael asked. Another tap of the touch pad and a picture appeared on the panel.

It showed a man. He was perhaps in his late forties, though it was impossible to tell for sure because his skin was wrinkle-free and there was a tightness around the eyes and the edges of his face that suggested he'd had plastic surgery to make himself look younger. His skin was naturally dark, his eyes brown and his perfectly black hair was greased back over his scalp. He neither smiled nor frowned: his expression was emotionless.

'This,' said Michael, 'is Cesar Martinez Toledo. Mexicans have two surnames – one from their father, one from their mother. Cesar is known as Señor Martinez and he is Mexico's biggest and most power-ful drug lord. About eighty per cent of the cocaine on the streets of Britain comes from his cartel. It's thought that he imports coca leaves from Colombia and processes them into cocaine in labs hidden in the Mexican jungle. He's impulsive and charming. He's also probably the most violent man in Central America – and if you understand anything about the politics of the area, you'll know that's really saying something.'

Michael tapped his keypad again. The image changed to a grainy, black-and-white photograph and it took a moment for Zak to work out what it showed. There was a dusty street with poor-looking shacks along either side. Lying on the ground, its body twisted, was a corpse. 'This photograph was taken about six months ago. The body belongs to one of Martinez's associates who saw fit to embezzle money from him. He was found shot by the side of the road.'

A third picture appeared.

It showed a tree with a low, overhanging branch. Suspended from the branch by their necks were five bodies, semi-rotted, two of them children. 'Martinez has a penchant for the hangman's noose,' Michael said quietly. 'The guy you just saw with a bullet in his head? These are the bodies of his wife, his two children, his sister and brother. They were hanged in their village as a warning for anyone else who thought it might be a good idea to cross Martinez. Nobody dared touch them until the flesh had rotted from the bones. Even then, nobody gave them a decent burial for fear of upsetting him.'

Zak stared in horror at the picture, his eyes lingering on the corpses of the children. It changed to an image of another man, who was almost as chilling as the picture of the corpses. He was incredibly skinny with a shaven head and a stubbly beard. But it wasn't his hair that fascinated Zak; it was his right eye – or lack of it. The skin had grown over the empty socket, so it looked as if the eye had never been there.

'Adan Ramirez,' Michael said. 'Nickname *Calaca*, which means "skeleton". I wouldn't call him that to his face, though. He's Martinez's head of security, the man who does his dirty work. Martinez is the business brain behind the operation, the kingpin. But Calaca's the brawn. It's impossible to say how many men he's killed. Chances are that he doesn't even know himself. I imagine you probably stop counting after the first couple of dozen.'

Calaca's good eye stared out from the whiteboard. 'He looks like a total psycho,' Zak said.

'That's not a bad description,' replied Michael. 'He is well suited for the jobs Martinez gives him. But he shouldn't be underestimated. Calaca is a very shrewd operator, in some ways shrewder than Martinez himself.' Michael was staring at Zak, who felt a bit uncomfortable.

'If Martinez is such a monster,' he said, 'why don't the Mexican government do something about him?'

'That's a good question, Zak. The answer is pretty simple: corruption. Martinez is one of the richest men in the world. That puts him in a very powerful position because it means he can bribe high-ranking members of the government. For years now, both the British and Americans have put pressure on the Mexican government to bring Martinez to book. But he has them in his pocket. As long as he keeps greasing palms in Mexico City, he's untouchable.'

'That's awful,' Zak said.

'Yes,' Michael replied. 'It is. Which is why something needs to be done about it.'

The old man stood up from his desk and started to pace the room between Zak and the whiteboard. 'Tell me, Zak,' he said. 'Are you a keen student of Greek mythology?'

'Er . . . no, not really.'

'That's a great shame. The ancients have a great deal to teach us. Let me tell you about the city of Troy. It's said that the Greeks laid siege to it for ten years, but because its walls were so tall and sturdy, they couldn't get into the city. So in the end, they stopped using force and started using their brains. One of their commanders was a man named Odysseus. He instructed his soldiers to build an enormous wooden horse. It was hollow, so that some of the Greeks could hide inside it. When it was finished, they left it at the gates of Troy as a gift, then the entire Greek army – apart from those who were inside the horse – retreated from sight. The Trojans thought the Greeks had departed for good and they brought the horse into the city. That night, when everyone was in bed, the soldiers hidden inside the horse crept out and opened the city gates. The Greeks flooded in and put every last man in Troy to the sword.'

'Messy,' Zak said.

'Yes. I rather think it would have been.'

'What's this got to do with Martinez?'

Michael raised one eyebrow slightly. 'Martinez,' he said, 'is like the Trojans. He has a wall around him too, in the form of an extensive personal guard. He lives in a compound approximately three miles south of Mexico City and his security is more robust than any world leader. To lead an assault on the Martinez compound would be like sparking a small-scale war; not to mention breaking I don't know how many international laws.'

He stared straight at Zak. 'What we need,' he said, 'is a Trojan Horse.'

The moment he said that, Gabs stepped forward. She and Raf had been standing next to each other behind Michael's desk, quietly listening to his presentation. Now her face looked concerned. 'Michael,' she said, 'you can't be thinking of sending Zak in—'

'*Gabriella!*' Michael spoke like a teacher. '*Please!*'

Gabs looked down at the floor, but she couldn't hide her anxiety. Nor could Raf who, although he had remained quiet, was frowning with uncertainty.

Michael turned his attention back to Zak. 'I want you to be our Trojan Horse,' he said.

Zak glanced back towards the image on the whiteboard. Calaca gazed back at him.

'Are you saying you want me to kill Martinez?' he asked.

Michael shook his head. 'No. You're not an assassin, Zak. And in any case, we want Martinez alive. Nobody in the world knows more about the cartels waiting in the wings to take over if and when he dies or gets brought to justice. If we're to stop someone just as bad from replacing him, we need that information. And we need it now. The British government want Martinez brought to book and they're prepared to risk a war with the Mexicans to do it. They're already making their preparations. If we can get our hands on him first, we can stop that.'

'This should be the Americans' job,' Gabs interrupted. 'Mexico's on their doorstep.'

'The Americans aren't willing to risk it,' Michael

said. 'A major diplomatic incident on their southern border is the last thing they need, and in any case they know how clever Martinez is. Evidence of his activities is impossible to find. He's a skilled operator who keeps himself totally separate from anything that would incriminate him. No, the only thing that can bring Martinez down is us. And the only way we can get close to him is if we have somebody on the inside. We plan to insert an agent into his compound in the hope that they can get proof of his activities. Once they've done that, they'll need to direct a special forces team into the compound to abduct him. If we have Martinez in custody *and* evidence of his drug trafficking, the Mexican authorities will hardly be in a position to complain. Do you understand everything I've said so far?'

Zak nodded. He didn't quite trust himself to speak and not sound terrified.

'Martinez is a very careful man. We've known for some time that he employs body doubles, much like Saddam Hussein used to in Iraq. Martinez's body doubles are better than Saddam's ever were. Our intelligence suggests that there are five of them, and they've all undergone extensive plastic surgery to make them indistinguishable from their master. Plus, they've studied his gait and his mannerisms. Our understanding is that it's extremely difficult to tell which is the real Martinez, but we're hoping that if somebody gets close enough, they'll be able to do it.'

Zak frowned. 'But . . . you can't expect me to break in to Martinez's compound without anybody knowing—'

'Zak,' Michael interrupted, 'you haven't been listening. Think of the Trojan Horse. The Greeks didn't have to send it into the city covertly – the Trojans brought it in themselves.' He pressed his keypad yet again and Calaca disappeared. A new face replaced him. It was a boy, about Zak's age, maybe a little older. With his black hair and dark eyes he looked very like Martinez himself. But there were differences. While Martinez's face had been emotionless, this one was more expressive. There was something sad about him. Something wary.

'This,' Michael said, 'is Cruz, Martinez's son. Look at his picture closely, Zak, because Cruz Martinez is about to become your new best friend.'

11

DECISION TIME

Zak stared at the picture.

'When I say that Cruz is to become *your* best friend,' Michael continued, 'what I mean is that he's to become Harry Gold's best friend. It's very important – and I can't stress this enough – that the moment we take you away from this island, you leave Zak Darke behind. You're fully familiar with Harry Gold's past, so you must be aware of his great-uncle Frank?'

It was like flicking a switch as Zak started to spout everything he knew. 'Frank Gold,' he said. 'Born 1931 in Blackburn, brother of Harry's paternal grandfather John. Never married, no children. Worked as a structural engineer until emigrating to Mexico in 1995.' His eyes narrowed. '*Mexico . . .*' he repeated

Michael was nodding in satisfaction. It clearly pleased him that Zak could remember this informa-tion so well. He brought up a new picture on the whiteboard: a thin, elderly man with a lined face, a bald head and sharp eyes. 'Meet your great-uncle,' he said. 'You look confused. What's wrong?'

'I don't know.' Zak shrugged. 'I guess I kind of thought all these relatives of Harry's were as made-up as him.'

'Some are,' Michael said, 'and some aren't. That's the art of deception. The best lies are the ones that have an element of truth in them. Remember that. Of course, it's probably crossed your mind that Frank Gold might not be everything he seems. He is, in fact, a long-serving MI6 field operative.'

'What's his real name?'

Michael sighed. 'This obsession with real names, Zak. You really must let go of it. If you think things through, you'll realize how important it is that you don't know Frank's "real" name any more than he should know yours. After all, there's no way you can give up information you don't have, is there?'

'No,' Zak replied. 'I guess not.'

'As you're aware, Frank Gold has been living in Mexico City for the best part of fifteen years. His cover is good and he's melted into the local community. He's part of the scenery, really. And as luck would have it, he's just extended an invitation to Harry to come and stay with him for a year. Frank was very upset by the death of Harry's parents, you see, and would like to do what he can for the lad –

especially as Harry's Spanish is excellent and he's shown a real interest in Mexican culture.' He looked over at Gabs. 'Harry's Spanish *is* excellent, isn't it?'

Gabs nodded mutely and Michael winked at Zak, looking rather pleased with his deception; but the mention of dead parents had been like a knife in Zak's guts, and he just looked down.

Michael continued talking. He didn't appear to notice Zak's pain. 'Of course, as Harry's guardian, Frank needs to make sure that his great-nephew continues his schooling, so he has enrolled Harry into the *Colegio de Mexico*, one of the finest educational establishments in the capital. This also happens to be the school that Cruz Martinez attends.'

'How convenient,' Zak murmured.

'Isn't it though? Harry needs to make friends with him, Zak. Good friends. Hopefully that will give you a reason for being in Martinez's compound, but after that it's up to you. Remember, your primary objective is to locate hard evidence regarding Martinez's involvement in drug trafficking. I can't tell you what that evidence will be. You just have to use your intuition. Once you've gathered enough evidence, you'll need to guide a special forces assault team into the compound, locate Martinez – *not* one of his body doubles – and help them abduct him.'

'Michael,' Gabs said. 'This is too much for his

first assignment. It's too difficult, too dangerous . . .'

Michael ignored her. 'You'll need this,' he said, and he handed something to Zak. It was an iPhone, slightly scuffed around the edges as though someone had already been using it. 'It's been modified,' Michael explained. 'You need to keep it on you all the time. It contains a highly advanced GPS tracking chip that we've attached to the SIM card cradle.'

'All phones have GPS chips these days,' Zak said.

'Not like this. It has its own built-in power source and can transmit much more powerful signals than most GPS devices. Special forces use these in the jungle where ordinary GPS chips get blocked by the canopy overhead.'

Zak glanced over at Raf. 'I thought I wasn't supposed to rely on GPS for navigation anyway.'

'You're not. This isn't for navigating, Zak. It's for us to know exactly where you are at any given moment. We have spy satellite technology – a dedicated satellite, just to follow you. This means that at a control centre in London we can have constant, real-time satellite images of where you are at all times. These images are very detailed – at least, they are during the daytime. It's like having your very own security camera pointing right at you. There will be a special forces team inserted in-country close to Martinez's compound. If you raise the alarm, they'll be there to pick you up in minutes.'

'How does he raise the alarm?' Gabs asked. She looked as nervous as Zak felt.

'By dialling one of two four-digit numbers. Six-four-eight-two means you're compromised and need to be extracted. Five-eight-six-nine means you're ready to guide in the SF team to abduct Martinez – but you can't do that *until* you have evidence of his criminal activities. The phone also comes with a high-resolution camera and scanning mechanism, as well as all the standard audio and video recording capabilities. There will be a constant data connection wherever you are in the world, which will allow you to upload any evidence to a secure server then delete it from the phone. You'll need to spend some time getting used to that device, Zak. It's your lifeline.'

Zak turned the phone over in his hand. It was cool and everything, but as lifelines went, it didn't seem like much. 'I don't suppose it makes phone calls as well, does it?' he asked.

Michael smiled. 'As a matter of fact, it does. But once you're inside the Martinez compound, you can't make any.'

'Why not?'

'The data connection is secure, but voice messages are easy to intercept. In any case, Martinez's compound is more than likely to be bugged to high heaven. You need to rely on the fact that we will know where you are at all times, and not contact us unless you're dialling the distress code.'

He handed something else to Zak. It was a credit card, platinum in colour, with the words *Coutts & Co* written on it in copperplate. 'Coutts are a private bank in London. When Harry's parents died, they left him a lot of money. An account has been set up in his name with a large sum deposited for you to draw on.'

'How much?' Zak asked, intrigued.

'A large sum. Should it start to dwindle, we'll replenish it. It's important for your safety that you should be able to get hold of money if you need it, but it would look suspicious if you went for weeks without spending anything and then suddenly let it be seen that you were wealthy. So you need to start spending from day one. Act like a rich kid. Buy whatever you want.'

'Anything?' Nobody had ever said this to him before – growing up, money had always been tight.

'Anything. Clothes, gadgets – if you see something you like, buy it. Even if you don't like it, buy it. It's an important part of your cover, and your cover is everything. You can't give anyone any reason to be suspicious of you. When Frank meets you at the airport, you greet him like a long-lost friend. You don't talk to him about your real reason for being in Mexico City unless you are absolutely sure nobody can overhear you or even watch your lips moving. Even when you're alone you'd be wise to keep quiet about it. The best way to make other people believe you really are Harry Gold is to act like you believe it yourself at all times.'

A silence descended on the room. It had all been a lot to take in and Zak felt confused. He was also alarmed by Gabs's reaction. She was no coward, so for her to be worried about the dangers of infiltrating Martinez's compound was unnerving.

'There's something else you need to know,' Michael said. He looked at Raf and Gabs. 'All three of you. The special forces unit will consist of six commandos, and will have an armed helicopter at its disposal with a special forces flight crew. Raphael, Gabriella, you're to join them. You've trained Zak and you know him. I want you there in case he needs any backup. The SF unit will be under your personal command.'

For the first time during that meeting, Gabs smiled. Not a smile of happiness, but of relief.

'The commandos will be taken from the Counter Revolutionary Warfare wing of the SAS,' he continued. 'This means they're highly vetted and the closest we can get to an entirely secure unit. They are also well used to deniable missions. And *this*, ladies and gentlemen, is very much a deniable mission. That means that if anything goes wrong, the British government will deny all knowledge.'

Michael looked at each of them in turn. 'And now,' he said, 'if you don't mind, I'd like a few words with Zak alone.'

Raf and Gabs looked a bit surprised, but they didn't argue. As she walked past Zak towards the door, Gabs gave him an encouraging little smile. And then he was alone with Michael.

The old man didn't speak for a minute. He just looked at Zak with those intense green eyes. In the end, Zak couldn't hold his gaze and he glanced downwards.

'You probably think,' Michael said finally, 'that I'm treating you rather badly.'

'I don't know what to think,' Zak said, and it was the truth.

'You need to understand that I wouldn't be activating you if I didn't think that you were up to the job. But that doesn't mean you have to go. There's no obligation. The choice is yours.'

Zak thought about that for a moment before replying. 'When I first came here, you said you'd tell me about my parents when the time was right. I think the time is right now. Tell me what you know and maybe I'll think about going to Mexico.'

Michael inclined his head. 'I don't blame you for trying to negotiate, Zak. It's what I'd do in your situation. But I'm afraid the answer's still no. The time will come when you'll understand why but that time hasn't arrived yet. You need to make a decision without any thoughts of your parents clouding your judgement. And you need to make it now, Zak.'

Zak stood up. He walked over to the tall windows and looked out over the island. The sun that had been so bright when he woke up was now clouded over. It didn't surprise Zak – the weather could change so quickly in this remote place and now it looked as windy and bleak as it always did.

'What happens if I say no?' he asked.

'Then you stay here with Raphael and Gabriella. Continue your training and wait for something more' – Michael sounded like he was searching for a word – 'more *appropriate* to come along. Of course, if you continue to refuse activation, there's a limit to how long you'll remain useful to us.'

'And what then?'

'What then indeed.'

Another pause.

'I'll do you a deal,' Michael said.

That made Zak turn around. 'I didn't think you were in the habit of making deals,' he said.

'I'm not. But in this instance . . . Go to Mexico. Infiltrate the Martinez compound. Try to find the evidence we need. If you don't, we'll pull you out and bring you back here. Either way I promise you – and it is a solemn promise – that next time we meet, I'll tell you what happened to your parents.'

Michael's face was serious. So serious that it didn't even occur to Zak to doubt him.

'You can pull me out any time?' he asked.

'Any time,' Michael replied.

Zak nodded then turned to look out of the window again. 'What if Cruz doesn't take a shine to me?' he asked. 'A lot of people don't at school. I mean, *didn't*.'

Michael walked up to where Zak was standing. He stood next to him and also gazed out across the bleak scenery. 'The secret to a successful operation,' he said in a quiet voice, 'is not to leave anything to chance.' He put one hand on Zak's shoulder. 'Cruz will take a shine to you. Martinez too, for that matter. I can absolutely promise you that. We've got it all worked out.'

It started to spit with rain, but compared to a drug lord's compound, this bleak island no longer felt so unwelcoming.

'What happens if this Martinez guy doesn't get brought to justice?' Zak asked.

'Families will continue to die. Innocent children. And not just in Mexico, Zak. The drugs that he sends into the UK ruin more lives than we can even count.'

Zak dug his fingernails into the palm of his hand.

He felt like he was on the edge of a cliff and didn't have the courage to take the final step.

'Yes or no, Zak. That's all you have to say. Your decision.'

Zak took a deep breath. He glanced over his shoulder at the picture of Cruz staring from the white-board into the room, then he looked back out of the window at the darkening sky.

And finally he spoke.

'Yes,' he said.

Michael nodded. 'Good. Then you need to listen carefully, Zak. I promised you that Cruz was to become your best friend. This is how we're going to do it . . .'

PART TWO

PART TWO

12

UNCLE FRANK

One week later

'Another Coke, Mr Gold?'

Zak smiled up at the air hostess. 'Yeah,' he said. 'Why not? Thanks.'

Harry Gold's booking on flight VS892 from London Heathrow to Mexico City International Airport was in first class, which meant his seat was large – and spacious enough to convert into a bed – and he could ask for pretty much anything he liked. Trouble was, although he thought he was doing a good job of pretending to be used to such luxury, inside he was churned up. He flicked through the films available on his personal TV set. Nothing grabbed him, so he forced down a meal of smoked salmon and rare beef, washed down with a couple more Cokes, then slept for the remainder of the journey.

137

Once they'd landed, he had to wait ages for his luggage – two expensive Louis Vuitton suitcases that he had bought on a shopping spree in Harrods just a couple of days ago.

It had been a strange week. The day after his long conversation with Michael, a helicopter had arrived to escort him off the island. Michael and Raf had shaken his hand; Gabs had been on the verge of tears. She'd handed him a present, wrapped up in blue tissue paper. Zak had unwrapped it to find a belt. 'But not an ordinary belt,' Gabs had said. 'Look.' She'd loosened the buckle to pull out a thin, exquisitely sharp blade. Zak couldn't help thinking the gift was a bit like Gabs herself. Stylish, elegant . . . but deadly. 'Be careful, sweetie,' she'd said. 'Remember everything you've learned.' And then she'd hugged him.

The chopper had escorted him back over the rough waters to the Scottish mainland, south into England and had set him down on a deserted helipad ten miles west of St Albans. There, a car was waiting. It was a black Daimler with tinted windows; the driver was grim-faced and didn't speak a word to Zak as he navigated to the M1, drove him into London and dropped him off outside a grand mansion block in Knightsbridge. Zak had known for some months that Harry Gold had a flat just off the Brompton Road, but he hadn't really expected to have full use of it. It was huge. The kitchen itself was bigger than the ground floor of his uncle and aunt's house and the fridge was stuffed full of food; there were three bedrooms and a games room with a full-size snooker table, a Wii, a PlayStation and an Xbox. Zak had felt a brief pang that he had nobody to share all this with. For an irrational moment he thought of calling Ellie – he even got so far as pulling out his specially modified iPhone to dial the number, but he stopped himself at the last second. He knew how stupid that would be. No, he'd just have to stick it out, anonymous, in this luxurious flat until the time came to travel to Mexico.

Whenever he did step outside – to go shopping or just to get some air – he kept his hood firmly over his head. London was a big place, but it was perfectly possible that someone from his previous life might recognize him. That would mean some explaining that he *really* didn't want to do.

The moment to leave had arrived quickly, and now here he was, suitcases in hand, walking into the arrivals lounge of Mexico City International Airport, Terminal 2. It was 5 p.m. on Sunday afternoon, but the place was busy. An echoing public address system piped flight information into the terminal in Spanish; Zak was slightly surprised to realize that he could instantly translate it. All around him his fellow passengers appeared eager to get into the terminal: there were serious-faced businessmen wearing suits and carrying briefcases; holidaymakers in bright shirts; families rushing towards each other to hug and be reunited. Zak felt separate from all of them as they hurried past him. He set his suitcases on the ground and scanned a small crowd of waiting cab drivers. There were about ten of them, all holding pieces of cardboard scrawled with the names of the passengers for whom they were waiting. Their skin was swarthy and sweaty, and they all wore rough clothes.

Beside this crowd of cab drivers, one man stuck out. He was taller than the others by a good head height, and older too with a lined face and sharp, narrow eyes. Unlike the cab drivers, his skin was white and his head almost entirely bald. Zak immediately recognized him from a picture Michael had shown him. Even if he hadn't, the knowing stare with which he fixed Zak would have revealed his identity. Zak gave him a nervous smile and walked in his direction.

'Young Harry!' the man said. His loud voice didn't suit his thin body. 'Let your old uncle Frank have a look at you, lad. Last time we met you were just a babe in arms.'

Zak felt like he was on stage. 'Hi, Uncle Frank,' he said, dropping his suitcases and holding out one hand.

Frank ignored it and embraced Zak instead, grabbing him in a big bear hug. 'Keep it up,' he whispered, barely loud enough for Zak to hear over the noise of the airport. 'We can talk in the car.' He let go of Zak. 'I'll take one of those, hey?' he said, his voice loud again. He picked up a suitcase and together they walked towards the exit.

The moment Zak walked out of the airport terminal, it was like stepping into a wall of heat. His skin tingled with sweat and humidity and he felt like he was breathing in a furnace. 'Warm day,' Frank observed. 'Not as hot as it has been, but I suppose it's a bit parkier in grey old London.'

'Yeah,' Zak replied. 'You could say that.'

Frank had parked nearby. His car was nothing special – an old Ford that looked as if it had seen better days. Zak's suitcases just fitted in the boot, and when he took his place in the front, his skin smarted against the hot plastic covering of the seats. Frank started the engine and flicked a switch on the dashboard. 'Important to have air conditioning in Mexico City,' he said. 'It's one of the most polluted places on earth.' And then, in a lower voice: 'In more ways than one.' He pulled out of the car park and joined a queue of traffic leaving the airport.

They sat in silence for a good fifteen minutes while Zak looked out of the window, checking out Harry's new home. Mexico City – at least the bit of it he'd seen so far – was a sprawling, dirty place. A choking cloud of fumes seemed to hover overhead, and the fierce sun glinted off the hundreds of cars that honked and snarled their way around the outskirts.

Frank put the radio on, then twisted the dial until he found a spoken-word station. Two men were arguing about something in Spanish, and it sounded pretty heated. When Frank himself spoke it was in a quiet voice. 'The voices on the radio should mask our conversation if anyone's listening in,' he said.

Zak peered nervously over his shoulder. 'Do you think anyone is?'

'No,' Frank shook his head. 'But I won't take any risks and neither must you. My house isn't very big and I sweep it for bugs twice a day. But when we're there, we don't say anything about your real reason for being in Mexico. All right?'

'All right.'

'You're enrolled at the *colegio* from tomorrow morning. You've got three days to settle in, then you make contact with Cruz on Thursday. Are you comfortable with the arrangements?'

Zak's face darkened. 'I guess so,' he said.

Frank nodded and he gave Zak a sidelong glance. All the good humour he had displayed back at the airport had fallen away and he was now rather severe.

'You're younger than I thought,' he said. 'I hope they know what they're doing, sending you out here. Martinez isn't the sort of guy you want to underestimate.'

Zak didn't reply. He looked out of the window again and thought of the dead bodies Michael had shown him – the family of Martinez's enemy.

They continued to drive in silence.

Frank's house was in an unassuming suburb of Mexico City. The house itself was a bungalow, identical to all the others that stretched along both sides of the street. There was a dusty yard at the front, and a shaded veranda with a wooden bench, a table and a hammock. Brown shutters on the windows meant that the inside was dark, but at least it was a little cooler, thanks to a series of rotating fans that hung from the ceiling. Zak's bedroom was small and simply furnished: a bed, a fan, a cupboard and a small table. The window looked out into a back yard which had a small patch of lawn. It was the only one, Zak noticed, as he pushed open the shutters and looked along the line of back yards, that had any greenery.

'An Englishman's home is his castle, eh Harry?' Frank was standing in the doorway of his room and his jolly nature had returned. 'Couldn't do without a bit of lawn. Course, it's not quite what you're used to, but I hope you won't mind slumming it with your old Uncle Frank for a bit.' He pointed at a new rucksack on the desk. 'School books in there, old boy. Everything you need – they sent me a list. Also paper, pens and pencils. Got you all kitted out for your big day tomorrow . . .'

That evening they ate a Mexican meal – tacos and refried beans – sitting out on the veranda. It was a relief when dusk came and the temperature grew a bit cooler. Children from the neighbouring houses came out to play football. They all noticed Zak, the new-comer; a few of them pointed at him. 'You'll soon become part of the furniture, Harry,' Frank said as he bit into a taco. 'I'm sure everything seems a bit un-familiar, but you'll soon find your feet. And I've no doubt you'll make some good friends at school.'

They exchanged a glance and Zak remembered the picture of Cruz Martinez. 'I hope so,' he said, and they finished their meal in silence.

13

CONTACT

Colegio de Mexico wasn't a bit like school as Zak remembered it. Situated in a street named Avenida Luis Peron in the heart of a southern district of Mexico City, it was a vast complex ringed by a three-metre-high grey concrete wall. It was a little before eight o'clock in the morning when Frank and Zak pulled up in front of the main entrance. Here, the name of the school was carved into the concrete wall, and crowds of students with rucksacks slung over their backs were already entering. 'Make sure you've got this area scouted out,' Frank said below the sound of the radio.

Zak nodded and looked around. In front of the gate was a pavement, about five metres deep. Avenida Luis Peron itself was twenty metres wide and on the other side, behind some iron railings, was a park – a pleasant place with benches and trees for shade. The road itself was busy, though not as log-jammed as some Zak had seen so far.

He turned his attention to the school gates and the nagging sense of panic that he'd had with him since he woke up grew stronger. The prospect of walking into this strange school, an unknown foreigner, wasn't very appealing. But he couldn't put it off. 'I'd better go,' he said.

'Wait,' Frank replied, and he looked meaningfully into the rear-view mirror. A convoy of three vehicles was arriving: a black Mercedes with dark windows and personalized number plates flanked by two black Range Rovers, the windows also blacked-out. The Mercedes pulled in to the kerb just in front of Frank's car; the Range Rovers remained stationary in the middle of the road. The drivers, whoever they were, were clearly ignoring the beeping horns of the vehicles jammed behind them because they were blocking the traffic.

Frank put a hand on Zak's arm. 'Watch,' he said.

The two front doors of the Mercedes opened at precisely the same time and a man emerged from each one. They were both dressed the same, in black suits and dark glasses, and Zak immediately identified the guns they were carrying – the MP5 Kurz – weapons especially designed for close-quarter urban battle. The man on the pavement side opened the back door and waited for a figure to emerge.

When he did, Zak caught his breath. He recognized the newcomer immediately. It was Cruz.

CONTACT

Cruz Martinez was very slight – gangly almost, with thin limbs and arms that looked a little bit too long for his body. His hair was black and he wore very ordinary clothes: blue jeans, white trainers and a green T-shirt. If it weren't for the armed guards, Zak reckoned he'd have passed him in the street and not given him a second look. Cruz looked awkward, though. As he stepped out of the car he barely acknowledged the armed chauffeur. It was almost, Zak thought, as if he hardly saw them.

Zak turned his attention back to the sub-machine-guns. 'That's what I call a chaperone,' he said.

'Martinez wouldn't have it any other way.' Frank scratched his nose as he spoke so that his hand was covering his mouth. 'It's how things are done in Mexico. He knows that if someone wants to get to him, they'll go for his family first. Cruz lives a danger-ous life. If he didn't have those bodyguards, he'd be abducted before he knew it.' The old man removed his hand from his face. 'Well, Harry,' he said with a bright smile, 'it's five to eight. Time for school. Have a good day, won't you? I'll pick you up later.'

'Yeah,' Zak said. 'Later.'

He stepped out of the car and into the hot morning air.

The two armed men accompanied Cruz to the gates. Zak noticed how the other students stepped

147

aside to let him through, their eyes lingering on the bodyguards' weapons. None of them spoke to Cruz. The bodyguards didn't cross over the threshold, however. One of them returned to the car; the other took up position at the school gates. Nobody argued with him, or suggested it was inappropriate for an armed man to be standing outside the school. Zak sensed that this was just normal. That nobody was going to quarrel with him . . .

By the time Zak got to the gates, Cruz had already gone into school and was nowhere to be seen. And as he walked into the school grounds, Zak sensed that Cruz and his guards were no longer the curiosity. *He* was. With his white skin and unfamiliar face, he attracted the stares of everyone he passed. He felt his skin prickle, but he kept his head up high and headed across the playground.

The school was a modern building. It was a place for the very rich, and looked like it. Three storeys high, it was surrounded by reflective glass which gleamed in the bright morning sunshine. Zak noticed that all the students, who were filing into an entrance in the middle of the ground floor, were well dressed in the latest trainers and expensive jeans. He was glad that he had taken Michael's advice and got himself kitted out back in London with several sets of Converse trainers and Diesel jeans.

As he entered the main building, he saw a reception desk to his left. A woman with half-moon glasses and tightly pinned-back grey hair sat there. Zak approached and, in his best Spanish, explained who he was. 'My name's Harry Gold. I'm new here . . .'

Five minutes later, the woman was leading him down a long corridor on the top floor of the school and into a classroom. There were twenty other pupils in there, each sitting at individual desks. Even though there was no teacher, they were quiet, their mathematics books open in front of them. When Zak appeared, they gave him curious glances – neither friendly nor unfriendly, but not exactly welcoming. And in the far corner of the room, at the window end of the back row, sat Cruz. Unlike the other students, he didn't seem all that interested in Zak's arrival. He just stared out of the window.

There were two spare desks in the room. One was next to Cruz at the back; the other was up front. It took a Zak a split second to take the front desk. He wanted to get close to Cruz, it was true, but he couldn't be obvious about it. Pretend to be the guy's best friend from day one and he might get suspicious. And besides, as Michael had said back in the UK, they had things all worked out . . .

The maths teacher arrived – Señor Valdez, a short, fat man with a splendid moustache. He noticed Zak, the new boy, immediately. 'Welcome in Mexico City,' he said in awkward English.

'Er, thanks,' Zak replied.

'You are liking mathematics, yes?' Señor Valdez's eyes twinkled and he reverted to Spanish. 'Write this down,' he instructed the class, before scrawling a list of calculations on the board.

Zak was surprised by how much Spanish he understood. When Señor Valdez started asking questions, Zak kept quiet. It wasn't that he didn't know the answers; he just wanted to keep a low profile.

The morning dragged. With the exception of an occasional 'ola', the other students largely ignored him, but that suited Zak fine. During the mid-morning break, when everybody went outside, he sneaked into an empty third-floor classroom overlooking the playground and watched through the protection of the mirrored glass. From his vantage point, he could see the entire playground. Little groups of people had formed, little cliques. But no clique formed around Cruz Martinez; on the contrary, people were avoiding him. He paced the length of the school wall like a prisoner pacing the prison yard. From this distance, Zak couldn't see the expression on his face, but he could see that Cruz's shoulders were a little hunched, his gait plodding.

'*Señor Gold!*'

Zak spun round to see Sanchez the maths teacher in the doorway.

'*Sí*, señor?' he asked, his Spanish accent almost faultless.

'It is not healthy to stay indoors on such a beautiful day.'

Zak gave him an apologetic look. 'I'm not used to this climate yet,' he said. 'It would be too hot for me there.'

'But Señor Gold, it is important for the new pupils to make friends.' The maths teacher stroked his moustache and his eyes sparkled.

'I will, señor,' Zak said. 'I promise.'

Sanchez gave a little shrug, then turned round and left. The truth was that setting himself up as a loner was all part of Zak's game plan. He went back to watching Cruz. It wasn't like Zak had even spoken to him, but he already felt he knew something about Cruz Martinez. Everybody knew of his father's reputation – how could they not, when Cruz was taken to school every day by an armed convoy? The other pupils in the school gave him a wide berth, not out of respect but out of fear. Perhaps their parents had told them to stay away from the Martinez kid; perhaps they didn't need telling. Whatever the truth, Zak sensed that Cruz was a bit dismissive of his schoolmates, but also lonely. He knew why the others avoided him, and he knew that wouldn't change any time soon. When the time came, Zak wanted Cruz to think of him as a kindred spirit.

For the rest of the morning, Zak spoke to nobody. He was quiet and studious in lessons; at lunch time he kept himself to himself.

In the mid-afternoon English lesson, the teacher – a tall woman with dark skin and honey-coloured hair – announced that they were to split into pairs and have conversations in English. Almost immediately, the rest of the class started shuffling around, quickly teaming up with their friends. Nobody offered to pair with Zak, and after about thirty seconds it was clear that there was only one other person left to be his partner.

'Harry,' the teacher announced, 'you can go with Cruz. Hurry up now, we haven't got all day . . .'

Zak felt his eyes twitch, but he tried to look unconcerned as Cruz stared at him from across the classroom. Zak stood up and walked over to where the Mexican boy was sitting. 'Hi,' he said casually, taking a seat. 'I'm Harry.'

'I know,' Cruz replied in surprisingly good English. He had a scowl on his face, and somehow Zak just knew it was because no one had wanted to partner up with him.

'I saw you arrive this morning,' Zak said in an innocent tone of voice. 'That was quite a convoy.'

CONTACT

Cruz shrugged. 'My father is a businessman,' he said. 'A wealthy one. There's a risk I might be kidnapped.'

'What sort of business?' Zak asked.

Cruz sniffed. 'Just business,' he said.

An awkward silence.

'I understand,' Zak said. 'My dad was a successful businessman too, before he died. We had to be careful.'

Cruz looked interested. 'Your father is dead?'

Zak nodded.

'It is my biggest fear, that my father should die,' said Cruz. And then he looked embarrassed by what he'd said.

'Your English is very good.' Zak paid him a compliment to keep the conversation going.

'And so is your Spanish,' said Cruz – in Spanish. 'How come?'

Zak shrugged. 'I learned it at school.'

'Why have you come to Mexico City?'

'To stay with family.' The lies rolled easily off Zak's tongue, and Cruz showed no sign of disbelieving him. 'And to see Mexico.'

'Some parts of Mexico aren't worth seeing,' said Cruz.

'I guess I'd better stick to the parts that are, then.'

'I could show you around,' Cruz offered. As he

153

spoke, he avoided Zak's eye, as if he wasn't comfortable with making friends like this.

Zak chose his words carefully. He didn't want to sound too keen, or say anything that would arouse suspicion. 'Yeah,' he replied with a little shrug. 'Maybe.'

All of a sudden the teacher was there, standing over Zak's shoulder. 'Cruz, Harry, how are you getting along?' she asked.

The two boys looked at each other. 'Fine,' Cruz said, almost smiling. 'We're getting along fine.'

Frank was waiting for Zak outside the gates at half past four. Cruz's armed guard was still there, standing motionless in the intense heat. As Zak approached Frank, he heard a voice from behind. 'See you tomorrow, Harry,' Cruz called in Spanish. Zak looked round to see his new friend emerging from the school gates. He smiled at Cruz, but instantly his bodyguard closed in on him and hustled him towards the waiting Mercedes.

Neither Zak nor Frank spoke until they were in the car. 'Looks like you made contact,' Frank said over the babbling radio as he pulled away.

'The bodyguard doesn't seem too pleased about it,' Zak noticed.

'Guess the stooge drew the short straw,' Frank said.

CONTACT

'What do you mean?'

'Well, I don't suppose standing outside the school all day waiting for someone to take a shot at Cruz Martinez is exactly what he signed up for.'

Zak glanced in the side mirror and caught a glimpse of the bodyguard escorting Cruz away from the entrance. 'Well,' he said, 'things will liven up for him on Thursday, right?'

Frank glanced at him and raised one eyebrow. 'Right,' he said.

For the next two days, Zak kept his distance from Cruz. He was friendly enough when they encountered each other, but not so friendly that anyone might suspect he was trying to get too close. 'Like fishing,' Frank said as they drove to school on the second day. 'Let the fish see the bait, not the hook. Otherwise you spook the little fella. Cruz has got to come to you – not the other way round.'

Their journey to school served a double purpose: to get Zak to lessons on time, and to become familiar with Cruz Martinez's routine. Zak remembered Michael's words: *The secret to a successful operation is not to leave anything to chance . . .*

On Tuesday morning, Cruz arrived at school at 07.55 hrs precisely. Zak and Frank were there to clock it.

155

On Wednesday morning, the same time. His minders had a timetable, and they stuck to it.

On Thursday morning, though, the routine was going to change.

Zak woke from a restless night's sleep before the sun was even up and he could hear Frank moving around the house already. They'd both been on edge the previous night and had gone to bed early. Zak got dressed: jeans, a black T-shirt and sturdy but comfortable, ankle-high Converse trainers. From his drawer he took the belt Gabs had given him and strapped it round his waist, and he slipped his phone into his pocket. For some reason it made him feel a bit better.

He went into the kitchen where Frank was drinking coffee. 'Harry, old boy. Have yourself some breakfast. Going to be a long day. Eggs OK? *Huevos?*'

There were two different Franks, Zak had decided. The affable one who appeared whenever there was even a remote possibility of someone listening in; and the abrupt one who appeared when they were talking in private. Zak thought of them as Fun Frank and Fierce Frank. The man speaking now was Fun Frank; but he had Fierce Frank's eyes and Zak understood why. To say that today would be a long day was the understatement of the year.

Frank cooked a plate of fried eggs while Zak sipped at some orange juice. He didn't really feel hungry but he ate anyway. He was going to need it.

They left the house at 07.20 hrs exactly. The journey to school only took twenty minutes, but it was important they built in time for any eventualities. 'You know what you're doing?' Frank asked over the noise of the radio.

Zak nodded.

They turned a corner into Avenida Luis Peron. Frank drove on for about twenty metres, then pulled over. They were fifty metres from the school gates, and the students were already filtering in. 'Anyone asks us why we're sitting here, let me do the talking,' Frank said.

Zak checked his watch. 07.43 hours. Cruz should be arriving in twelve minutes. He wiped his sweating palms on his jeans and kept his gaze firmly in the rear-view mirror while Frank kept the engine turning over.

07.50 hrs.

'They should be here in five minutes,' Zak said.

'Don't tell me when they *should* be here,' Fierce Frank replied. 'Tell me when they *are* here.'

07.52 hrs. Zak ran through their plan in his head for the tenth time that morning. He licked his dry lips as the minutes ticked down.

07.54 hrs. In the rear-view mirror he saw a black Range Rover turn the corner into the street. 'That's them,' he said.

Frank didn't hesitate. He indicated right and pulled out immediately into the line of traffic, cutting up an open-top BMW who honked his horn at them. Zak kept his eyes on the mirror. He could see the whole of Cruz's convoy now, plus the five cars that were between Frank's Ford and the leading Range Rover. They drove for ten seconds, then Frank pulled over again about twenty metres from the school gates.

'*Go*,' he said under his breath as the convoy drove past them. Zak opened the door just as Cruz's Mercedes slipped past the Ford. The moment he slammed it shut, Frank pulled out again and did a U-turn, joining the line of traffic heading in the opposite direction and avoiding the snarl-up the convoy caused as it stopped.

Zak walked slowly towards the gates, carefully taking everything in. There were approximately fifteen students outside the gates, none of whom seemed particularly surprised by the approaching convoy – to them it was totally normal. The Mercedes pulled over, flanked as usual by the Range Rovers. Suddenly a white Transit van appeared. It stopped between Zak and the Mercedes.

The doors of the Mercedes opened and the two bodyguards stepped out. The one on the pavement side opened the rear door and Cruz appeared.

CONTACT

It all happened incredibly quickly.

The bodyguard was escorting Cruz towards the school gates when the back door of the white van swung open and a man exited, just in front of Zak. He was carrying a Colt pistol, matt black, and his head was covered with a balaclava. Nobody outside the school appeared to notice him as he raised the gun and pointed it directly at the second bodyguard who was walking around the back of the Mercedes.

Someone screamed: '*Get down!*' It was one of the students by the gate, a girl. She had seen the gunman, and at the sound of her voice everyone stopped and looked round.

Gunshot. It cracked above the noise of the cars.

The .45 round from the Colt entered the bodyguard's leg just above the knee, making a brief squelching sound. There was a sudden splash of red and the man collapsed, like a puppet when the strings have been cut. Two seconds later he started to shout in agony. The other bodyguard was five metres from the Mercedes now. He looked around in panic, clearly unsure whether to run back to the safety of the car or do something else.

More screaming from the students around the gate. Three of them rushed into the school grounds; the remainder just stared in horror, unable to move. The shooter aimed his Colt just above them and fired a round into the concrete wall, which spat dust all over the pavement.

Everyone, including Cruz and his bodyguard, hit the ground. Two of the students cowered with their knees bent; about ten others lay flat on their fronts, covering their heads with their hands. A few of them screamed. The gunman, who was only five metres in front of Zak, aimed at Cruz.

Zak moved quickly. He ran towards the gunman and barged into his back, knocking him to the ground. The man's gun clattered to the pavement. Zak dived towards the weapon and grabbed it.

The shooter started shouting, calling to colleagues inside the white van in Spanish. 'Cruz is on the ground! Repeat, the target is on the ground! *Get him now!*'

Another masked figure jumped out of the Transit, but instead of aiming at Cruz, the second shooter trained his gun on Zak. Zak didn't hesitate. He fired a single round, which ripped into the shooter's chest. There was another flash of blood from the area around his heart; the impact flung the man back a metre and he went down.

After that, it was total chaos. Eight armed men jumped from the two Range Rovers flanking the Mercedes. One of them – clearly the boss – shouted instructions as four of the men grabbed the wounded guard and carried him into one of the vehicles. The other four ran round to where Cruz and his body-guard were hugging the pavement. They pulled the boy to his feet and, surrounding him completely, hustled him up to the second Range Rover, which instantly pulled into the traffic and screamed away.

Four balaclava'd figures jumped from the back of the white Transit van. Two of them picked up the limp body of the man Zak had shot, while the other two covered them, pointing their weapons towards the school as the first shooter scurried back. When the body was safely inside the van, the others piled in, closed the door and the Transit shot away in the opposite direction to Martinez's convoy.

Which left Zak.

He was standing on the pavement, a Colt in his right hand and a look of total shock on his face. He turned round. All the students who had been pressed against the pavement were now on their feet; when they saw the gun in his hand, they backed away from him in alarm.

Sirens. They were close. The convoy and the white van had only been gone for thirty seconds when Zak saw two white police cars, one coming from either end of the road. The traffic pulled over to let them pass; seconds later they had screeched to a halt, each one no more than twenty metres from where Zak was standing.

The doors opened. Armed police with helmets and body armour emerged – seven or eight of them, all with their weapons pointed in Zak's direction. The air became filled with shouts in Spanish: 'Drop your weapon! *Drop your weapon!*'

Zak didn't resist. He knew that if he gave them even the slightest reason, these cops would shoot. And so he bent down, laid the Colt on the floor and put his hands up. Seconds later he was lying on his front, his hands Plasticuffed behind his back and his cheek pressed against the tarmac. Three cops pointed assault rifles directly at him.

Frank, of course, was nowhere to be seen.

Zak was on his own.

In the rear of the white Transit van, a figure in a balaclava was stretched out on his back. His front was saturated and sticky with a thick, red liquid. The vehicle's seats had been ripped out which meant there was enough space for the four people crouched around him. The van swung round a corner and they all swayed slightly.

By the time the van straightened out again, however, the figure on the floor was sitting up.

He removed his balaclava first, to reveal a thick head of blond hair, a square, frowning face and a flat nose. As he pulled off his polo neck, he uncovered a sticky

CONTACT

plastic pouch that had once been filled with the
stinking pig's blood that had now seeped into his
clothes. The pouch was strapped over thick body armour,
the canvas of which had been ripped away by the
impact of the heavy bullet.

One of the figures surrounding him removed her
balaclava. It was a woman in her twenties with white-
blonde hair and large blue eyes.

'You OK, Raf?' she asked.

Raphael winced as he removed the body armour.
His chest had already come up in bruises, but the
bullet hadn't pierced his body. 'Yeah,' he said. 'I'm
OK.' He looked at the woman. 'He did well, Gabs. All
those mornings on the firing range paid off.'

Gabriella smiled. 'You knew he would,' she said.
'Otherwise you wouldn't have volunteered to take the
bullet.'

Raf inclined his head, then winced again. He was
glad Agent 21 was such a good shot, but he knew he'd
be sore for a good few days to come . . .

14

JAIL

Like everyone, Zak had sometimes wondered what jail might be like. He had never thought it would be as bad as this.

The police had been rough – all shouts and pushes. Once they'd made the Colt safe, they'd bundled him into one of the white police cars and taken him – sirens blazing – to a facility in the north of the city. In order to get there, they travelled along the elevated freeway that stretched through the capital from south to north. Zak was in the back of the car, his wrists still cuffed; apart from the driver there were two other armed cops with him. They neither spoke nor smiled.

Zak couldn't keep his mind off Raf. He'd recognized his guardian angel even though he couldn't see his face; but the explosion of blood from his chest was so realistic that Zak couldn't help worrying that he'd actually shot him. The thought made him feel sick, and he did everything he could to put it from his mind.

From the car window he could see Mexico City in all its variety. It was an enormous, sprawling place. There were shabby brownstone tenement blocks, and concrete buildings plastered with graffiti; but there were also green, open spaces and, dominating the sky-line, shining skyscrapers glittering in the sun. You only had to take one look to see that rich and poor lived side by side in Mexico City.

The northern district where they took Zak was not a rich one. They stopped outside a bland, functional concrete building. A sign outside read 'Comisaria' – police station – and the officers hustled him through the door. A woman at the reception desk gave Zak a bored glance as he was frogmarched into the building and down a long corridor that smelled of antiseptic. Minutes later his police escort released him into the custody of a surly prison guard who stank of sweat. This man removed his Plasticuffs with a big pair of sharp scissors. The guard led him to a processing area – little more than a small room with strip light-ing, a big metal cabinet and a wooden table – and spoke four words to Zak: 'Belt, watch, wallet, phone.'

'Aren't they going to ask me any questions?' Zak had assumed that because he had fired in self-defence, the

Mexican police would be sympathetic. Looked like he'd assumed wrong.

'What do you think you are? Important? We've got fifty more like you downstairs. Belt, watch, wallet, phone.'

Zak handed each item over with reluctance – especially the phone, but he wasn't in a position to argue. He noticed his hand shaking as he did so. The guard locked them away in the metal cabinet, then patted him down to check he wasn't carrying any concealed weapons. 'Come with me,' he said, and took Zak down into the basement of the facility to lock him up.

The cell was ten metres by ten, and was home to twenty-three people including him. They were all men – many of them with intricate tattoos inked onto their skin – and Zak was comfortably the youngest. In the far corner there was a toilet without a seat which gave off a foul stench. The others had already crowded in those parts of the cell that were furthest from the toilet, and the only place Zak could find to crouch was against the far wall, three metres from it. From here he could look out of the iron bars that fronted the cell. There was a second unit opposite and this housed the women prisoners. If anything, they looked even more threatening than the men.

The smell that leached from the toilet mingled with

the heat and the sweat to create an odour which made him want to retch. His wrists still hurt from where the police had cuffed him. His knees stung too, because when the prison guards had hurled him inside he had stumbled and scraped himself against the concrete floor. A swarm of flies buzzed not only over the toilet but also around all the prisoners. For the first ten minutes, Zak tried to swat them away with his hand, but he soon realized how pointless that was. He'd just have to put up with them crawling over his skin.

The other men in the cell looked as if they were used to places like this. When Zak entered they all gave him unfriendly stares, but their interest in him almost immediately petered out when they realized he wasn't a threat to any of them, that he simply intended to sit quietly against the wall like they all did. It was too hot for anything else. Not that this made Zak feel any better. This was never part of the plan. Cruz could hardly thank him for saving his life when he was banged up in a stinking cell like this, alone and terrified.

To stave off the fear, he told himself that Frank would be along any minute to get him out. In the meantime, he put his head down and tried to merge into the background. All he could do now was wait . . .

* * *

London.

In a block of flats on the south side of the River Thames near Battersea, three men and a woman watched a large bank of computer screens. One of the men was Michael, but the other two didn't know him by that name. To them he was Mr Bartholomew. Or 'sir' for short.

One of the computer screens showed a map of Mexico City with a moving green light flashing on it.

'Agent 21 on the move sir,' said the younger man.

'Thank you, Alexander, I can see that. Tell me when he stops again, please.'

Michael turned and looked out of the window across the river. It was 1.30 p.m. here, but it had already been a long day and he was nervous. Their plan was finely tuned, and he hoped he hadn't put too much faith in young Zak Darke.

An hour passed. All was silent in the flat until . . .

'He's stopped again, sir,' said Alex.

'Where?'

The girl – her name was Sophie – spoke. Sophie zoomed one of the computer screens in on a satellite image. 'A police station, sir.'

'Good. Sophie, get in contact with Frank Gold. Tell him where Agent 21 is. He needs to get him out on bail immediately.'

'Yes, sir,' Sophie said, and Michael went back to staring out of the window.

Zak had been in the cell for half an hour when the door opened and a sour-faced prison guard threw three plastic bottles of water inside, before locking the door again. There was a scramble as seven or eight of the prisoners tried to grab the bottles. The lucky three cradled their treasure like they were holding their own babies. It was immediately clear that they had no intention of sharing the water with anyone else in the cell. Most of the unlucky prisoners returned to their places with dark looks, but one of them – he was wearing open-toed sandals, black jeans and a lumberjack shirt, and had a lean, desperate face, several days' stubble and a tattoo on his neck – remained on his feet. He took a step towards the smaller of the three bottle-holders, who had scraggly black hair around his shoulders. 'Give me some,' he said.

The guy with the bottle took a step back towards the bars. He shook his head.

The thin man moved as quickly as a cat. Zak didn't see where he pulled his knife from, but it must have been somewhere well hidden to have escaped the prison guard's notice. It had a short, stubby blade, but it was shiny and sharp and the thin man held it threateningly at head height, ready to stab.

The long-haired man immediately dropped the bottle. 'Take it,' he said, and his eyes darted around nervously.

That should have been an end to it, but the thin man was after more than water. He wanted a fight. He didn't drop his knife. He just kept advancing.

Zak sensed all the other prisoners shifting away from the area of conflict. They knew what was about to happen, and they didn't want to get involved.

A little voice in Zak's head told him to do nothing, to avoid drawing attention to himself. But he couldn't stand by and watch a man being stabbed. He pushed himself up to his feet and in three big strides crossed the cell, coming up behind the knifeman just as he was about to bring his blade down on his adversary. '*No!*' Zak shouted. He barged into the knifeman with his shoulder, forcing him away from his victim so that he fell against the railings. The knife clattered into the corridor outside.

There was a horrible silence in the cell. The knife-man turned slowly to look at Zak. His eyes flashed and there was a nasty sneer on his face.

'A hero, are you?' he whispered. He started flexing his fingers and took a step in Zak's direction.

'I don't want any trouble,' Zak said. But he felt himself tensing his body at the same time, preparing for a fight.

'It's a bit late for that, *niño*.'

Zak looked around the cell. Nobody was about to help him.

'*Enough!*'

The voice came from outside the cell and Zak saw the prison guard. The knifeman's eyes narrowed. 'Just you wait, *niño*,' he hissed, and he turned slowly to look at the guard.

The warden, however, wasn't interested in him, or the fight, or the knife on the floor. He pointed at Zak. 'You,' he said. 'Come with me. Looks like it's your lucky day.'

Relief crashed over Zak. *Frank must be here*, he thought, *ready to bail me out of this hellhole*. The warden unlocked the cell door. Zak stepped around the knifeman, whose face grew even darker now he realized he wouldn't be allowed the pleasure of laying in to Zak, and hurried out of the cell. The warden locked the door again and led Zak away.

'Friends in high places, have you?' he asked in a gruff voice as they climbed the stairs again.

Zak shook his head. 'No,' he replied, wondering what the guy meant.

It was only when they were back in the processing area that he understood.

The person waiting for them was most definitely *not* Frank. He was incredibly thin, but sweated like a fat man in the sun. He had a couple of days' stubble, and was wearing a pair of jeans and a green Mexico football shirt with a number nine on the back. The shirt covered an angular bulge at his hip: it was clear this man was carrying a firearm. But it wasn't his physique or his clothes that made Zak's blood run cold. It wasn't even the barely concealed gun. It was his face. His eyes.

Or rather, his eye.

There was only one. His right eye was missing, and the skin had grown over it so smoothly that it looked as if the eye had never been there in the first place. Zak recognized him, of course. He had seen his picture on Michael's whiteboard back on St Peter's Crag. Adan Ramirez. *Calaca.* Zak remembered what Michael had said about him. *It's impossible to say how many men Calaca has killed. Chances are that he doesn't even know himself.*

He looked around, half hoping to see Frank walk into the room. But it didn't happen, and Zak felt fear rising like acid in his stomach.

'The boy, Señor Ramirez,' said the warden.

Zak shook his head. 'My uncle . . .' he stuttered.

'Shut up,' said Calaca. 'You have his things?'

The warden nodded. He unlocked the cabinet and pulled out a wooden tray containing the items he had confiscated from Zak. Calaca examined them. He rifled through Zak's wallet, checking the name on his credit card and noting the wodge of cash that was stashed inside; he put the watch to his ear and turned the phone over in his hands. Zak held his breath, hoping Calaca would not want to study the phone *too* closely. Finally, however, satisfied that the items were of no concern to him, Calaca turned to Zak and nodded. 'Take them,' he said.

Zak did as he was told.

Calaca handed a handful of brand-new Mexican pesos to the warden. 'From Cesar Martinez Toledo,' he said, his voice flat and quiet. 'He is pleased to know he can always rely on your loyalty.'

Zak was looking at the warden carefully so he saw his expression when Calaca mentioned the word 'loyalty'. His eyes widened and his lazy arrogance fell from him. He was, quite obviously, scared – although that didn't stop him from taking the money.

Calaca turned to Zak. 'You,' he said, 'come with me. Señor Martinez has business with you.'

Zak exchanged a glance with the prison warder. 'Where am I going?' he asked. And then, when the warden didn't answer, 'I need to call my uncle. *Please.*'

'You will call nobody,' Calaca said in a dangerously low voice. 'Get moving, now.'

It was clear Zak didn't have a choice.

* * *

A vehicle was waiting for them in the street outside. It was a Range Rover with blacked-out windows, just like the ones that escorted Cruz Martinez to school. Calaca opened the back door. 'Get in,' he said.

Zak turned to him. 'Where are we going?'

Calaca's one good eye bored into him. 'Get in,' he said again.

There were two other men in the car: a driver and one other sitting in the passenger seat. They both wore suits and dark glasses. Neither of them even looked at Zak as he climbed into the back seat. After the rank heat of the cell, the air conditioning was blissful. The car moved away immediately.

They were back on the elevated freeway, heading north to south, when Zak finally spoke.

'Thank you for coming to get me,' he said.

Calaca gave him a cool look. 'Do not thank me,' he said. 'You may find that a conversation with my employer will make you wish you were back in that prison cell.'

Zak thought of the picture of the dead bodies Michael had shown him, and swallowed hard. But he didn't let his fear show in his face. Instead, he pretended to be ignorant. 'Who *is* your employer?' he asked.

Calaca gave him a dismissive look. 'You'll find out soon enough,' he said.

They drove on in silence, through the centre of the city and out to the south. The elevated freeway became an ordinary main road; that in turn became a smaller road. The vehicles grew less numerous, and about ten minutes later, they turned onto a dusty track that didn't feel like it was doing much for the Range Rover's suspension. They were no more than half an hour from the southernmost district of Mexico City now, but it looked like a different world. Looking out of the tinted window, Zak saw that the surrounding area, for as far as he could see in either direction, was covered with tree stumps.

'Who cut all the trees down?' he asked.

Calaca didn't reply.

The car slowed down and up ahead Zak saw a wall. It was easily six metres high, was topped by rolls of barbed wire and, at intervals of approximately thirty metres, there were observation posts, each with two armed men keeping guard. They reminded Zak of pictures he'd seen in history books of prisoner-of-war camps. He realized that the lack of trees meant the lookout guards were able to see the surrounding area clearly. If anybody approached, they'd know about it.

The Range Rover stopped in front of a pair of massive metal gates. Calaca pulled his phone from his pocket and dialled a number. 'It's me,' he said. Seconds later the gates opened outwards, very slowly.

The vehicle moved inside and the gates made a booming, metallic bang as they closed behind them.

Calaca turned to Zak. 'Get out,' he said.

The second he was outside the vehicle, Zak looked around to get his bearings. He blinked a few times to check he wasn't seeing things. The area inside the perimeter wall could not have been more different to the featureless former-forest outside. Here, everything was green. Zak was standing on a well-surfaced road that extended about a hundred metres ahead. On either side of the road were enormous expanses of perfectly mown grass, kept lush by the ten or twelve sprinklers that were filling the air with sparkling, silver water. At the end of the road was an enormous house. It was extravagant – gaudy, almost – built in a classical style with columns along the façade, like a smaller version of Buckingham Palace.

Calaca said, 'Walk.'

It was unbelievably hot as Zak approached the house. Light spray from the lawn sprinklers landed on him as he walked, but it evaporated almost immediately so by the time he was ten metres from the front of the house, the only moisture on him was the sweat from his skin. Calaca accompanied him all the way, but stayed a good five metres behind until they were almost at the house. Four guards with assault rifles stood at the entrance.

'He's expecting us?' Calaca demanded.

'Yes, Señor Ramirez,' one of the guards replied. 'He knows you are here.'

Calaca turned to Zak. 'Follow me,' he said. 'And only speak when you're spoken to.'

'Thanks for the advice.'

'It's not advice. It's an instruction.'

The thin man walked into the house. Zak followed.

The interior was as grand as the outside. Calaca led him into an atrium the size of a tennis court. It had cool marble flooring and an internal water fountain easily as big as the statue of Eros in Piccadilly Circus. Chandeliers hung from the ceiling and against the far wall was a lavish staircase which wound up to the left, leading to an open hallway – more of a mezzanine – overlooking the atrium with a low wall at the front. On either side of the stairs were enormous floor-to-ceiling windows, in front of which stood two guards with assault rifles. Along the left-hand wall of the atrium, just under the mezzanine wall, there was a cage, about three metres deep, two metres high and five metres wide, filled with a remarkable array of brightly coloured songbirds. They chirruped brightly. And standing in front of the cage, with their backs to Zak and Calaca, were three men, each identically dressed in loose-fitting white linen clothes.

'Wait here,' Calaca said under his breath.

The thin man stepped towards the birdcage and approached the middle of the three figures. He stood behind him and, from a distance, Zak could hear the low murmur of his voice.

Calaca stepped back. 'Come here,' he called to Zak.

Zak walked forwards nervously. When he was only a few metres from the birdcage, he stopped.

The three figures turned round.

Zak blinked.

The were identical. Not just similar. *Identical*, down to the shape of the nose and the line of the jaw. Each man had wrinkle-free dark skin, brown eyes and black hair greased back over his scalp. Each man was entirely unsmiling. Each man looked exactly like the picture of Cesar Martinez Toledo that Zak had seen.

The birds twittered in their cage.

It was the middle of the three men, the one to whom Calaca had been talking, who stepped forward. He stared at Zak with a flinty gaze.

'You are Harry Gold?' He spoke in Spanish.

'Yes, señor.'

'It is you who shot the man outside the school this morning?'

Zak nodded. He was aware of Calaca standing to one side, fixing him with an unpleasant leer.

'Why? Why would you risk your life and your freedom for someone you do not know?'

Zak felt his mouth going dry. All eyes were on him, waiting for his response.

'I kind of did it without thinking,' he lied. 'The man looked like he was going to open fire on everyone. And on me . . .'

'And yet you killed him.'

'I didn't mean to . . .'

'You shot him in the chest and you didn't mean to kill him?'

Zak shook his head vigorously. 'I'm not . . . I didn't . . . I swear . . .'

A pause.

And then the man to whom Zak had been talking stepped back, and the identical figure to the left took his place.

He stared at Zak.

His eyes narrowed.

Then he put his hands on Zak's shoulders, looked him in the eye and then embraced him in a rough bear hug. 'You,' he said, 'you saved my son's life. The friendship of Cesar Martinez Toledo is now yours. Anything you want, you only have to ask.' He released Zak from the hug but kept his hands on his shoulders.

'Anything, Harry Gold,' Martinez continued. 'You understand that? *Anything.*'

15

LA CATRINA

'I'm scared of the police,' Zak said in his best Spanish. 'I thought they would see that I fired in self-defence, but they put me in prison and . . .'

Martinez – Zak could only assume that the man who had just hugged him was the real one – was taken aback. He looked at Calaca, then round at the two body doubles, and finally back at Zak.

And then he laughed, as if Zak had just told him a very good joke. A deep belly-laugh that echoed round the marble-floored atrium. 'Do you know where you are, Harry?' he asked.

Zak shook his head.

'Come with me.' With one hand on Zak's back, Martinez walked him towards the main entrance of the house. They stopped on the veranda, and Martinez pointed towards the observation towers on the perimeter wall. 'You see those, my young friend?' he said. 'There are two marksmen at each post twenty-four hours a day. Nobody can enter without my permission. You are safer here than El Presidente himself – with whom, I should say, I am well acquainted. Ramirez – you know, with the one eye: everyone calls him "*Calaca*" behind his back, but if you want my advice don't say that word to his face – has done some research on you, Harry Gold. I know you have only recently arrived in Mexico, so you probably don't know that I have influence in these parts.'

'Are you a businessman?' Zak asked, trying to sound as innocent as possible. 'Like my dad was.'

Martinez laughed again. 'Yes!' he said, rubbing his eyes. 'Yes, a businessman! A very successful business-man. I can put a good word in for you. You don't need to worry about the police. But it would be better if you stayed here for a little while. Until everything has settled down. While you are under my protection they will not come near you. My people will explain to the school that you and Cruz will not be joining them for a few days.'

Zak swallowed hard. The plan had been to get close to Cruz and Martinez, but he'd never expected to get *this* close *this* quickly. A guest in the compound.

'My uncle will be worried,' he said.

'Then you must call him,' Martinez said. 'Now. You have a telephone?' He folded his arms and waited for Zak to get his phone out. 'Just one thing, Harry. It would be better if your uncle did not know where you are.'

'Why not?'

Martinez gave him a bland smile. 'It would be better,' was all he said. He nodded at Zak to indicate that he should make the phone call now.

Zak dialled Frank's number. His uncle answered immediately. 'Harry, old boy, what on earth's happened? I've heard terrible things. I went to the police station and you weren't—'

'Everything's all right, Uncle Frank.'

'But where *are* you?'

'I'm, um . . . I'm just safe, OK?' Zak felt Martinez's eyes on him.

'Harry, you've got to tell me what's—'

'I've got to go now, Uncle Frank. I'll call you again.'

He hung up. Martinez appeared satisfied with the conversation but as Zak glanced at the heavily guarded main entrance to the compound, he couldn't help feeling trapped.

'Come with me,' Martinez instructed. They walked back into the atrium of the house. Calaca had gone, and so had the two body doubles; but the guards were still there. 'Find Cruz,' Martinez said, and one of them slipped away.

A silence. 'You realize, Harry, that those men were after my son?'

'I don't understand why. Is it because you are rich?'

'In a way, Harry. In a way. You see, it is impossible to become wealthy in this life without making enemies,' Martinez said. 'My enemies know that I love Cruz more than all the money in the world. That is why they target him. Most probably it was a kidnapping attempt.'

'Do you know who it was?'

Martinez licked the tips of his fingers and used them to smooth down his hair. 'I will find out. And when I do, the people behind it will wish they had never crossed Cesar Martinez Toledo.' His eyes lit up as he looked across the atrium. 'Here is Cruz! Come here, my boy. Harry, Cruz told us about you even before today's unfortunate events.'

Cruz walked across the atrium. His long arms and lanky legs were ungainly and he avoided Zak's gaze as he approached. He avoided his father's gaze too, for that matter, and looked firmly at the marble floor.

'Cruz! Shake Harry's hand. You have a great deal to thank him for.'

Cruz's handshake was unenthusiastic and limp. He glanced up at him. 'Thank you,' he said.

Before Zak could reply, Martinez interrupted. 'Harry will be staying here for a while. Show him around, Cruz. Give him a bedroom. Tonight, we will share a meal together. Harry, my home is yours.' He nodded at them and left the atrium.

It was an awkward moment. The two boys just stood there, with Cruz staring at the floor.

'Why did you do it?' Cruz asked.

'I don't know,' said Zak. 'It just . . . I wasn't really thinking, I guess. Your dad said he could keep the police off my back.'

Cruz frowned. 'Yes,' he said. 'He can do that. I suppose you want to see round the compound.'

'Sure,' Zak replied.

The tour took an hour. Cruz showed Zak the gym and the sauna just off the atrium; a shooting range outside. The first floor consisted of a long corridor surrounding the central atrium and consisted mostly of bedrooms, but one of the doors opened into a TV room that was more like a small cinema. None of it seemed to impress Martinez's son. He appeared slightly bored by it all. At the back of the house there was a helipad and a swimming pool, but it was not the inviting, clear water that attracted Zak's attention. It was the two brightly painted stone statues at the far end. They were about three metres high and took the form of women dressed in highly decorated robes of gold and purple. Each woman carried a bunch of yellow flowers and wore an elegant, multicoloured headdress. Both faces, however, were nothing but a skull, fixed in a gruesome, exaggerated grin. The sight made Zak shiver.

'Not exactly Michelangelo,' he said.

Cruz glanced at the statues as if they were the most natural thing in the world. '*La Catrina.*'

'Who?'

'It's a Mexican thing. You see it mostly on the Day of the Dead in November, when we remember friends and family who have died. *La Catrina* is supposed to remind us that even the rich and beautiful will die one day.'

Zak wondered who wanted to be reminded of *that* when they were lounging by the pool.

He changed the subject by pointing at the pool itself. 'Do you use it much?'

Cruz shook his head. 'Not really.'

'That's right,' a voice said from behind them. 'Cruz doesn't like taking his top off. He's afraid we might laugh at how thin his arms are.'

Zak saw Cruz's face darken. He turned round to see a boy a little older than them, and he instantly started mentally recording details of his appearance. He wore fashionable sunglasses and the top few buttons of his shirt were open to reveal a small, golden medallion hung around his neck. The smell of Brylcreem lingered around him and his tight, curly black hair glistened. This was a teenager doing everything he

could to appear like a grown man. It wasn't a great
look.

'Who are *you*?' the boy demanded.

Zak was wondering the same thing. He'd been fully
briefed on Cruz, Martinez and Calaca. This was someone Michael obviously didn't know about – an
unnerving reminder that the intelligence could never
have been complete.

'Harry Gold.' Zak didn't offer his hand.

'What are you doing here?'

'I'm a friend of Cruz's.'

The boy made a snorting sound. 'Cruz doesn't *have*
any friends. He spends too much time reading books.'

'Well, he does now.'

The boy removed his sunglasses and gave Zak a
poisonous look. 'Do you know who I am?' he asked.

'Er . . . Brylcreem salesman?' Zak suggested, looking meaningfully at his hair.

The boy sneered. 'You think you're funny?' He
looked around the place as if he owned it. 'I'm Raul,'
he said. 'Remember the name.' He put the glasses
back on. 'You're not Mexican,' he observed.

'Spot on.'

'So how come you speak Spanish?'

Zak smiled at him. 'From a book,' he said. 'You
should try reading one. It's amazing what you can
pick up.'

Raul looked like he was thinking up a response, but nothing came. So he just sneered again and walked away with a lazy gait.

'Who's the goon?' Zak asked when Raul was out of earshot.

'My cousin,' said Cruz. 'The son of my father's late brother. You shouldn't wind him up.'

'Do you always let him talk to you like that?' Zak carefully examined the uncomfortable look on Cruz's face.

Cruz looked away. 'It doesn't matter,' he said.

'Yeah, it does. How come he's so impressed with himself?'

Cruz shifted from one foot to another. 'It's my father,' he said. 'He knows I'm not interested in the family business.'

'You don't like what he does?'

'No, it's not that. I would be a hypocrite. My father's business has given us everything. I just want to do something different. He's a proud man. It was hard for him to accept, but now he knows that I am serious. He would never think of passing the business on to somebody who wasn't family – that's the Mexican way – so he brought Raul in to live with us. Raul knows that puts him in a powerful position round here.'

Zak looked over to where Raul was disappearing

inside. He wondered if he'd been wise to make an enemy of Martinez's nephew. He turned his attention back to Cruz. 'So if you don't want to go into business with your dad,' he asked, 'what *do* you want to do?'

Cruz looked faintly embarrassed. 'I like science.' He frowned. 'It's not something Raul would really understand.'

'I get it,' Zak said. 'Back in England I used to—'

And then he stopped himself. He was getting a bit too close to talking about his own life, not Harry's. And anyway, he sensed that Cruz didn't want to talk about it any more, so he let it drop and they continued the tour.

'This place is pretty cool,' Zak said when they'd returned to the atrium. As he spoke he found himself naturally checking that he could correctly remember the layout of this big hallway, the position of the big central staircase and the location of the exits.

Cruz shrugged. 'I guess,' he said.

'You don't sound like you mean it.' Zak remembered his cover. 'You should see the place where I have to stay with my uncle,' he said with a rich kid's sneer.

Cruz looked around with a frown. 'The man you shot was coming to kidnap me, wasn't he?' he asked, changing the subject.

'That's what your father thinks.'

'My father tells *you* more than he tells *me*.' Cruz

didn't sound bitter, exactly. Just sad. With a pang, Zak thought about his own father. 'You should try to get close to him, Cruz,' he said. 'One day he won't be there, and . . .' Zak's voice tailed off.

'He's not interested in me any more.'

'I bet that's not true.'

Cruz shrugged. 'Maybe,' he said. 'But look, thank you for this morning.' Cruz put his hand out and Zak shook it for a second time, trying not to think about the blood that had spurted from Raf's chest.

Cruz clearly noticed something in Zak's face. 'You shouldn't worry about killing him. He was a dead man the moment he tried to kidnap me.' Cruz's eyes were hard.

'Doesn't that bother you?'

'Doesn't it bother *you*?'

Zak shook his head.

'Everybody dies sooner or later,' said Cruz. 'Why does it matter if it's sooner and not later?' He gave Zak a chilling stare. 'Remember *La Catrina*,' he said.

How could I forget, Zak thought.

'Er . . . those body doubles,' he said, trying to probe for more information. 'They're pretty good likenesses.'

'They're perfect,' said Cruz. 'Even I can't tell the difference sometimes.'

'Must be pretty confusing.'

'You get used to it. It's no secret that there are many

people who want to kill my father.' He looked around. 'So, it doesn't look like either of us are going to school for a bit,' he said. 'Do you want to watch a movie or something?'

'Great,' Zak said with as much enthusiasm as he could muster. 'Lead the way.' Together they headed to the TV room.

Zak didn't mention it to Cruz, but as they left the atrium he noticed Calaca, standing almost hidden in a doorway, watching them, noting their movements and listening to every word they said.

Ten miles from Cesar Martinez Toledo's compound, in the grounds of a long-deserted farmstead, there were two old barns. One of them – the larger of the two – had a collapsed roof so it was open to the elements. Anybody looking at it from outside might expect it to be filled with rubble, or old farming tools, or nothing. They certainly wouldn't expect it to contain a UH-60 Black Hawk helicopter.

But that's exactly what it contained.

Maximum speed, 183 mph. Capacity, 2 flight crew and 14 troops. Rate of climb, 700 ft per minute. On either side of the fuselage there was an M134 Minigun capable of firing 7.62 mm rounds at a rate of up to 6,000 rounds per minute. All in all, not the kind of thing the average Mexican farmer would expect to see in one of his outbuildings.

The second barn had a roof, but its contents were no less surprising. Just outside, semi-hidden by an abandoned truck, was a small signalling dish, its antenna pointing at the sky. Inside, there was a small generator in the corner, powering a bank of computer screens. Along the walls were a series of low beds – four of them occupied by sleeping men. Two other men had taken up position by the main door, assault rifles in hand. And at the bank of computer screens stood Gabs and Raf, both wearing comms earpieces and mikes.

They were staring at a high-definition, real-time satellite image of the Martinez compound. It was very clear: you could see the compound walls, the magnificent house, the lawns and even the sprinklers. They could tell Zak was inside – a flashing green dot superimposed on the house indicated his exact position.

'Are you getting this?' Michael's voice came over the comms all the way from his centre of operations in London.

'Roger that,' replied Raf. 'Looks like he's in.'

'He just made contact with Frank and confirmed he was safe.'

'Any signs of coercion?'

'Negative. Our working theory has to be that

he's there as Martinez's guest, not his prisoner.'

Gabs glanced at the satellite image. Look carefully enough and you could just see the observation posts dotted around the walls. 'Given the security around that place,' she said, 'I'd say there's not much difference between the two.'

'Agreed,' said Michael. 'Stay on high alert. We need to be ready to extract him the moment he gives a distress call.'

Raf and Gabs exchanged a long look.

'And well done, you two. I didn't expect him to be inside so soon. You did a good job on him.'

A pause.

'We'll know just how good,' Gabs said, 'when we see if he comes out alive, won't we?'

Michael didn't answer and they went back to staring at their computer screens.

16

CHINESE WHISPERS

The afternoon sun was hot.

Calaca was in the habit of meeting with his employer to discuss business by the swimming pool. Martinez would always have a long, cold rum punch with plenty of ice, the rum imported especially from Havana. Calaca drank water. He knew that an attack on his master could come at any time. For that reason, two body doubles lounged at the far end of the pool, also drinking rum punches, there to confuse any hitmen. But body doubles or not, Calaca's head needed to be clear, so he never touched alcohol.

'Something isn't right,' he said as they stood by the pool.

'You worry too much, Adan,' replied Martinez.

'That's what you pay me for.'

Martinez shrugged and took a sip of his drink. What Calaca had just said was true.

'It's too neat,' the one-eyed man continued. 'This

new kid just *happened* to be there at the time someone tried to kidnap Cruz? I don't believe it.'

Martinez stared at his head of security. He put his rum punch down on a little table covered with a neatly starched tablecloth, then put one arm around Calaca's shoulders. He extended the other to indicate the vast and magnificent grounds all around him.

'You see all this?' he said. 'It is mine for a reason. And do you know, Adan, what that reason is?'

'The business,' Calaca replied.

'The business, yes,' said Martinez. 'But the business is only a success because we are willing to do what others will not. Young Harry Gold killed a man this morning, Adan. You and I know that life is cheap, but the authorities?' He shook his head. 'It is not in their nature to sacrifice a pawn to catch the king. Harry Gold is a brave boy. If we keep him here, he could be of use to us. And besides, Cruz owes him his life. For that I am grateful.'

'But—'

'No more buts, Adan.' Martinez's genial voice had become sharp and Calaca knew not to argue with him. 'Harry Gold stays here. If nothing else, he will be a friend for Cruz. Do you understand me?'

Calaca bowed his head. '*Si*, Señor Martinez,' he said. 'I understand you.' He turned and left the swimming pool, leaving his boss to enjoy his rum punch and the sight of the setting sun.

Deep inside the headquarters of the CIA in Langley, Virginia, there is a wall. It is called the Memorial Wall. Ninety black stars are engraved on it, along with these words: *In honour of those members of the Central Intelligence Agency who gave their lives in the service of their country.*

The stout, middle-aged man who walked past the Memorial Wall paid it no attention. He never did. And as he left CIA headquarters via the concrete and glass archway that was the main entrance and exit, he caught nobody's eye. Not that anybody wanted to stop and talk to him. They were all too busy for that, and he was a man of little importance.

It was 5 p.m. The man always left at this hour. He wasn't an important cog in the intelligence wheel. Far from it. His job was simply to file intelligence, to make sure that the right nuggets of information were kept in the right place. Because, as he always told anyone who would listen, a piece of intelligence mis-filed is a piece of intelligence lost.

He walked to his car. It was nothing all that special – a Toyota Prius that his wife had nagged him to buy because she said it was better for the environment. He didn't care about that. What he really wanted was a

Lotus, but he hadn't bought one because he knew it would be stupid to flash his money around. It would be far too glamorous a car for somebody on his pay grade. When he retired, maybe he'd treat himself; and if things carried on going the way they were, retirement could be just around the corner . . .

At the perimeter gates he slowed down and handed his biometric ID card to the policeman in his booth. 'Watching the ball game tonight, Bob?'

Bob grinned. 'Had the beers chilling all day. Another half an hour and I'm out of here.' He inserted the ID card into his card reader then handed it back. 'See you in the morning, Lou, bright-eyed and bushy-tailed.'

'Not if you drink too many of those beers.' Lou winked at him and drove off.

Lou and his wife lived in a condo in downtown Washington. Journey time from Langley at this time of day, approximately one hour. But Lou wouldn't be going home just yet. In fact he was driving northwest, ten miles along the 193 before he pulled off and drove another couple of miles to a little settlement that was too small even to have a name. There was a diner here – the sort of place only frequented by truck drivers. Lou had scoped the place out a year before. It had no security cameras of any kind, which meant he could be sure his presence would not be recorded. He knew how the intelligence services worked, so he was able to keep one step ahead.

He pulled up outside the diner and walked in. A friendly waitress took his order – a coffee and a slice of blueberry pie – and while he waited for the food to come, Lou stepped over to the phone box on the far wall. He dug into his pocket for a couple of quarters, then dialled a number.

It rang eight or nine times before an unfriendly voice answered in Spanish.

'*Si?*'

'It's me,' said Lou.

No reply.

'I have information.'

'I'm listening.'

'The British are planning to swipe Martinez. They've got someone on the inside. Thought you'd like to know.' Lou couldn't help looking pleased with himself, even though there was nobody to see.

A pause.

'You have a name?'

'Nope. Highly classified. All I have is a codename. Agent 21.'

'Anything else?'

'That's your lot,' said Lou. 'You have a good evening now.'

He hung up and went to sit down at the table. He

looked at his watch. A quarter to six. Maybe he should just go home now. But then he smiled. His wife was expecting him home late, and the blueberry pie really did look too good to miss.

In the federal offices of the Mexican government an enormously fat man placed his phone back on its cradle. His name was Juan Michel, and despite the fact that his office was air-conditioned, he was sweating like a man in a sauna.

He sat quietly for a moment and considered what his CIA contact had just told him. To swipe Cesar Martinez Toledo was impossible. The Americans knew that, and they'd given up asking the Mexicans to help. It was the worst-kept secret in Mexican politics that Martinez was bribing half the government; and the idea that the British were equipped to do anything was a joke. No, this information from Langley sounded like a red herring. Perhaps he should discard it in the rubbish bin of his mind where it belonged.

But then he shook his head.

Martinez paid him well for his services and he didn't want the payments to stop. Even if this intelligence was nonsense, he'd be a fool not to pass it on – just to show he was on the ball. He wiped his sweaty palms on his clothes, picked up the phone again and dialled a number.

Somebody answered almost immediately.

'This is Juan Michel,' said the fat man.

'Good for you.'

Insolence, thought Juan. *I shouldn't have to put up with it.* But he thought of the money and kept quiet.

'What do you want?' the voice at the other end said.

'I want you to put me through to Adan Ramirez. Tell him who it is. And tell him I have some information in which Señor Martinez will be most, most interested.'

17

A FEW SIMPLE QUESTIONS

'Calaca wants you in here. He says it's secure.'

The bedroom which Cruz led Zak to was even more flash than the one in Harry Gold's flat in Knightsbridge. It had an enormous four-poster bed and an intercom he could use to call down to the kitchens. 'Anything you want,' Cruz said, 'just buzz.' There was an en-suite bathroom, of course, with a Jacuzzi, and one of the doors led to an enormous walk-in wardrobe filled with expensive new clothes and shoes. It was like an amazing hotel, with one difference. The corridor outside had a security camera, which was pointed directly at Zak's door.

'What's with that?' Zak asked Cruz.

'Don't worry about it,' Cruz replied.

Zak looked down the corridor. His was the only room to be under camera surveillance.

'I don't think anybody really uses them,' Cruz continued.

Yeah, right, thought Zak.

All he really wanted was a moment to himself. It had been a gruelling day, and everything had happened so quickly. He was exhausted and worried. He didn't know if Raf was safe after that morning's theatrics; or if his phone was broadcasting its signal to indicate where he was. He hoped that Raf and Gabs had managed to insert their unit somewhere nearby. But contact was out of the question, and he felt very alone.

He couldn't allow himself to fade now, though. Martinez was expecting him for dinner and Zak had to keep up his pretence. His life depended on it.

He showered and changed, by which time it was seven thirty. Time to go down, so he slipped his phone into his pocket and left the room. Martinez and Cruz were waiting for him outside by the pool, and Raul was with them, along with two butlers. There was a neatly laid table, piled with more food than the four of them could possibly eat. Cruz was sitting down, a book open on his lap. Raul had a bottle of Coke in his hand, which he sucked at slowly through a straw while watching Zak approach.

'Harry!' Martinez sounded genuinely pleased to see him. 'Come and join us. What will you drink?'

'Coke, please,' Zak said. Martinez nodded at one of the butlers, who fetched a bottle from an outdoor fridge next to the table and handed it to Zak, who couldn't help glancing towards the skeleton-like statues at the end of the pool.

Martinez noticed this. 'You like *La Catrina*, Harry?'

'Er, yeah,' said Zak. 'They're great.'

'Excellent! Excellent!' He put one hand out towards Cruz's cousin. 'This is Raul,' he said.

'We met already,' Raul said, one eyebrow raised.

'Yeah,' Zak added. 'We have the same taste in literature.'

Martinez looked from one to the other. 'Is there something I'm missing, gentlemen?' he asked. The edge of his mouth was curled into a little smile, as though the thought of Zak and Raul being at each other's throats rather delighted him.

'Nothing,' Raul said. He went back to sucking and staring.

Martinez put an arm round Zak's shoulders like an affectionate uncle, and took him over to the table. 'What will you eat, Harry? Roasted lamb? Beans? Bread?'

Zak was starving and he piled his plate high. Just as he was sitting down next to Cruz, however, Calaca appeared. It rather took the edge off Zak's appetite. Martinez's head of security was still wearing his green Mexican football shirt which covered the firearm at his hip, and he was clearly here to speak to his boss, but he couldn't help his one good eye flickering in Zak's direction, shooting him a look of pure poison.

'And here is Adan!' Martinez announced. He winked at Zak. 'If *La Catrina* were a man, he would look like my head of security, no? Yes, Adan? What is it?'

'We need to speak. In private.'

A broad smile crossed Martinez's face. 'Adan, we are eating together—'

'It's important,' interrupted Calaca. And there was something in his face that chilled Zak's blood . . .

Martinez nodded. 'Harry,' he announced. 'You will excuse me, I hope.' He smiled. 'Perhaps you and Raul can discuss literature while I'm gone!'

Adan Ramirez led his boss back into the atrium.

'What is it, Adan?'

Calaca looked around to check nobody was listening. 'I've just had a call from one of our contacts inside the government.'

'And?'

'He has a source in the CIA. The source says that the British are preparing to target you.'

'Pffff . . .' Martinez was scornful. 'Abduct *me*? The *British*? They wouldn't dare. The source is mistaken.'

But Calaca wouldn't be put off. 'They have details,' he said. 'The intelligence suggests that they already have somebody close to you. Codename, Agent 21. The information is very specific. I think we would be foolish not to take it seriously.'

Martinez nodded slowly. 'Perhaps you are right.'

'What about this Harry Gold,' said Calaca. 'Everybody else in this compound has been personally vetted by me. He is the only weak link.'

'Harry Gold is only a kid. And kids don't make good secret agents.'

'Maybe. But he's a kid who has already killed one man today.'

Martinez frowned. 'Does he have a weapon?'

'Not that I know of.'

'And he has already been alone with me today. If he planned to kill me, he could have tried then. Anyway, I can recognize assassin material. Harry Gold isn't it.'

Calaca sniffed. 'I think you should let me ask him a few simple questions.'

Martinez appeared to think about that for a moment. 'No,' he said finally. 'I know what your interrogations are like, Adan. I would like Harry to retain the use of his fingers.'

'It's never worried you before.'

'This is different. I like the boy. He has guts. He stands up to Raul for one thing, which is more than Cruz can do. I can see that my son likes him too.

Perhaps if he spends time with Harry, he will learn to be more of a man.'

'Or perhaps,' said Calaca, 'Raul will be inheriting your empire sooner than you think.'

A pause.

'You forget yourself, Adan,' said Martinez.

Calaca bowed his head. 'Forgive me. I only want to be sure that your enemies are not closer than you think.'

Toldeo nodded slowly. 'Very well,' he said. 'I want you to find out everything you can about Harry Gold. He has an uncle in Mexico City. Start with him. If anything doesn't add up, tell me. But in the meantime, the kid must have no idea that we're investigating him.'

'You shouldn't be in his presence without a guard,' said Calaca 'I will send someone now. And the body doubles should be with you at all times – just in case.'

'Very well, Calaca. Do what you need to. But remember – Harry must know nothing of this.'

Calaca nodded and watched as his boss stepped out of the atrium towards the swimming pool again. He heard his voice booming outside. 'Harry! Eat some more! We need to build you up, like a Mexican . . .'

He left them to it. From his pocket he pulled a radio. He pressed the transmission button and ordered two guards and two body doubles to join the party by the pool. Then he went down to the basement of the house.

Calaca had an office here. Opposite the office there was a cell with thick iron bars. This area was off-limits to everybody else in the household except Martinez, but his boss had no interest in it. The office was large – ten metres by ten – and well equipped with tele-phone lines, fibre-optic Internet connections and high-powered computer terminals. Adan Ramirez was a simple man from a simple background, but he had worked out long ago that to keep his boss safe, he needed to understand the technology that his enemies might use against him. These computer terminals gave him a direct link, among other things, to the files of the *Centro de Investigación y Seguridad Nacional* – the Mexican intelligence service. Whatever information he needed would be at Calaca's fingertips in minutes.

Calaca sat at his screen, logged on and typed the words HARRY GOLD.

A brief pause. And then the information started to come.

The first thing he brought up was Harry's birth certificate. Born 3 September 1995 at University College Hospital, London. Parents Oliver and Fenella Gold, recently deceased. He found two passport photographs, one taken when Harry was five years old and the second when he was ten – and they were him all right. There was a list of every flight Harry had ever taken, ending with his most recent journey from Heathrow to Mexico City. Calaca made a note of his arrival time, then continued to sift through the information. It was a disappointment: nothing suspicious, nothing to suggest Harry had any skill with a firearm, or was anything other than a bereaved rich kid with time and money on his hands.

After half an hour, Calaca changed his search.

FRANK GOLD.

The picture of an old man appeared on the screen. According to the notes he was born in 1931 in Blackburn, Lancashire. He had been in Mexico for fifteen years. Before that he had been a structural engineer whose work had taken him all over the world. But now there was nothing to suggest he was anything other than one of the many British ex-pats in Mexico City.

Calaca logged out of the intelligence service's mainframe and directed his browser to a different IP address: airport security at Mexico International. He typed in a username and password that he had acquired by bribing a member of the airport security team, and seconds later he had access to the closed circuit security camera footage for the last week. He checked the flight arrival time that he had scribbled down while looking at Harry's details, then opened up the files for the Terminal 2 security camera. A grainy black-and-white image of the airport appeared on the screen, with a white time code. Calaca navigated to a point twenty minutes after Harry's flight arrival, then sat back to watch.

Harry appeared ten minutes in, with two suitcases which he set down beside him as the crowds jostled past and he looked around. After a moment he spotted someone, picked up his suitcases again and walked forward. The angle on the security camera was awkward, but Calaca could just make out that the person he'd approached was Frank Gold. Harry put out his hand, but Frank embraced him. It appeared to Calaca that he was truly pleased to see him. Either this was splendid acting, or it was a genuine reunion.

He paused the film and stared for several minutes at the still picture of Harry and Frank Gold. Were they authentic? They certainly appeared to be so. Maybe his boss was right. Maybe Harry Gold really was who he said he was. Calaca didn't know why, but for some reason the thought disappointed him.

There was one more thing he could do. He couldn't be sure that his boss would approve, but Martinez didn't have to know. Calaca left the basement room, locked it and went back upstairs.

It was dark outside now. From the atrium he could just hear his boss talking to the kids, so he left them to it and exited from the front of the house. The Range Rover he had used to collect Harry was still parked by the main gates. He climbed into the front and turned the ignition. Moments later, he had passed through the security perimeter of the compound and was driving through the night towards Mexico City.

It was 10 p.m. and Frank Gold was getting ready for bed. His night-time routine was always the same: he would lock all the doors and windows to his house, then check all the most likely places for bugs – down the back of radiators, behind pictures. He knew he was being ultra-cautious, but it was the habit of a life-time. Only when he was sure the place was secure did he go to the bathroom to brush his teeth.

He was just squeezing the toothpaste onto the toothbrush when he heard a noise. A creaking sound. He looked up and saw his reflection in the mirror.

Silence.

Frank turned on the tap and moistened his toothbrush.

The creaking of a door. He looked in the mirror again and his blood ran cold.

There was someone behind him. Frank saw a monstrous face with only one eye. The man was wearing a green Mexico football shirt and he had a handgun pointed straight at the back of Frank's head.

'Make a single move I don't like,' the man said in a rasping voice, 'and I shoot.'

Very slowly, Frank laid his toothbrush and tooth-paste tube by the sink, turned off the tap and raised his hands above his head. 'Easy, old boy,' he said, a tremor in his voice. He watched in the mirror as the one-eyed man took a step backwards.

'The bedroom,' said the intruder. 'Now.'

Frank sat on the edge of the bed, his hands on his head. The one-eyed man moved an armchair so he could sit opposite him, about two metres away. He kept the gun pointing at Frank's chest.

'Now then,' he said, 'I'm going to ask you a few simple questions and you're going to give me a few simple answers. Who is Harry Gold?'

Frank stared directly at the intruder. He knew that if he gave any sign that he was lying, young Harry would be dead before the night was over.

'M . . . my nephew,' he stuttered. 'Actually, my great-nephew.'

The intruder gave a thin smile. 'You're lying. By the time I've finished with you, you will be telling me the truth. Why not save yourself the pain and tell me the truth now?'

Frank shook his head. 'I don't understand. There's been a mistake. I . . . I heard about what happened this morning, but the police won't tell me where he is.

Do you know? He called me, but wouldn't say where—'

He didn't finish his sentence. The man lowered his gun towards Frank's leg, and fired. The weapon wasn't suppressed, so the noise was ear-numbingly loud. Frank jumped, fully expecting to have been shot. But all he felt was a rush of air as the bullet whizzed past his left knee and landed harmlessly in the mattress of the bed.

'I never miss, old man,' said the intruder. 'The next shot will hit you in the knee. Do you have any idea how painful that is?'

Frank shook his head. His mind was turning over like a cement mixer. He knew who this man was, of course. He recognized his face from the briefing papers and he knew what he was capable of. Adan Ramirez clearly had his suspicions about Harry. But suspicions were all they were: if he had anything concrete, Harry would already be dead. So would Frank, for that matter.

He had to keep up the pretence. Even if Ramirez kneecapped him, he had to keep up the pretence . . .

'Please don't shoot me . . .'

'Then tell me who Harry Gold is.'

'I swear,' Frank whispered. 'I don't know what you're talking about. I'm just worried about him.'

It was impossible to read the expression on

Ramirez's face. 'I will count to three,' he said. 'One . . .'

'I don't know what you're talking about.'

'Two . . .'

'Please, señor, you have to believe me.'

'Three.'

The men looked at each other. Frank was wide-eyed with genuine terror, but Ramirez looked puzzled. As though this interrogation had not gone the way he expected. He stood up. 'Very well,' he said. 'We will leave it there for now. Do not try to contact Harry, if you want him to stay alive. Do you understand?'

Frank nodded.

'We have eyes everywhere, Señor Gold. If you call the police, I will know about it within minutes. Don't make the mistake of not believing me.'

'Yes, señor,' Frank whispered. 'Just tell me, is he safe?'

'For the moment,' Ramirez said. He flicked his gun hand. 'Open the door and let me out. Now.'

Frank watched Ramirez's Range Rover leave from behind the safety of his window. His hands were shaking and his stomach churned. Only when the rear lights had disappeared from view did he make the call on a secure, encrypted sat phone which he kept under a loose floorboard in his bedroom.

'It's me,' he said.

'What is it?' Michael's voice was alert, even though it was half past three in the morning in the UK. 'You sound out of breath.'

Frank recounted what had happened. 'They're on to him,' he said. 'We should pull him out.'

A pause.

'Negative,' said Michael.

'That's insane.'

But Michael stood firm. 'If they truly suspected him,' he said, 'you'd both be dead by now. You know that. Stay on high alert and do what Ramirez tells you. We need him to think he's got you running scared.'

He has *got me running scared*, Frank thought to himself as he finished the conversation. He hid the sat phone away again then walked into the kitchen, where he fetched a bottle of malt whiskey from the cupboard. He was getting too old for this sort of thing, he decided, and right now he *really* needed a drink.

18

EAVESDROPPING

Dinner felt like it had gone on for ever. It had been an awkward affair, full of long silences and dark looks from Raul. Martinez himself had seemed to enjoy it – he was almost jolly as he kept the conversation going – but Zak's mind was somewhere else.

What was it that Calaca had needed to speak to his boss about? And why had the body doubles and guards appeared just after their little chat? Something told Zak that their secret conference concerned him. Now he was back in his bedroom, he decided he *had* to find out what was going on. If they were on to him, he needed to know so he could make the distress call and get out of there . . .

He couldn't just walk out of the room. The security camera was on him and if anyone noticed him leaving at this time of night, he'd have some difficult questions to answer. But stuck here in his room he wasn't going to gather any information about anything.

Instead, he looked up.

The ceiling was made up of plaster panels, each one about a metre square. Zak jumped up onto the table, from where he could just reach one of the panels. He pushed, and it moved. Sliding the panel to one side, he grabbed the edges of the opening and pulled himself up. The muscles in his arms burned as they took all his weight, but Raf and Gab's training sessions had paid off and moments later he was above the rafters and replacing the plaster panel. He used his thumbnail to mark the panel so he would remember which one it was when he returned.

It was dimly lit up here. His bedroom ceiling had down-lighters, the backs of which glowed faintly in this gloomy attic space. Zak looked over towards the ceiling of the neighbouring room. This room's down-lighters were switched off.

It meant the room was unoccupied. He hoped.

Zak crept across the rafters, careful not to tread on the panels. A foot through the plaster would be a tricky one to explain . . . When he thought he was above the room next door, he carefully moved one of the panels – just a few centimetres – and peered down.

The room was dark. And empty.

He lowered himself down and managed to swing onto the bed, which broke his fall. He quickly moved to the door, opened it a little and checked the corridor was empty. He saw the security camera, firmly directed towards his own room. But nothing else, so he slipped out in the opposite direction and carefully started to creep towards the stairs that overlooked the atrium. The sound of the songbirds in their cage reached his ears as he crouched low behind the banisters of the hallway that looked over the atrium. Zak breathlessly peered round the top of the staircase. He saw Calaca's figure. The bony man was staring into the birdcage. Zak crept back along the banister again and stopped when he was just above Calaca and the birdcage, his back pressed to it.

He listened.

Calaca had been waiting in the atrium for a full fifteen minutes by the time Martinez turned up. He was wearing a thick velvet dressing gown and was flanked by two guards and two body doubles. All three versions of Martinez smoked fat cigars, and even Calaca didn't know which was the real Martinez until the entourage held back, leaving the two men to speak in hushed tones by the cage full of songbirds.

'Well?' asked Martinez.

'Where is the boy?' Calaca countered.

'In bed. Fast asleep, I should think. It's been a long day.'

Calaca nodded. 'Maybe you were right,' he said.

'His story stands up. He seems to be who he says he is.'

Martinez took a deep drag on his cigar, surrounding himself in a cloud of smoke. 'You did well to be suspicious,' he said. 'I thank you for it.'

Calaca inclined his head.

'But if Harry Gold is not Agent 21,' Martinez continued, 'then you must look to your own security personnel.'

Calaca bristled. 'I trust them all,' he said.

'Of course you trust them,' said Martinez. 'That is why they are such a risk. If I were to plant somebody in this household, I would start with them. They have the run of the house, and they carry firearms.' Martinez gave Calaca a meaningful stare. 'You are my head of security, Adan,' he said. 'I trust you. But I want to know you are capable of investigating your own people. Otherwise I will be forced to find another head of security who can. Am I understood?'

Calaca's one eye twitched. 'Yes, Señor Martinez,' he said, his voice emotionless. 'You are understood.'

'Then do what is necessary.' Martinez puffed once more on his cigar and peered towards the floor-to-ceiling windows. 'A beautiful night!' he announced to nobody in particular. 'Sleep well, Adan.' He turned and left the atrium. Seconds later, Calaca followed.

* * *

Zak remained pressed against the banister wall. He'd heard enough of their conversation to realize he'd had a lucky escape. Somehow they knew about Agent 21, but they'd decided it wasn't him.

He waited for silence in the atrium below him, then prepared to return to his room. But just as he was pushing himself to his feet, he heard a sound that he'd been dreading.

Footsteps.

They were coming back along the corridor that led to his room. For a moment he froze. If anyone found him here, he'd never be able to explain it; but his only escape route was down the stairs into the atrium. And so, moving as quickly and as silently as possible, he headed for the top of the staircase. The atrium looked empty, so he rushed down, looking for a place to hide. There was nowhere in the atrium itself – it was all too open – and he stood at the bottom of the stairs for a moment, paralysed with indecision. But then he heard the sound of people talking up on the landing, and he knew he *had* to move. He sprinted across the atrium and into a narrow corridor that led to a flight of steps into the basement. It wasn't ideal – he didn't know where these steps ended up and he could be fixing himself into a corner – but he was there now and was running out of options . . .

The staircase was dark. It led down to a long

corridor. On the right-hand side there was a steel door with a numeric keypad on the outside. Opposite the door was a sight that made him feel slightly sick. It was a cell, not unlike the one he'd been in that morning, with sturdy iron bars and big lock on the door. It was empty, but Zak didn't even want to think what happened to anybody who ended up in there.

This, Zak thought to himself, would be a *very* bad place to be caught.

He gave it two minutes, no longer, before tiptoeing back up the stairs. He took a deep breath, then looked out into the atrium.

It was empty.

All he could do now was move across the open space to the stairs and hope he didn't bump into anyone. Best not to run, because if anybody *did* see him, it would look suspicious. If he was walking, maybe he could talk himself out of the situation.

It took an age to reach the staircase, and another age to climb it. Zak could hear his heart pumping in his ears and he was breathing like he'd just run a mile. He turned left at the top of the stairs and walked along the corridor until it turned a corner round to the left.

And then he stopped.

There was a guard standing five metres away – a young man, no more than twenty years old, wearing a khaki uniform with a rifle slung over his shoulder. Zak stared at him.

The guard stared back.

He had something in his hands, but Zak was too scared to clock what it was. His mind started turning over as he tried to work out an excuse for not being in his room.

The guard looked over his shoulder. Then back at Zak. 'Please,' he said, his eyes wide. 'Do not tell Señor Ramirez you saw me here.' To Zak's astonishment, the guard looked terrified.

'Where should you be?' Zak asked, trying to sound full of authority.

'Outside. Guarding the perimeter with the other guards.' He looked guiltily down at the objects in his hand, and Zak saw what they were. Photographs.

Zak drew himself up to his full height and looked stern. 'What's your name?' he demanded.

'Gonzalez, señor.'

'And what are you looking at, Gonzalez?'

'Pictures of my family, señor. I miss them when I am here. The other guards, they laugh at me . . .'

Zak felt a twist of sympathy for this young guard, but didn't show it. Gonzalez was clearly feeling so guilty about his own actions that he hadn't thought to be suspicious of Zak wandering around the house.

That meant Zak had the upper hand, and he needed to use it.

'You'd better go,' he instructed. 'Now.'

The guard nodded quickly. 'Thank you, señor.' His face filled with gratitude and he hurried away.

Once Gonzalez was gone, Zak hurried back to the room next to his, his veins pumping from his close shave. He jumped on the bed and pulled himself up into ceiling again.

One minute later he was back in his own room, sweating and dizzy with fear. That, he decided, was the last time he went for a midnight wander in this place, no matter *what*.

19

A SUGGESTION

It might have been the most comfortable bed in the world, but Zak slept badly. He nodded off towards sunrise, but was woken again by the dawn chorus, and by his worries. His mission here seemed impossible. Nobody had even mentioned the word drugs and Martinez, for all his jovial nature, was surely too smart to do anything that would incriminate himself in front of Zak. And as for distinguishing him from his body doubles, it was impossible. They weren't just alike; they were identical.

There was no way he was going to sleep again, so he got dressed and left his room. The camera was still directed at his door, but at least there was nothing suspicious about him getting up early.

It was pleasant down by the pool. Martinez's butlers had cleared away all the food from last night and there was a fresh breeze blowing. On the lawn beyond the water, a flock of birds that Zak didn't recognize were pecking for worms. One of them was perched on the headdress of a *La Catrina* statue, but despite those grisly effigies, it was peaceful here. You could almost forget that you were surrounded by observation posts manned by heavily armed militia.

Almost, but not quite.

Zak sat in silence for a while, trying to enjoy the stillness. But he'd only been down for ten minutes when he heard footsteps behind him.

'You are an early riser, like me, Harry?' It was Martinez.

'I couldn't sleep,' Zak said.

Martinez came and sat next to him. His eyes were serious; the playfulness he had shown last night was gone.

'You are still worried about the police, perhaps? You shouldn't be. The police are mine to control. Maybe it is something else. The first time you take a man's life is always the most difficult, you know. After that it becomes easier.'

Zak looked at him sharply, but Martinez was staring out across the grounds.

'You understand what it is that I do, Harry?'

Zak felt his pulse racing. 'Not exactly,' he said. 'I mean, I've got an idea . . .'

'You are a clever lad. A very clever lad. And tell me, what is it, this idea of yours?'

Zak licked his lips, which had suddenly gone dry. 'I think it's something to do with drugs,' he said.

Martinez smiled. 'And do you think I am a bad man, Harry?'

It was all Zak could do to keep his voice level. 'I'm just glad you got me away from the police,' he said.

'Many people think I *am* a bad man. But then, they are not as intelligent as you. I come from a poor village, you know. My parents had barely enough money to clothe or feed my two brothers and me. In Mexico, if you are born poor, you stay poor – unless you can find a way of beating that poverty. Do you understand me, Harry?'

'Yes, señor,' Zak said politely. But in the back of his head he remembered something Michael had told him before he left. *Martinez can charm the birds out of the trees, Zak. Don't let yourself be taken in by him.*

'The economy of Mexico depends on the drugs trade, Harry. Without me, it would collapse. The men who import the coca leaves from Colombia – what do you think would become of them if I did not pay them for their labour? You think there are so many jobs in Mexico that they would find work again? And the poor people in villages like the one where I grew up, you think the government looks after them?'

Zak shook his head.

'*No.*' Martinez's eyes were alight. 'It is up to *me* to

give back to these communities. It is I who builds their churches and their schools. It is *I* who provides money for their sick.'

And it's you, thought Zak, *who kills their families*. The picture of the hanged bodies Michael had shown him burned in his mind.

'People say terrible things about me, Harry. But they do not understand the truth. They do not understand what a man has to do to get on in this world. Do you see what I am saying?'

Zak nodded.

'You are a good lad,' Martinez continued. 'Cruz could do with somebody like you around. Raul bullies him. He thinks I do not see this, but I see more than he knows.' He tapped his forehead with two fingers.

'Why do you let Raul do it?' Zak asked.

'Because I hope it will teach Cruz to be more of a man. To stand up for himself.'

'If someone's being bullied,' Zak said, 'it's difficult for them to do anything.'

Martinez threw his arms into the air. 'Then what am I to do?' he demanded. 'Sit idly by while he becomes an ineffectual nobody?'

'You could just try letting him be himself.' Zak didn't quite know if it was him talking, or Harry. 'He might surprise you.'

'Surprise me? Pff . . .' Martinez stood up and made

a sweeping gesture with one arm. 'I have worked hard all my life to build this empire. How can I leave it to Cruz when he has no interest in business? No interest in *making* something of his life. All he wishes to do is keep his nose in a book. What did books ever teach anybody? Raul, at least, has hunger. He may not be the cleverest boy I've ever met, but he wants to succeed. Maybe the brains will come later, hey?' He looked out again over his land.

Martinez sounded to Zak like he was trying to persuade himself of something, and Zak thought he spotted an opportunity. While Martinez's back was turned, he pulled his phone from his pocket and switched on the voice recorder, before hiding it again.

'What happens to the coca leaves,' he asked, 'once they are picked?'

Martinez turned to look at him, and for a moment there was suspicion in his eyes. He seemed to master it, but he chose his words carefully. 'Some people say there are facilities. Processing centres. The coca leaves are harvested two or three times a year, imported from Columbia, then taken to laboratories in the Mexican jungle where they are turned from raw material into crude cocaine.'

'It must be a complicated process,' Zak observed.

'It is,' Martinez replied. 'The men who know how

to do it are paid well for their efforts. Why are *you* so interested all of a sudden?'

Zak looked away. 'Nothing,' he said. 'It's just . . .'

'Just what?'

'Just something Cruz said to me.'

'What has the boy been saying?'

Zak sighed, pretending that he was reluctant to betray Cruz's confidence. 'He told me he wants to be a scientist,' he said.

'What money is there to be made in science, of all things?' Martinez demanded.

'Well, I don't know. What goes on in these laboratories – that sounds like science to me.'

A pause. Martinez blinked at Zak, who could tell he had the drug lord's attention.

'I mean, it's just a thought, but maybe if you showed Cruz what goes on in these places, it might interest him.'

'You think so?'

Zak shrugged. 'It's worth a try, isn't it?' He couldn't quite believe what he was suggesting. Most boys his age went to football matches with their dads. Here he was trying to persuade Martinez to take his son to a cocaine processing facility. Talk about messed up . . .

'Stand up, Harry Gold,' said Martinez.

Zak stood.

Martinez stepped towards him and Zak couldn't

shake the feeling that the drug lord was examining him, searching his face for any sign of a trap. But then, without any warning, he embraced Zak just as he had the previous day.

'I *knew* you would be a good influence on my son,' he said. 'I could tell the moment I saw you. You will come with us. Together we will turn my son into a Martinez worthy of the name!'

He released Zak and turned towards the house.

'Wake Cruz!' he bellowed at the top of his voice, so loud that the flock of birds on the lawn rose up into the air. 'And bring me Adan! Arrange a helicopter. We are going to take a trip. Now! Harry, come with me!'

Impulsive, Michael had said of Martinez. He wasn't wrong.

On the drug lord's command, guards were suddenly scurrying around the house. Martinez himself jogged towards the atrium. Zak switched off his voice recorder and ran after him.

Two minutes later, Zak was back in his room. His pulse was racing – this was all happening quicker than he'd expected, and he needed to think clearly. He pulled out his phone and pressed an onscreen button. The phone displayed a game and played a jaunty little tune. But after ten seconds it changed: a blank screen with space for a six-digit PIN. Zak entered his code; a moment later a small icon indicated he was connected to Michael's satellite network. He started to upload the voice recorder file. A graphic indicated the status of the upload: 10%, 20%, 50% . . .

While the file was uploading, Zak laid the phone on his bed, opened the cupboard and quickly rifled through the clothes that were hanging there. He soon found what he wanted – a pale blue short-sleeved shirt. Not the sort of thing he'd normally wear, but it had one advantage: a breast pocket on the left-hand side. He estimated the pocket's depth: about ten centimetres. Perfect for what he had in mind . . .

A knock on the door.

'Just a minute,' Zak called. He ran to the phone. 60% . . . 70% . . .

'Zak, it's Cruz? Do you know what's happening?'

80% . . . 90% . . . He quickly changed shirts.

'I'll be right there.'

100%.

Zak disconnected from the satellite network just as a sound he recognized filled the air outside. A shadow crossed over his bedroom window and a chopper started descending onto the lawn outside.

Zak hurried to open the door. Cruz was there. 'Sorry,' said Zak. 'Just using the bathroom.'

'What's happening?' asked Cruz. 'My dad's summoned us – you and me.' He looked over Zak's shoulder. 'What's the helicopter here for? Is something wrong?' There was a slightly panicked expression in his eyes.

Zak did his best to look relaxed. 'Nothing's wrong. I think your dad wants us to go on a little trip, that's all.'

'A trip? What sort of trip? Where to?'

Zak smiled. 'I'll let him explain that,' he said. 'I think he's got something to show you.' He closed the door behind him. 'Come on. We'd better go.'

20

THE LAB

'Señor, this is *not* safe.'

Calaca stood with his boss in the atrium, sweat pouring from his skin. He could smell his own body odour. 'You *never* visit the labs. You *never* visit anywhere that is anything to do with the business, and for a good reason. If anyone *sees* you there . . .'

Martinez held up one hand. 'Adan,' he said. 'This is important to me.'

'If you must go, leave it for a day. Let me put the proper security arrangements in place.'

'Pff . . .' Martinez dismissed his suggestion with a wave of his raised hand.

'Then take a couple of body doubles with you. Or at least, let me come too.'

'It is not necessary. I have my concerns, Adan, you have yours. When we return this evening, I want to know how your investigation is progressing. I want to know who our traitor is.'

Calaca felt his lips thinning. 'You know I will do whatever is necessary. But I wish you would listen to me, señor. What if this is some kind of trap?'

'A trap?' Martinez smiled. 'How can it be a trap, Adan, when it was *my* idea in the first place, just half an hour ago? Unless I am mistaken, our enemies are not mind readers.'

'Then leave Harry Gold here,' Calaca said. 'There is no reason for him to go.'

Martinez's face darkened. 'Adan, we have already had this conversation. Harry Gold is a friend of ours. It is he who has given me this opportunity to get closer to my son. Would you deny me that?'

Calaca said nothing.

'*Would you deny me that?*'

'No, señor.'

'I am very pleased to hear it. *Tonight*, Adan. I want our traitor *tonight*. Otherwise I might start wondering if you are as loyal to me as you say.'

Calaca felt himself frowning. 'Yes, señor.'

'Cruz! Harry!' Calaca looked round to see the two boys entering the atrium. Martinez put one arm round each of their shoulders. All of a sudden it was as if Calaca wasn't even in the room. 'The helicopter is waiting!'

'Where are we going, Father?' asked Cruz.

'Just you wait and see. Somewhere you'll find interesting I think, hey, Harry?'

'Yeah,' said Harry Gold. 'Very interesting.'

It was only momentary, but Calaca thought that as the boy spoke, he gave him a guilty, sidelong glance.

The chopper's doors were open, its blades spinning. Two guards stood five metres from the aircraft, their hair blowing in the downdraught; they were carrying M16 assault rifles. Martinez ran with Cruz and Zak towards the chopper and was the first to climb inside. Cruz went next. Before Zak got on, he looked over his shoulder.

He saw Raul running towards them. 'Wait! Where arc we going?'

'I don't think you're invited.'

Raul gave Zak an evil stare, but appeared lost for words.

Zak winked at him. 'See you later,' he said, and he jumped up into the chopper.

Martinez's helicopter was much more comfortable than the one Zak had taken to and from St Peter's Crag. The seats were made of leather and each one had a personal TV screen; and when the door was shut, the noise of the rotary blades grew much quieter, as if the cabin was soundproofed. Once the two guards had climbed in and taken their positions by the doors, the chopper rose into the air. Within seconds the Martinez compound appeared small and faraway. Zak anxiously put his hand in his pocket to check his phone was there. He wondered if his location was being monitored. He sure hoped so. What he was about to try was dangerous. If he got caught, Raf and Gabs would have to pull him out sooner than they thought. Provided he was still alive, that is.

'You still haven't told me where we're going,' Cruz said.

'There's something I want you to see,' Martinez replied, and he smiled at Zak.

Their flight time was one and a half hours. Cruz had brought a book with him and he sat reading it while Zak looked out of the window. He saw the land underneath change. At first they passed over cities and smaller *pueblos*, but as they headed further south, the terrain became greener and more dense. To the east, Zak could see a mountain range – 'The *Sierra Madre del Tur*,' Martinez told him. 'Very beautiful.' When they finally started to lose height, Zak saw that they were flying over intensely thick jungle, with blue lagoons dotted among it. The chopper zoomed just five metres over the top of the trees, its tail raised slightly, until it stopped and hovered above a clearing, just large enough for it to land. The pilot carefully lowered the aircraft to the ground.

The guards got out first, carefully scoping the area around the chopper to ensure there were no unexpected surprises.

'Is this safe?' Cruz asked. He couldn't hide the nerves in his voice.

Martinez's face was serious. 'We are in the Lacandon Jungle,' he said. 'It is very large. The authorities cannot locate our activities here. Satellite imagery is no good because of the canopy, nor are spy planes or helicopters. And this clearing – it is like a pinprick on a map. Harry, you look worried.'

Zak shook his head and tried to look unconcerned by what Martinez had just said. 'No.'

'Good. Let's go.'

The three of them disembarked. It was unbelievably hot and humid outside, and Zak's skin was moist within seconds. Four swarthy men emerged from the edge of the clearing. They carried AK-47s and had bandoliers of ammo strapped round their bodies.

One of the men approached. He wore body armour and a green military helmet, and he eyed the three of them warily. 'Señor Martinez,' he said. 'This is an unexpected pleasure.'

Zak couldn't help thinking that he didn't look all *that* pleased.

'My name is Andreas. Señor Ramirez called an hour ago and asked me to look after you.'

'You have a family, Andreas?' Martinez spoke slowly. Slyly. All the friendliness he had shown to Zak had disappeared.

A proud look crossed Andreas's face. 'Yes, señor. My wife has just given birth to twins.'

Martinez nodded. 'You have my congratulations. This is my son Cruz and his friend Harry from London.' He licked his fingers and used them to smooth his hair. 'If anything happens to them today, your twins will pay for it with their lives.'

Zak tried not to look shocked as the muscles in Andreas's face tensed up. 'Yes, señor,' said the man.

'I wish to show my son one of the processing laboratories. How far is the nearest one?'

Andreas looked nervous. 'Señor, I do not think it is a good idea for you to . . .'

He stumbled over his words as Martinez gave him a withering glare. 'I didn't ask for your opinion,' he whispered.

'No, señor.'

'How far is the nearest lab?'

'From here, señor, two kilometres. But the helicopter has put you down in a safe zone. There are no roads in from here. We must make the journey by foot.'

Martinez nodded. 'Lead the way.'

They walked in convoy: two guards at the front, then Martinez, Cruz and Zak, and two guards taking up the rear. The moment they stepped out of the clearing and into the jungle, Zak felt like he was in a different world. It was much darker, the only light coming from thin sunbeams that splintered through the canopy overhead. The humidity doubled and after only a minute Zak found that he had to wipe the moisture out of his eyes. Strange squawkings and slitherings curled through the jungle – it was impossible to say what made them, or how near or far they were. The ground underfoot was sometimes mossy and soft, at other times hard and knotted with tree roots. Occasionally, Zak would catch flashes of colour in the green thickets around and above him – an orchid-like flower, or a bright, beautiful parrot on a branch.

Despite the heat, he felt a chill. Everything had happened so quickly, but somehow he'd managed to lure Martinez towards the heart of his drug-processing operation – a place Michael had said he was never normally to be found. This was Zak's chance – a chance to get incriminating footage of the drug lord, but how was he to do it? It wasn't like he could ask Martinez to stand by a pile of cocaine and say 'cheese' . . .

They walked in silence. Occasionally they stopped and one of the guards would run ahead to recce the path. It was slow going and took about an hour.

Eventually, however, they reached another clearing. Unlike the area where the helicopter had landed, this one was not entirely devoid of trees – there were enough to provide cover and to keep the place hidden from the air, but they were more thinly distributed. The convoy stopped and Zak peered into the clearing.

It was like a small encampment, made of cheap buildings that could be easily abandoned if necessary. There were five huts with pitched metal roofs. A track ran through the middle of them and, at right angles to it, there was a fast-moving stream with wooden planks crossing it as a makeshift bridge. Between the bridge and the huts, off to one side, there was a huge electricity generator, the size of a large caravan. It gave off a grinding hum and the smell of burning diesel. There were seven or eight more armed guards positioned at intervals around the clearing, but there were other people too, some of them with clipboards. One of them, a man easily in his sixties, approached them. He wore a white lab coat and square glasses; he avoided looking Martinez in the eye.

'It is an honour to have you here, señor,' he said.

Martinez nodded. 'Dr Sanchez. This is my son, Cruz. I would like you to show him what you do here.'

'Of course, señor.' He smiled rather nervously at Cruz. 'Please, come this way.'

Cruz looked up at his father, who nodded. He followed Dr Sanchez into the little encampment. Zak and Martinez went too, and a moment later they found themselves inside one of the huts.

The huts were shabby on the outside, but inside they were surprisingly modern. The floor and walls were made of burnished steel, and bright halogen lamps hung from the ceiling. In the middle of the room, on a series of sturdy tables, sat several large ceramic containers, each the size of a bath. Dr Sanchez cleared his throat. 'This is the cocaine base lab,' he said, as though talking to a class of students. 'The coca leaf is harvested in Colombia, where it is processed by the addition of cement powder.'

'Cement powder?' asked Zak. 'Why?'

Dr Sanchez opened his mouth to speak, but it was Cruz who answered him. 'Because it's alkaline,' he explained. 'The alkali in the cement powder enables the alkaloid in the leaves to be extracted . . .'

Zak glanced at Martinez. The drug lord's eyes were suddenly shining with pride.

'Quite,' said Dr Sanchez. He looked rather impressed. '*Quite*. Once the alkaloids are extracted, the leaves are turned into coca paste. This is easier to transport than the leaves themselves, so it is in that form that we receive it here.' He walked over to one of the ceramic baths. 'The coca paste is mixed with hydrochloric acid . . .'

'The acid acts as a solvent?' asked Cruz.

Dr Sanchez looked at him over his glasses. 'Indeed it does, young man. We then add a solution of potassium permanganate. This is necessary to extract any remaining alkaloids, otherwise the crystallization of the finished product would be most difficult.'

Zak took a step backwards. Two armed guards were at the door to the lab and they looked alert. Zak wanted to get his phone out and take some photographs of Martinez in this compromising location; but it was just impossible.

Dr Sanchez was still talking. 'We allow the mixture to stand for several hours, then filter it. We discard the precipitate – you understand what the precipitate is, do you, Cruz?'

Cruz nodded.

'He is a very sharp young man, Señor Martinez,' Sanchez observed. 'To the solution we add ammonia and another precipitate is formed. We dry this under heating lamps.' He looked up at Martinez. 'I can show him, if you would like.'

Sanchez led them out of this hut into another. This second lab was equipped with four lines of tables that had long, narrow heat lamps suspended above them. On the tables were trays full of a white powder. 'This is cocaine base,' Sanchez explained. 'It vaporizes at a low temperature, so is suitable for inhalation. But most cocaine is snorted – inhaled up through a tube, like a rolled-up banknote. So we must convert it to a form that is water soluble and can pass through the mucus membrane of the nose. Therefore we have a final stage to convert the cocaine base to cocaine hydrochloride.'

He led them into a third lab. It was different from the others, because one wall was entirely covered with approximately thirty microwave ovens. The floor space was taken up with more ceramic vessels on tables. 'We dissolve the cocaine base in acetone,' explained Sanchez, 'then we add more hydrochloric acid. This causes the cocaine to crystallize as a salt. The resulting HCl is dried in these microwave ovens. It is a very skilled job, because if the HCl is over-cooked, its properties are destroyed and it has no value. Three men have already been—'

He looked at Martinez and stopped himself just in time, leaving Zak to wonder just what *had* happened to these three men. 'Is there anything else you would like me to show you, Señor Martinez?'

Martinez looked at his son. 'Would you like to see more, Cruz?' he asked.

Cruz nodded. For the first time since Zak had seen him, he looked enthusiastic about something. Dr Sanchez led them out of the third lab and they walked for a couple of minutes through this strange jungle encampment. Zak could feel people watching them, but everybody kept away. They clearly knew who their visitor was, and they knew of his reputation. Zak kept his hand in his pocket, his fingers round his phone.

They came to a much larger building – not high, but wide and deep. There were about fifteen people inside and in the middle there was a large machine, about two metres high and one metre wide. In one corner, to the right as they walked in, were five big oil drums. And on the far side of the room was a blue wooden pallet, piled high with what looked like pale bricks.

Martinez put his arm around Cruz's shoulder and walked with him towards the machine. Zak loitered by the door for a moment. Everyone's eyes were firmly on the drug lord and his son. Nobody was paying any attention to Zak. He looked up to check for security cameras. Nothing, so he wandered idly over to where the oil drums were standing and stood behind them.

He pulled his phone from his pocket and activated the video camera.

Zak's hands were shaking and he took a deep breath to steady himself before he slipped the phone into the breast pocket of his shirt, with the eye of the camera pointing outwards and just peeking out of the pocket. He stepped casually out from behind the oil drums, towards Martinez and Cruz.

'This,' Martinez announced, 'is where we press the

cocaine hydrochloride.' He turned to one of the men standing by the machine. 'Show him.'

The man nodded vigorously and clicked his fingers. Another worker scurried up and handed him a plastic container the size of an ice-cream tub. The machine operator poured this into an open-topped box in the middle of the machine before pulling a lever on its side. There was a grinding sound as a hydraulic compression plate eased down onto the powdered cocaine. A dial on the face of the machine started turning: just as it moved into the red, the operator lifted the lever and the compression plate raised, to reveal a neat brick of pressed cocaine.

Martinez stepped forward, picked up the brick and turned to face Cruz. Zak positioned himself so that the camera's eye was pointing directly at him.

'Leave us,' Martinez commanded everyone in the room. The assembled company didn't need to be told twice. They swarmed towards the door as Zak stepped backwards, doing his best to keep Martinez in the frame for as long as possible.

'Harry, you may stay.'

Only when all the others had left the building did Martinez speak again.

'Cruz, do you know what this is?'

'Cocaine, Father.'

Martinez shook his head. 'No. It is much more than

that. It is wealth. It is power. It is what has stopped our family from being paupers. It was Harry's idea that I should bring you here today, to show you that there are parts of our business that might interest you. My dearest wish is that we should control this empire together, you and me. I do not want Raul by my side. I want *you*.'

Martinez put the brick of cocaine back on the machine, then faced Cruz. They stared at each other without saying anything.

And then, a sob.

It came from Cruz, who stepped forward and allowed his father to embrace him.

'Harry,' said Martinez. 'I think you should leave us for a minute.' The drug lord was misty-eyed.

Zak left quickly. Outside the building, the former occupants had gathered in little groups. They looked up as Zak walked out, but lost interest in him immediately when they saw he wasn't Martinez. Zak walked away from them as calmly as he could, past the labs and a few metres into the jungle. Checking over his shoulder to see that nobody was looking, he removed the phone from his breast pocket and tapped the screen to pause the video recording. He rewound through the footage, stopping a couple of minutes in to play it.

. . . *Cocaine, Father.*

. . . No. It is much more than that. It is wealth. It is power.

The image was grainy and juddery, but Martinez's face was as clear as his words, and the footage showed the brick of cocaine. If this wasn't sufficient evidence for Michael, nothing would be . . .

He tapped the screen again and waited for thirty nervous seconds while the phone attempted to locate Michael's satellite network. When finally it did, he started to upload the video.

5% . . .

10% . . .

It was painfully slow. He heard activity back in the village.

'Come on,' he muttered. 'Come on, *come on* . . .'

15% . . .

20% . . .

And then a voice. Shouting.

'*Harry? Harry, where are you?*'

It was Martinez.

Zak's felt his heart in his throat. He *had* to get this file uploaded and wiped from his phone, and he had to do it *now* . . .

Martinez emerged from the building with his arm round his son. It had been an emotional moment, but he didn't intend to let his staff see that. 'Get back to work,' he instructed. He looked around. '*Harry?*' he called. '*Harry, where are you?*' And then to Cruz: 'Where is Harry? It is time for us to leave.'

But Harry Gold was nowhere to be seen.

Martinez's eyes narrowed. He grabbed one of the men who was re-entering the building. 'The boy,' he demanded. 'Where did he go?'

The man pointed away from the building, towards the edge of the encampment. 'That way, señor.'

Martinez turned to Cruz. 'Follow me,' he said.

They found him almost immediately. Harry Gold had his back to the encampment and his head was bowed as though he was looking at something. Martinez walked up behind him and stopped when he was just two metres away.

'What are you doing?' he asked in a quiet, danger-ous voice.

The boy span round. His phone was in his hands and he had a guilty look on his face.

'Nothing,' he said. 'Nothing, I promise.'

'Give me the phone.'

Harry's eyes darted from left to right, but he handed it over.

'Cruz, you understand these devices. Check what's on it.' Martinez handed the phone to his son, then licked the tip of his fingers and patted down his hair. He didn't take his eyes off Harry.

Thirty seconds of silence. An animal shrieked somewhere behind them.

Cruz stepped forward. He had clearly brought something up on the screen and he handed it to his father.

Martinez stared at the screen.

He blinked.

He was looking at a photograph of a brightly coloured bird. A parrot. Glancing over Harry's shoulder, Martinez saw the exact same bird, perched on the branch of a tree.

'There is nothing else on this phone?'

'Nothing, Father.'

'I . . . I'm sorry,' Harry Gold stuttered. 'I didn't mean to go off. I just wanted a picture of the wildlife. I've never been to the jungle before.'

Martinez paused, and then a fat, relieved smile crossed his lips. 'Of course,' he announced. 'Of *course*! But Harry, we must go. The helicopter is waiting for us, and this isn't a good place for us to stay too long.' He handed the phone back and put one arm around Zak's shoulders. 'Come,' he said. 'You have done well, Harry. Cruz and I have much to discuss. We leave in five minutes.'

21

THE TRAITOR

Calaca sat in his basement office, his skin sweaty and his one good eye red with tiredness. All day he had been examining the files of the security personnel in the Martinez compound, searching for something – anything – that might tell him who the traitor was. But he found nothing.

And now, he knew, he had a choice to make.

His boss was unstable. Jolly one moment, psychotic the next. He rewarded loyalty generously; but anyone suspected of treachery paid for it with their life. If Calaca told Martinez that he suspected one of the guards of being a traitor, he knew what would happen: the guard would be taken from the compound into the surrounding countryside and he wouldn't come back. And then his family would be hung from a tree.

But if he *didn't* come back to Martinez with a name, what then? That morning his boss had said he would consider Calaca himself to be a traitor, which meant *he'd* be the one to get the noose round his neck.

And he wasn't about to let *that* happen.

No. He needed a name. Any name would do. It didn't matter if they were *really* a traitor. What mattered was that Martinez thought Calaca was on top of things.

He started going through his files again until he pulled the details of a guard called Gonzalez. He was a young man of twenty, quite new to the compound. He had a wife, three children and two elderly parents to support. Seven close family members. Calaca nodded quietly to himself. He knew how Martinez's mind worked. The more people he killed, the safer he thought he was. If he ordered Calaca to kill Gonzalez and his family – to hang them from the trees of their village – the one-eyed man's loyalty would never be in doubt . . .

He looked at his watch. 5 p.m. They would be back any minute. He stood up and loosened the weapon in its holster beneath his Mexico football shirt. By the time Martinez returned, he would have Gonzalez in custody.

After that, his boss only had to say the word.

The return flight seemed to take twice as long. Maybe it was Zak's nerves. He'd only just managed to upload the video, delete it from his phone and take a picture of the parrot. If Martinez and Cruz had returned thirty seconds earlier, he'd have been toast.

But somehow he wasn't. Somehow he was even closer to Martinez and Cruz than he had been when they left that morning. The drug lord was beaming; his son was full of questions about the cocaine lab and how it worked. Every so often Martinez would glance at Zak with a grateful look on his face. *I have you to thank for this*, he seemed to be saying.

It was a quarter past five when they touched down on the compound's helipad. Zak was looking forward to rushing up to his room to get some much needed time alone. But his heart sank as they disembarked and he saw Calaca waiting for them just ten metres away, his green football shirt ruffling in the downdraught.

'We need to talk!' Calaca shouted over the noise of the rotary blades.

Martinez nodded.

'Alone, señor.'

Martinez appeared to think about that. 'No,' he said finally. 'Things have changed. It is time for Cruz to be involved in our decisions. Harry, you come too.'

Calaca looked like he was about to argue, but Martinez gave him a dangerous look and he kept quiet.

The room in which they met was an ornate office

just off the atrium. In some ways it reminded Zak of Michael's office back on St Peter's Crag, with its big wooden desk and large windows looking out onto the compound grounds. Martinez sat at the desk, on which there was a large, ornate vase full of yellow roses, only half open. He folded his hands in front of him. Calaca stood on the other side, while Cruz and Zak remained discreetly by the door.

'So, Adan?' Martinez asked. 'You have news for me?'

'There is a traitor, señor, and I know who he is.'

Zak felt his heart in his mouth. Immediately he started scanning the room for his best exit. The main door would be no good because there was an armed guard outside; the only other way out was through the windows. It would mean breaking through them, but . . .

'His name is Gonzalez,' Calaca continued. 'I have him in custody now.'

Zak tried to control his breathing. He remembered the guard, of course, who had stealthily been looking at pictures of his family while Zak was conducting his midnight search of the house. He remembered how grateful he was. How scared.

Martinez's face was expressionless. 'You are sure it is him?'

'You want to see the evidence?'

Martinez shook his head. 'No, Adan,' he said. 'I

trust your judgement.' He turned to Cruz. 'There are people who want to destroy our family, Cruz. They will do it, if we let them. We have learned that there is a traitor in the compound. For a moment, Adan even thought it was young Harry here.'

Zak took a step back as he felt all eyes on him. Martinez seemed to find this funny; Calaca most certainly didn't.

'Relax, Harry,' Martinez announced. 'The spotlight of suspicion has moved to someone else.' His smile changed instantly to a frown and he looked back at Cruz. 'You understand, my son, that we must stamp on these threats the moment they appear?'

Cruz nodded. 'Yes, Father,' he said.

Martinez looked satisfied. 'Good. Adan, what do we know about this Gonzalez? About his family.'

'He is married, señor, with three young children – two girls and a baby boy. His parents live with them.'

Martinez's eyes were dead. 'He denies everything, of course.'

'Of course, señor.'

A pause.

Martinez stood up and slapped his hands together as though brushing crumbs away. 'Tonight,' he said to Zak and Cruz, 'we eat together once again. I shall see you by the pool at seven o'clock. And now, gentlemen, Adan and I have things to discuss. You will excuse us, I hope.'

Zak didn't need any more encouragement to leave the room. His head was spinning, and he and Cruz were halfway across the atrium before either of them spoke.

'What will happen to that guard?' Zak asked.

Cruz shrugged. 'My father treats those who are disloyal to him severely. Do you have a problem with that?'

Zak shook his head. 'No,' he said. 'It's not my business.' They reached the stairs. 'I need to shower,' he said. 'I'll see you later, OK?'

'OK.'

Up in his room, Zak paced like a madman. Gonzalez was a good man, even though he was one of Martinez's guards. Zak could tell that easily enough. He kept thinking of what Calaca had said. *Two girls and a baby boy.* He had no doubt what lay in store for them. A bullet if they were lucky. The hangman's noose if not. What should he do? he wondered. Sit back and let it happen, all in the name of preserving his cover? That would probably be Michael's instruction.

But Michael wasn't here, and Zak couldn't have the murder of an entire family on his hands. He wasn't going to sit by and watch it happen. Not when there was something else he could do . . .

He took his phone from his pocket. Rummaging in one of his bedside drawers he found a propelling pencil. He clicked the lead out several notches and inserted it into the small hole at the top of the handset. The SIM card holder clicked out. It was longer than most, and held two cards – the actual SIM card, and the self-powered GPS chip the guardian angels were using to track him. He secreted the GPS chip in the sock of his right foot and replaced the SIM card holder into the phone. If he could find Gonzalez and give him the GPS chip, he could alert the guardian angels. They could swoop in and rescue the guard. Zak would be left in the compound – without his tracking device, it was true, but with a bit of fast talking he might be able to stop the mission from being compromised . . .

For a moment he considered leaving via the ceiling to stop himself being viewed on the security camera. But there was no time for that. He needed to find this Gonzalez quickly, before they took him away. Instead, he grabbed a pair of swimming trunks and a towel from the wardrobe full of clothes in his room. If anyone saw him, he'd say he was going for a swim.

He took a deep breath and left the room.

Zak walked slowly along the corridor towards the landing which overlooked the atrium. The chirruping of the songbirds in their cage grew louder and soon he was walking down the staircase. Once he was in the atrium itself, he scoped the place out.

A guard walked through and frowned at him. Zak smiled, held up his swimming gear and headed towards the pool. But as soon as the guard had disappeared to the front of the house, he double-backed on himself.

He didn't know for sure where Gonzalez was being held, but he had a pretty good idea. Zak crossed the atrium towards the basement stairs down which he had hidden the previous night.

It was still dark and gloomy down there. Zak hurried down the stairs, his skin prickling as he went. And sure enough, in the cell along the left-hand side of the basement corridor, he saw a man.

He was huddled in the far corner of the cell, clutching his knees, and he looked pretty bad. His dark eyes were wild with terror and he had a great purple bruise on one side of his face. He'd clearly taken a beating. He looked at Zak.

'Kill me,' he said in a hoarse, painful voice. 'Do whatever you want to me. But leave my family, I beg of you.' There were tears in his voice.

Zak looked over his shoulder, then approached the bars. 'Listen carefully,' he hissed. 'I'm not killing anyone. I *know* you're not a traitor to Martinez. I'm here to help you.'

Gonzalez stared at him, a glimmer of hope in his eyes.

'Who are you?' he asked.

'It doesn't matter who I am,' whispered Zak. 'They're going to kill you and your family. If you want any chance of getting out of this alive, you have to do *exactly* as I say. OK?'

Gonzalez stood up. He wasn't much taller than Zak himself, but he was stocky and strong. He approached the bars. 'You would really risk this?' he asked, his eyes slightly wide.

'Yes. But we *have* to hurry.'

Gonzalez was right by the bars now. He held out his hand. 'My brother,' he said, his face shining with gratitude.

'Yeah, whatever.' Zak impatiently took Gonzalez's hand. But the moment they touched, he knew he'd made a terrible mistake.

Gonzalez clutched Zak's hand, squeezing it hard and pulling his arm through the bars. He grabbed hold with his other hand and his eyes lit up with triumph as he started to shout at the top of his voice.

'GET DOWN HERE,' he yelled. 'GET DOWN HERE NOW. I HAVE FOUND YOUR TRAITOR. HE IS WITH ME. I HAVE HIM! *GET DOWN HERE, NOW!*'

22

THE DEVIL'S CHOICE

Panic surged through Zak. He struggled to get away, but Gonzalez kept a firm grip on him, pinning him to the bars of the cell. And in less than a minute he was surrounded by three more guards, all armed, all pointing their weapons in his direction. Only then did Gonzalez let go.

'He tried to help me escape,' the prisoner said in an urgent voice. 'Tell Calaca. Tell him what he did!'

'He's lying,' Zak protested. 'He's trying to save himself . . .'

But the guards didn't want to listen. They hustled him away from the cell and up the stairs. Calaca, who had clearly heard the commotion, was striding across the atrium. One of Zak's guards approached and they spoke quietly.

Calaca's face was expressionless as he listened. When the guard had finished, he paused for a moment, fixed Zak with his single eye and wiped some sweat from his forehead with the back of his hand. Then he spoke.

'Bring him with me.'

Calaca moved purposefully, across the atrium towards the door of Martinez's office. He didn't bother to knock – he just burst straight in, and Zak was thrown in behind him.

Martinez was at his desk, smoking a cigar and reading through some papers. The yellow roses on his desk that Zak had noticed the previous day were fully open now. Martinez looked up in irritation. 'What is it, Adan? I don't wish to be disturbed right now . . .'

'Harry Gold was caught trying to help Gonzalez escape. He was found outside the cell. *He* is your traitor. *He* is Agent 21.'

A horrible silence filled the room. Martinez calmly laid his papers on the desk in front of him. When he spoke, it was in little more than a whisper. 'Is this true, Harry?'

'No, señor.'

'Then what were you doing outside the cell?' Martinez appeared perfectly calm.

'I . . . I was just being nosy, señor. I was on my way to the pool and I wondered what was down those stairs. I got talking to Gonzalez and he grabbed me and started shouting for the guards.'

Martinez nodded. 'A reasonable explanation, wouldn't you say, Adan? This Gonzalez would try to pin the blame on anyone. We have seen people do worse things to try and save their skin, after all.'

Calaca looked like he was going to spit. 'Señor,' he said. 'You are not seeing things as they are . . .'

Another silence. Martinez looked from Zak to Calaca, then back again. He looked like he was deciding which one to believe.

'Bring Gonzalez here,' he said finally.

Calaca barked an instruction and two of the guards disappeared. Zak felt sweat trickling down his back. Nobody spoke and it was impossible to read the expression on the drug lord's face.

Two minutes later, the guards reappeared. They had Gonzalez with them, his hands tied behind his back. They pushed him further into the room so that he was standing a couple of metres away from Zak, just in front of Martinez's desk.

The drug lord examined them both.

'It seems,' he said, 'that I have to choose between you.'

He stood up, walked around the desk and behind the two prisoners. 'Gonzalez, Adan tells me you are a traitor. That there is no doubt about it.'

'No, señor . . . I swear . . . I would not dare . . .'

'*Silence.*'

He continued to pace behind them.

'And you, Harry. Yesterday you saved my son, today

you saved my family by bringing us closer. I have much to thank you for.'

Zak kept his head held high. He didn't trust himself to answer.

'And yet . . . and yet . . .' Martinez mused. 'Perhaps Adan is right. Perhaps I would be foolish to ignore these warning signs.'

He walked back to his desk, gently touched one of the yellow roses and bent down slightly to smell its fragrance. 'Do you know, Harry, what the yellow rose represents in Mexico?'

Zak shook his head.

'It represents death.' He pulled one of the long stems out of the vase then returned to his seat and continued to smell the rose for a little while longer, his eyes closed.

'Adan,' he said finally. 'Give me your gun.'

Calaca approached and removed his handgun from underneath his green football shirt. He placed it on the desk in front of his boss and took a step backwards. Martinez laid one hand almost tenderly on the handgun. He picked it up and pointed it at Gonzalez. The handcuffed prisoner started to shake. 'No, señor . . .' he breathed.

Martinez ignored him. He moved his aim towards Zak, who just jutted his chin out a bit further.

'Maybe,' Martinez whispered, 'I should just kill you both, to be on the safe side.'

He waved the gun at Gonzalez, then at Zak again.

And then he laid it once more on the table.

Zak felt like a mouse being played with by a cat. Half of him considered taking his phone out there and then and dialling the distress number. But that would just give him away and the chances were that Martinez would shoot him immediately.

No. He had to brave this out. He had to keep up the pretence.

'Harry,' Martinez said. 'I am a fair man. I shall give you the benefit of the doubt.'

Gonzalez's legs buckled. 'Please, señor . . . my little ones . . .'

'*Silence!*' shouted Martinez. He took a deep breath to calm himself, then looked back at Zak. 'As I was saying,' he continued, 'I will give you the benefit of the doubt. I shall give you the chance to prove that you are not a traitor or a mole. That you are loyal to me and nobody else.' Martinez's face twitched. 'Take the gun,' he said.

Zak gave him a confused look. 'I don't understand.'

'It's very simple, Harry. I told you to take the gun.'

Zak's eyes flickered nervously between Martinez and Calaca. He stepped round the side of the desk and picked up the weapon. The handle felt slippery in his sweaty palm.

'Good,' said Martinez. 'Now then. Kill Gonzalez.'

Zak blinked. It was the Devil's choice: kill an innocent man, or save his skin.

'Perhaps you didn't hear me, Harry. Kill him. Now.'

Gonzalez started to shake – '*Please, señor . . .*' – but Martinez was deaf to him. All his attention was on Zak. 'I know it does not worry you to kill a man,' Martinez almost purred. 'You showed me that yesterday. Now I am giving you an opportunity to prove that your loyalty to me has not been an act.'

Zak licked his lips. He raised the gun towards Gonzalez.

'That's right,' whispered Martinez. 'Do it now.'

Zak felt sick. His brain burned. He tried to work out what Michael would tell him to do. What would Raf say? Or Gabs? Would they tell him to kill this man? To turn his children into orphans and his wife into a widow?

Was that the sort of person he'd turned into?

Gonzalez started to whimper. His head was bowed and his shoulders were shaking. Zak imagined Calaca and his men turning up at Gonzalez's house, ready to kill his family. Could he really let that happen?

But then he imagined what they would do to him if he failed to shoot this man. He remembered something Michael had said months ago. *There are a great many people out there who don't play by the same rules as ordinary folk.* Cesar Martinez Toledo was, without doubt, one of those people. His retribution would be violent . . .

All eyes were on him. His hand didn't shake as he kept the weapon pointed at Gonzalez.

He looked the terrified man in the eye.

And then he lowered the gun and placed it back down on the table. The game was up.

'I won't kill an innocent man,' he said in a hoarse voice. He turned towards Martinez. 'I'm not a murderer, unlike you.'

A strange expression crossed Martinez's face: a brief look of pain, as if Zak's betrayal had truly hurt him.

But it didn't last long.

'Search him,' he instructed.

It was Calaca himself who patted Zak down like an airport security official. He found Zak's phone immediately, of course, and confiscated it; but he failed to locate the tiny GPS chip which Zak had secreted in his sock. That wasn't much comfort. Now that Zak couldn't let his controllers know he was in trouble, all the GPS chip would do was lead them to his corpse . . .

'Lock him up,' Martinez said in a flat voice. 'Keep a guard outside the cell.' He looked up at Zak. 'I treated you as a friend, Harry Gold,' he whispered. 'I treated you as *family*. You saw fit to betray that trust, and now you will feel the anger of Cesar Martinez

Toledo. We will wait until after dark. Then my men will take you from the compound and deal with you.' He turned to Calaca. 'I want *you* to be the one who executes him, Adan. Leave his body hanging, so that the birds start to peck at his flesh. Then, when he can still be recognized, dump his body outside the house of this Uncle Frank. I want the old man to know what awaits him after we kill him too. Report back to me when the boy is dead. Now get him out of my sight. I never want to see this fool again.'

A nod from Calaca, and the guards roughly man-handled Zak out of the office. Just as he was leaving, he heard Martinez's voice again. 'And kill this Gonzalez, just to be sure . . .'

'No!' Zak shouted. '*No!*'

But too late. The office door closed behind him just as there was a shot. A shot that meant Gonzalez's children had just been orphaned.

Out in the atrium, he saw Cruz. He was coming down the stairs as Zak was being forced towards the basement. Their eyes met, and Cruz looked confused. He didn't do anything, though. He just stood on the stairs and watched as the guards forced Zak down towards the cell.

One of them opened the cell door; another hurled Zak inside. He heard the door being locked almost before he hit the ground with a thump. He winced, wondering for a minute if his arm had been broken. But he could move it all right – not that it would do him much good, locked in here, waiting for Calaca to come and finish him off. Perhaps there would be an interrogation first. He thought back to his ordeal on the island. Calaca, he knew, would not show the same restraint as his guardian angels. He could be in for a very unpleasant few hours – if he even lasted that long.

There was no time for self-pity, though. He thought of Gonzalez. The man had double-crossed him, but that wasn't his family's fault. Zak was filled with a new sense of urgency. He had to bring Martinez to justice. He *had* to . . .

There was one guard outside. He stood against the far wall and was carrying an MP5. He looked at Zak with a sneer but didn't say anything.

Terror surged through Zak's veins. Panic. He heard Gabs's voice in his head. *If you can admit you're scared, that's the first step to controlling it. And if you can't control your fear, it can get in the way of you making the right decisions.*

Control his fear. That was what he had to do. As long as he was still alive, he had a chance . . .

He stepped up to the bars. The guard nudged his MP5 in Zak's direction.

'Help me,' Zak whispered. 'I'm rich. Get me out of here and you'll never have to work again.'

The guard's cheek twitched, but he didn't say anything.

'I mean it,' said Zak. 'I can give you more money than Martinez will pay you in a lifetime. You'd be a wealthy man, and I can stop Martinez or Calaca from *ever* finding you.'

The guard didn't even look tempted. 'Calaca can find *anyone*,' he said.

'Not you,' said Zak. 'I can see to it.'

'You don't know what you're talking about,' whispered the guard. He looked around guiltily, as though just speaking to Zak was a criminal offence. 'They'd kill me even for thinking about it. You can keep your money. It's not worth risking my family's life for.'

Zak could tell he was beaten. He gritted his teeth and looked down at the ground. 'Will they really kill Gonzalez's wife and children?' It was important that he knew.

The guard almost seemed to find this question funny. 'They don't care *who* they kill,' he replied. 'The more the better.' He looked around again. 'A year ago,' he said, 'there was a rumour that an American journalist had evidence against Martinez. You know what he did?'

'What?'

'He got hold of the journalist's schedule. Found out

that he was going to a conference in Nigeria. And then, in order to eliminate just that one man, he killed *all* the guests at the hotel. Just for *one man* . . .'

Zak felt like he'd been kicked in the stomach. The guard continued to talk, but Zak didn't hear a word.

A hotel in Nigeria. All the guests killed.

The faces of his parents rose in his mind, and he clenched the bars of the cell hard – so hard that his knuckles went white. His breath came in short, sharp bursts. In one part of his mind he realized the guard was looking at him strangely, but he didn't care, because at that moment there was really only one thought in his head.

And that thought was very clear: Cesar Martinez Toledo had killed his parents. And now he was about to kill Zak too.

23

THE HANGMAN'S NOOSE

Time passes quickly when you're waiting to die.

They came at midnight: Calaca and three others. The one-eyed man carried a long, thick rope with a noose neatly tied at one end. They found Zak curled up in a corner of the cell, clutching himself with his arms and staring out at them with hatred in his eyes.

Calaca turned to one of the guards – a short, stocky man with a shaven head and square shoulders. 'Carlos, tie him.'

The guard Zak had tried to bribe opened the door and Carlos entered. He was carrying a small bag, from which he removed a set of Plasticuffs. 'Put your hands behind your back,' he instructed.

'Or what?' spat Zak.

Carlos didn't hesitate. He just booted Zak hard in his belly so that he was immediately gasping for breath. The stocky man bent down, pulled Zak easily to his feet and threw him against the wall. He forced his hands behind his back and tied them. Zak was still trying to get a lungful of air when Carlos pulled a hood from his bag. He covered Zak's head.

The hood was made of a coarse, scratchy cloth. It would have been difficult to breathe through even if Zak hadn't been winded. Nobody cared about that, though. Carlos grabbed him by his right arm and walked him out of the cell and up the stairs. When Zak stumbled, Carlos didn't slow down. His knees scraped against the stairs as he tried to scramble back up to his feet.

And then they were outside, because it was slightly cooler. Zak heard Calaca issue a muffled instruction. About twenty seconds later he heard the sound of a vehicle drive up. Several vehicles, in fact, but he couldn't tell exactly how many. Carlos made him move again. Zak felt a hand on the back of his head, which was forced downwards. It felt like he was being shoved into the boot of a vehicle; seconds later he felt the boot shut above him, and heard the clunking sound of the lock.

He wanted to shout out for help, but he knew how futile that would be, here in the centre of Martinez's compound. *Keep calm*, he told himself. *Just keep calm.*

He thought through his options. Calaca had taken his phone, so there was no way he could dial the distress number; he just had to hope the GPS chip was still transmitting. Zak awkwardly used his left foot to kick off his right shoe, then managed to worm his foot out of the sock. He shuffled around so that he could pick up the sock and remove the chip. It was impossible to be sure that the signal would penetrate the metal of the car, but it had a better chance now it was out of his shoe. All he could do was pray that the guardian angels were tracking him, and that he could somehow raise the alarm.

Keep calm, he repeated to himself. *Keep calm* . . .

But it was almost impossible, stuck in the back of this vehicle which he now felt moving away.

Impossible, because he knew that when the boot was opened, he could be only seconds away from a horrible, painful death.

In the London control centre, Michael stared at a live satellite feed. A flashing green dot was moving along the road that led away from the Martinez compound. He turned to Sophie, the girl who was operating the equipment. 'Can you get a closer look?' he asked.

'The signal's weak,' Sophie said, but she typed a few commands on the screen and the satellite image zoomed in. It was dark, and difficult to make much of this grainy image; but Michael thought he could just see three sets of headlamps.

'He's moving,' Michael murmured. 'Three vehicles in convoy. But we can't tell why or who with.'

He looked up at a wall where a clock showed Mexico time. Five past midnight. He sucked his teeth. Why would Zak be moving out of the compound at this time of night?

Michael picked up the phone and dialled a number. The first ring hadn't even finished when Gabs answered.

'Are you watching this?' Michael asked.

'Of course.'

'Make any sense to you?'

'None. I don't like it. We should go in, Michael. Pick him up. You've got your evidence. This has gone far enough.'

Michael thought about that for a moment.

'No,' he said.

'He's just a kid, Michael . . .'

'*No*. The fact that we can track his signal means he has his phone with him. If he has his phone, he can dial in the distress call.'

'What if it's not him? What if somebody else has his phone?'

'Then this is a trap, and we're not going to fall for it. We'll monitor his movements carefully, but for now do nothing.'

'But—'

'That's an order, Gabriella.'

Michael hung up the phone and went back to watching the screen.

There was hardly any wriggle room in the boot – certainly not enough for Zak to get up onto his knees – and every time the vehicle went over a bump in the road, he felt like he got a new bruise. His body ached, but he had to forget about that. His captors might stop the car any minute, and when they did, he had to be ready.

His hands were tied behind his back but he was able to feel for his belt – the one Gabs had given him on St Peter's Crag. He needed to get access to the buckle, and to do that he had to twist it round so the buckle was at the back. It was hard work. Every time the buckle hit a loop on his trousers it got caught, and he had to coax it through slowly.

Not easy, when he knew that time was running out.

But eventually his fingers could grasp the buckle. He gripped it at both sides and pulled it open to reveal the hidden blade. The vehicle bumped and shuddered along the road while Zak, in the darkness, attempted to slice the sturdy plastic of his handcuffs.

'*Ow!*' He let out a muffled cry as the blade dug into his wrist and he felt blood seeping over his skin. He had to ignore it and he kept on at the Plasticuffs, sliding them gently against the blade, until finally they snapped open.

As quickly as possible, Zak replaced the blade and unhooded himself, before putting his sock and shoe back on and making sure the GPS chip was firmly in his hand. It was still pitch black, but at least he could breathe a bit better. He felt for the locking mechanism of the boot. Maybe if he could get it open . . .

But no. It wouldn't budge. There was no way he was getting out of here until somebody opened it up from outside.

When that happened, he'd just have to be ready.

Zak positioned himself so that his back was facing the front of the vehicle and his legs were bent at the knee, pressed up against the rear of the boot. Quite how long he stayed like that, he couldn't have said. Maybe ten minutes, maybe twenty.

Soon, however, he felt the vehicle slowing down.

His muscles ached from his uncomfortable position. His pulse raced and he was sweating with fear. But he knew he had to ignore all that if he was going to get through this.

The vehicle stopped.

Calaca's voice from outside. 'Tie up the rope.'

Zak tensed up, like a tightly coiled spring.

He put the GPS chip in his pocket and waited.

Footsteps outside the boot.

The sound of a key in the lock.

And then the boot opened up.

Light flooded in.

He had to time it well. Too early and he wouldn't be effective; too late and he'd lose the element of surprise. The boot door was open just over halfway when he struck, jabbing his feet out sharply into the belly of the man standing there. There was a moment of solid contact and a low groan.

This was his chance. He had to move. Now.

Zak jumped out of the boot to see that he had hit Carlos. The stocky man was doubled over in pain. Zak didn't hesitate. He raised his right knee with as much force as he could manage, whacking Carlos underneath the chin. The Mexican guard's head flew back just as Zak clenched his fist and delivered a fierce punch to the side of his face. Carlos hit the ground.

Zak saw now that the guard was carrying an MP5, which he grabbed before giving himself a couple of seconds to take in his surroundings. There were two other trucks in front of him, each of which had a set of three bright headlamps fixed to its roof. The headlamps were shining directly at Zak, dazzling him slightly and stopping him from seeing anyone else in or behind the trucks. Although he couldn't see them, he could hear their shouting.

He looked to left and right. They were on a thin,

straight road – more of a track, really. On one side was a sheer drop. How far down it went, Zak couldn't tell, but it was too steep to use as an escape route. On the other side was a line of trees starting about twenty metres from the road and extending as far as he could see in both directions.

'*Shoot him!*'

Zak recognized Calaca's voice immediately, but he didn't have time to be scared. A shot rang out, and he felt a rush of air as it whizzed past his head. A pinging sound as it ricocheted off the open boot door.

'*SHOOT HIM!*'

There wasn't even time to think. Zak flicked the safety catch on the MP5, raised it above the level of the trucks, and fired a burst of covering fire.

Then he ran.

He sprinted towards the line of trees just as the air was filled with the crack of gunfire. Rounds landed on either side of him in the dust, missing him by inches. He kept his attention firmly on the trees, and could see the noose hanging from a low branch.

Fifteen metres to go. More rounds.

Ten.

Five.

'*KILL HIM!*' Calaca screamed, but now Zak was a metre away from cover. A round ripped into a tree, throwing bark splinters into his eyes. Then he was beyond the tree line. It was dark, and treacherous underfoot, but Zak didn't slow down.

He *couldn't* slow down.

His whole life depended on how fast he could run.

Calaca slammed his fist against the hard metal of the truck. He walked round to where Carlos was groggily pushing himself up from the ground.

'*Idiot*,' he hissed.

'Señor Ramirez, I . . .'

But Calaca didn't want to hear it. He pulled his handgun out from under his green football shirt, aimed it at the guard's head and fired. Blood and brain matter spattered over Calaca's football shirt as Carlos fell dead to the ground. By that time, though, Calaca had already turned away. He waved his gun around in the general direction of the other guards – four of them – that he had brought with him. 'I'll kill the rest of you *and* your families if you don't find him.'

The guards looked nervously at each other.

'*WHAT ARE YOU WAITING FOR?*' Calaca roared. '*FIND HIM! NOW!*'

24

OUT OF THE WOODS

Zak sprinted through the trees, trying to keep to a straight line so that he at least knew where he was. Twice he stumbled and fell to the ground, grazing his knees and his forearms; twice he pushed himself back up and forced himself to keep running as fast as he could, even though his muscles and lungs were burning. After all, a bit of pain now was a lot better than the alternative.

Two minutes passed.

Three.

The trees stopped suddenly. Zak found himself looking out over a vast open area. By the bright light of the moon, he could see that it was dotted with wild, thorny-looking bushes about the height of his chest, and boulders, some of which were bigger than him. The line of trees ran left to right. For how far, he couldn't tell.

He was gasping for breath, and as he gave himself

twenty seconds to rest against the trunk of a tree, he attempted to think clearly. To carry on running blindly would be suicide. Eventually they'd find him, and when that happened . . .

No. He needed to get out of the range of these guards and their guns. And to do that, he needed a strategy. Some way of getting them off the scent. A plan formed in his mind. It was risky, but he couldn't think of anything better. For it to work, he needed some idea of where he was. Of direction and location. Not easy, here in the middle of nowhere.

He remembered one night, six months ago on St Peter's Crag. His first night. He looked up into the sky and the stars looked back at him. His eyes searched for the familiar patterns: the saucepan shape of Ursa Major, and the W of Cassiopeia. And between the two of them, twinkling brightly, Polaris – the North Star. It was directly ahead of him as he had his back to the forest, which meant the line of trees was running from west to east.

'Nice one, Raf,' he murmured as he turned to the west and started to sprint along the tree line. He counted his strides as he went. Once he'd covered two hundred westward paces he stopped.

He waited ten seconds, then started to shout.

'Help!' he bellowed at the top of his voice. '*Help me!*'

He paused and allowed his shouts to echo away, before shouting again – injecting a note of panic into his voice. *'HELP ME!'*

He listened carefully. There was no sound of Calaca's guards, but he knew not to be fooled by that. They would be moving towards the sound of his voice, quickly and quietly.

He headed north, away from the tree line and into the area of wide open bushes and boulders, occasionally checking Polaris to make sure his bearing was straight. He estimated he had covered about fifty metres before he stopped and looked back. The trees were barely visible from here – all he could see was a silhouette of their tops against the bright, starry sky. He felt confident nobody along the tree line would be able to see him either, especially as he was mostly hidden by the height of the thorny bushes and the boulders.

He checked Polaris and turned again, east this time, and continued to run, counting his strides and stopping every twenty paces to double-check his bearing. He was dripping with sweat by the time he'd done two hundred, at which point he turned south and headed back towards the trees. This, according to his calculations, was exactly where he'd started off from. All he needed to do was run in a straight line back through the woods and he'd come out where the vehicles had stopped. Calaca's guards would still be looking for him where he'd been shouting for help. At least, that was the plan.

Zak clutched his MP5 firmly, took a deep breath and plunged into the forest once again.

'Michael, what's going on?' Gabriella sounded panicked.

The truth was, Michael didn't know. From the control centre overlooking the Thames in London, he had watched the green dot trace its way across the screen, moving in perfect sync with the three sets of vehicle headlamps. When the convoy had stopped, the green dot had moved away from the road. As Michael had watched it move, he thought at first that Zak was performing some kind of defensive manoeuvre and was on the point of sending in Raphael, Gabriella and the unit. But at the last minute, Zak had started moving quickly back towards the convoy. It didn't make any kind of sense.

'Are you on standby?'

'I've been on standby for the last forty-eight hours, Michael. When are you going to send us in?'

Michael watched the green dot. It was by the road again.

'Not yet,' he said quietly, as a bead of sweat trickled down the side of his face. 'Not just yet . . .'

* * *

As Zak ran through the trees, he strained his ears to listen for any sounds that weren't of his own making. There were none, and in a couple of minutes he saw lights up ahead.

The vehicles.

He stopped, breathless, about half a metre behind the tree line. In a corner of his mind, he heard Gabs's voice. *There'll be times when you need to hide. To camouflage yourself, either because someone's hunting you down or because you're observing them. You can't do that effectively unless you know why things are seen.*

Shape, shadow, surface, spacing, movement . . . His training came back to him with perfect recall. He moved himself so that he was half hidden by a tree to break up the shape of his body. He was casting no shadow because there wasn't any light on him; his spacing was uneven; he kept perfectly still. Zak could look out towards the vehicles without fear of being seen.

He saw Calaca. The one-eyed man was standing by the three vehicles, all alone. He was pointing his handgun out towards the trees and panning round, searching for trouble. But it was perfectly clear that he couldn't see Zak.

Zak raised his gun. Only when he had Calaca firmly in his sights did he speak.

'Drop the weapon, Ramirez,' he called. 'Otherwise I put you down.'

Calaca froze, but he didn't let go of his gun. He looked in the direction of Zak's voice, but plainly couldn't see him.

'I mean it,' said Zak. 'Drop the weapon. *Now.*'

Calaca had no choice but to obey. He laid the gun on the ground then stood up straight, took several steps back and held his arms in the air.

Zak moved forward quickly, keeping the MP5 trained on his enemy. When Calaca saw him, he sneered, but he kept his hands above his head. Zak pointed at the truck furthest up the road to his right. 'Where are the keys?' he demanded.

'In my pocket,' hissed Calaca.

'Walk there. Any sudden moves and I'll shoot.'

'You would not dare.'

Zak raised an eyebrow. 'You want to bet?'

Calaca's sneer grew more pronounced, but he didn't reply. Instead, he turned and walked towards the truck. Zak followed.

'Open the door, keep it open and start the engine.'

Calaca lowered his right hand and pulled a set of keys from his pocket. He leaned into the body of the car; seconds later, the engine was turning over.

'Step back,' Zak told him, 'and move towards the trees.'

The one-eyed man turned. Zak was standing five metres from him. 'Get behind the tree line and you'll live.'

Calaca's face was brimming with hate. 'You should kill me now,' he whispered, 'while you have the chance.'

'Maybe I should,' Zak replied. 'It's not like you haven't had it coming. But that would make me just the same as you, and I'm better than that.'

The older man looked like he was thinking of a response, but in the end he said nothing and just spat on the dusty ground.

'The trees,' Zak repeated. 'Keep walking.'

It was thirty seconds before Calaca reached the tree line. 'Keep your back facing me,' Zak called as he stepped towards the vehicle. Calaca kept on walking, disappearing beyond the tree line. Zak was about to step inside the truck when he heard his flat, emotionless voice drifting over the night air.

'I *will* kill you, Harry Gold.'

Zak narrowed his eyes. 'Yeah?' he muttered. 'Well, you'll have to catch me first.'

He jumped into the vehicle, shut the door and knocked the gearstick into reverse. The wheels screeched as he performed a half turn, before thrusting the gearstick into the forward gears and accelerating back along the road, the way they had come.

As he glanced in the rear-view mirror, he just caught sight of Calaca, running towards the remaining vehicles with his phone pressed to his ear.

The one-eyed man was out of the woods. And that meant Zak wasn't. Not yet.

25

...━━━...

Zak zoomed up through the gears until the speedo-meter was hitting 120 kph. The MP5 was on the passenger seat next to him, safety on. His brow was furrowed as he concentrated on keeping the vehicle on the road, which was lit up brightly by the headlamps on the top of the vehicle. This was nothing like the driving lessons Raf had given him on St Peter's Crag. His brain shrieked at him to put as much distance as possible between himself and Calaca and his men. They'd be chasing him soon. He knew, though, that he needed help. So he gave himself five minutes before he hit the brakes.

The vehicle screeched and performed a small skid before it finally stopped. Zak moved like lightning. He opened the driver's door, stood on the edge of the vehicle and hauled himself up onto the roof. The three headlamps were attached to a rack, and they were hot to the touch. Zak pulled his sleeves over his hands then started to grapple with them, twisting each one so that now they pointed upwards.

He swung back down into the driver's seat, shut the door and started to drive again. Slower this time, because he had to concentrate on something else. He switched off the vehicle's lights and the road ahead was plunged into darkness.

Zak glanced in the rear-view mirror. Nothing, but he knew it was only a matter of time before he saw the lights of Calaca and his men behind him. When that happened, they'd open fire, so Zak just had to pray that his strategy was going to work . . .

Michael looked like he had aged ten years in the last hour. His skin was grey, his eyes bloodshot. He kept his phone pressed to his ear – an open line between himself and the unit in Mexico; but he kept his eyes on the screen; the green dot moving back along the road, superimposed on the real-time satellite image that showed nothing but the faint glowing headlamps of a single vehicle.

And then, to his horror, the headlamps disappeared.

Michael stared at the screen.

Thirty seconds passed. It felt like an hour. Michael found he was holding his breath. He only let it out when the lights appeared again – more clearly, like

... --- ...

they were pointing upwards from the top of the vehicle.

Pointing towards the satellite that was tracking Agent 21.

And they were flashing.

A pattern.

Morse code.

... --- ...
... --- ...
... --- ...

'SOS,' he muttered under his breath. He shouted into the phone: 'Distress call! Distress call! Move in to get him. Now, Gabriella. *Now!*'

Zak checked the rear-view mirror. Lights behind him. That was it. He had to stop the SOS signal. It was slowing him down too much. Either his guardian angels had picked up on his distress call, or they hadn't. Right now, he couldn't hang around.

He put the lights onto full beam and his foot to the floor.

The vehicle juddered over the stony road.

80 kph.

100 kph.

120 kph.

The road continued straight for about a mile, but as Zak kept glancing in the mirror, the other vehicles looked like they were getting closer. He wished he knew some way of making the truck go faster, but this was its limit. This was all it could do.

The road swerved round to the left and Zak had a moment of horror.

Headlamps up ahead, coming towards him.

The road was too narrow for them both to pass, but to slow down would be suicide. The other driver needed to get out of the way.

Zak gripped the steering wheel hard, kept his foot on the gas and continued to zoom along the road. The headlamps grew closer alarmingly quickly. Straight towards him. They were only fifty metres away and they didn't look like they were going to move . . .

Forty metres.

Thirty.

Twenty.

The angry sound of a car horn filled the air. Zak kept his nerve.

Ten metres.

The other car swerved to the edge of the road and spun around in the dust. Zak checked his mirror. Calaca's men were closer. They were gaining on him.

They were *too close*.

A sudden cracking noise inside the car: the sound of

glass splintering. *'What was that?'* Zak hissed, but a quick look over his shoulder told him. The rear window looked like a spider's web, with a point of impact in the centre. *They were firing at him.* A bullet had just hit the window.

Moments later a second shot. The whole window crumbled and shattered. Zak slipped down lower in his seat to protect his head. The back of the vehicle was totally exposed now. All they needed was one lucky shot and he'd be history.

The road ahead was straight again. Straight and dark. Zak wished with all his being that he could see something that suggested people – house lights, a gas station, anything. But all he saw was darkness up ahead and the lights of Calaca's convoy behind him, no more than twenty metres back now.

Another bullet ricocheted off the chassis of his vehicle; he felt the truck swerve to the right slightly, but managed to keep hold of it. He swerved the vehicle left then right, so that he was a more difficult target. That just slowed him down, though, and Calaca's men gained ground. So he continued to drive straight, and two more bullets hit the vehicle: one shattered his side mirror; the other ripped into the passenger seat, passing straight through it and into the dashboard.

That's it, Zak told himself. *They're too close. You can't get away. Any second now you're going to feel a round in your back . . .*

Sure enough, the air was filled with a deafening thunder of gunfire. Zak braced himself.

But then he frowned.

The gunfire hadn't come from behind. It had come from above.

He checked the mirror. Calaca's convoy was suddenly lagging behind. He saw a searchlight beaming down to his right, and heard the low judder of rotary blades.

A chopper.

Another burst of fire, and Zak realized that a gunner in the helicopter was firing on Calaca's men again. *The guardian angels. It was Gabs and Raf and their unit. It had to be . . .*

The chopper zoomed away, following the line of the road while Zak kept his foot on the accelerator. About a hundred metres ahead, it lowered to the ground, coming to rest at right angles to the road.

Zak gritted his teeth and kept his foot to the floor. A round pinged into the vehicle from behind. It missed Zak's head by no more than an inch and slammed into the front windscreen, which splintered, making it impossible for Zak to see clearly through it. He wound down the side window and looked out. The chopper was fifty metres away.

He kept his foot hard on the gas.

More impact from behind. The vehicle swerved and Zak had to pull it back on track.

Thirty metres to safety. Twenty metres.

Zak slammed his foot on the brakes, just as a round from Calaca's men burst one of his rear tyres. The car spun round ninety degrees, and for a horrible moment Zak thought he would collide with the chopper. He skidded to a halt, though, just metres from where it was waiting, its side door open and two figures waiting for him.

Zak opened the driver's door and heard a voice.

'*RUN! GET IN THE CHOPPER – NOW!*' shouted Gabs.

Zak didn't need telling twice. He jumped out of the car, leaving the MP5 in the passenger seat, lunged towards the chopper and hurled himself inside. He didn't even have his legs fully inside as the chopper lifted into the air. Gabs was pulling him in; Raf was operating a Minigun, which peppered its 7.62 mm rounds towards Calaca and his men as the chopper veered sharply away from the road. From the corner of his eye, he saw two men jump from the side of the vehicle. It was the last thing they ever did. The rounds from the Minigun slammed into their bodies and sent them flying to the ground, dead.

Zak lay flat out on the floor of the aircraft, trying to

catch his breath. He was aware of other people around him. They all wore dark helmets cut away around the ear, blue body armour and carried M16 assault rifles.

'Zak?' she shouted over the noise of the chopper. *'Zak, are you OK?'*

It was Gabs. She kneeled down beside him, her face etched with worry.

Zak frowned. 'Yeah,' he said. 'I'm OK. But do me a favour, would you?'

'What?'

He gave her a weak smile. 'Next time someone's trying to kill me, don't wait quite so long, huh?'

Gabs smiled. 'We're getting you to safety now, sweetie,' she said. 'The operation's over.'

Zak sat up.

'No, it isn't,' he said.

'What do you mean?'

'The plan was to grab Martinez. Michael's got his evidence. I uploaded it from a cocaine lab in southern Mexico.'

'I know. He got it.'

'But if we don't get Martinez now, he'll go to ground. He knows we're on to him. This is our only chance.'

Raf crouched down beside Gabs. 'It's too dangerous, Zak,' he said. 'His men have probably already called through to the compound. They'll be expecting us.'

'Then we'll just have to be smarter than them, right? Calaca's his head of security. With him and the guards he had with him out of the picture, Martinez is vulnerable.' Zak looked at his two guardian angels. They didn't seem convinced. He lowered his eyes. 'Martinez killed my parents,' he said.

Gabs looked astonished. '*What?* How do you know?'

'I just do, OK. And if we let him get away now, who knows if I'll ever have a chance to bring him to justice?' He looked around everyone in the chopper. 'This is the best chance we'll ever get, and I *can't* let him get away. You've *got* to help me do this.'

Gabs's eyes were uncertain as she exchanged a glance with Raf. 'Michael wants us back at base,' she said.

Raf raised one eyebrow. 'Michael's not here.'

Something seemed to pass between them. They nodded at each other.

'The body doubles,' Raf said. 'You think you can tell the difference between them?'

Zak thought of the doubles – perfect replicas of his enemy. Indistinguishable in every way. Even Cruz didn't know which was which.

'Yeah,' he said. 'I think I can.'

'And you know the layout of the compound?'

He nodded.

'All right, then. We'll do it. But Zak?'

'What.'

'No heroics, OK. We've already nearly lost you once today. Let's not have a repeat performance.'

26

GOING NOISY

'*Three minutes out*,' Gabs shouted at the unit. She handed Zak a set of body armour and a helmet. 'Put this on.'

As he strapped the gear to his body, Gabs looked around the aircraft slightly guiltily. She pulled something out of her black ops waistcoat. A small pistol. 'Self-defence only, right?'

'Right.' Zak checked the safety and lodged it in his belt.

'OK, everyone,' Raf shouted over the noise of the chopper. 'Listen up. The target is Cesar Martinez Toledo and we want to take him alive. He has five identical body doubles, so we need to make sure we have the right one. As you know, Agent 21 has been inside the compound, so he can give us a rundown of what to expect.' He nodded at Zak.

'Er . . . right,' said Zak. 'The compound is surrounded by a circular wall, about six metres high and about two hundred metres in diameter. There's only one entrance, on the northernmost edge. Either side of the entrance are two observation posts with armed guards. There are seven more OPs set at thirty-metre intervals around the wall, all manned. From the entrance there's a long road – about a hundred metres – leading up to the house which is in the middle of the compound. Armed guards at the entrance. Behind the house there's a swimming pool and a helipad. Oh, and a shooting range. The rest of the place is laid to lawn. Nowhere to hide in the grounds.'

Raf took over. 'We need to make the main exit impassable,' he shouted. 'Then deal with the OPs. This is going to go noisy.'

'*One minute out!*' shouted Gabs.

Raf turned to Zak. 'You see the webbing on the side of the aircraft?' he shouted.

Zak nodded.

'Hold onto it. Things are going to shake up a bit before we land.'

Zak edged to one side of the chopper and grabbed hold of the criss-cross of ropes fixed to it. He looked down through the window. Below him, in the distance, he could just see Martinez's compound: searchlights shone from the observation posts around the perimeter wall and the house itself, bang in the centre of the circle, glowed in the night.

The chopper swooped down, like a hawk closing in on its prey. In only a few seconds, it was cruising over the house and heading towards the perimeter wall. It hovered about ten metres from one of the observation posts and the Minigun operators opened fire.

Rounds thundered into the thick stone wall and Zak couldn't stop himself from letting go of the webbing and moving himself so that he could see through the front window of the chopper. He just caught a glimpse of two guards jumping from the OP out of the compound – the only way they could stop themselves being minced by the powerful Miniguns – before the chopper swung round and started blasting the next OP.

'Two down,' Raf shouted. 'Seven to go. Once we've neutralized the OPs, we can go in. Hold on tight!'

Zak did just that.

Cesar Martinez Toledo woke with a start. His mobile phone was ringing and only one person had the number: Calaca. He sat up in the darkness of his bedroom and answered.

'What is it, Adan?'

'Harry Gold, señor. He has escaped.'

Martinez blinked in the darkness. 'What do you mean?'

'He got away from us, señor. He had back-up. A

helicopter. It fired on us. Three of my men are dead.'

Martinez didn't care about that. 'How could you let this happen, you fool?'

'You need to leave the compound. Remember, our source said the British were trying to abduct you. You need to go now. I will call our contacts in the Mexico City police force. I'll instruct them to send a helicopter to extract you.'

Martinez was already out of bed and getting dressed. 'Do that,' he said, and hung up his phone, too angry to talk any more to his head of security. He made for the door, stopping only to grab a loaded pistol from his table. Two guards stood outside. They looked surprised at his sudden appearance.

'Get me the body doubles. In the atrium. Now.'

The guards stared at him.

'*Now!*'

Immediately one of them ran off. 'Follow me,' Martinez told the remaining guard, and he hurried down the corridor until he reached another door. He didn't knock, but just burst straight on through it into Cruz's bedroom. 'Wake up,' he shouted, but he needn't have. Cruz was already sitting up. 'Get dressed and get down to the atrium.'

'Why, Father?'

'Don't argue. Just *do it*.'

Sixty seconds later, Martinez was in the atrium with

his five body doubles and two guards. He pointed at the guards. 'You and you. We're leaving the compound, now.'

'*Si*, señor. Where to, señor?' one of them asked.

Martinez saw red. He placed his pistol up against the guard's head. 'Interrupt me again,' he shouted, 'and I'll kill you.'

The guard gulped.

Martinez turned to the body doubles. 'You will all stay here. Spread yourself around the house. Someone might come looking for me. If a single one of you reveals that you are not the true Cesar Martinez Toledo, the families of every man in this room will die a painful and lingering death. Do you understand?'

The body doubles looked anxiously at each other.

'*Do you understand?*'

'*Si*, señor,' they said in unison.

There was a noise from outside – faint at first, but it grew louder very quickly. It was mechanical. Juddering. Like . . .

'A helicopter,' Martinez whispered. The Mexican police?

He heard short, sharp bursts of gunfire.

The birds in the birdcage started screeching. Martinez's face went white. He ran to the back of the atrium and out towards the swimming pool. There he saw it: a Black Hawk, hovering over his land, pumping bullets towards an observation post on the western side of the perimeter. He watched in anger and shock as the guards on the observation post jumped outwards from the wall to save themselves, before the chopper moved onto the next post. This was not Calaca's police helicopter. But where was it?

Martinez spun round. One of his guards was standing there, gaping. 'Give me that,' Martinez instructed, and pulled the guard's M16 from his hands. He aimed it towards the chopper and fired two rounds. The chopper's guns fell silent for a moment; but then it turned and, with a deafening noise, started spraying rounds in an arc, blowing the skull-like head off one of the *La Catrina* statues round the pool, and forcing Martinez and his men to sprint back inside.

Cruz was waiting for him, alarmed but steely-eyed; and so was Raul, who looked terrified. The noise of gunfire continued outside, moving round the perimeter. 'They are taking out all the observation posts, señor!' shouted a guard.

'I know that, you idiot. Is there a vehicle out front?'

'Yes, señor.'

'Go and get it started.' He turned to the body doubles. 'Spread around the house and remember what I told you. I will start with your children.'

The body doubles didn't wait. Two of them sprinted up the stairs, another went down to the basement, one into Martinez's office and one hunkered down by the birdcage. Martinez himself led Cruz, Raul and the remaining guard towards the front of the house. A black 4 by 4 with darkened windows was waiting for them, but as they stepped out into the open, Martinez realized he had a problem. The Black Hawk had completed its circle of the perimeter, which meant the observation posts had been cleared of armed guards. Now it was setting itself down right in front of the only exit to the compound. If they were going to leave, they had to get past the chopper first. And that was never going to happen.

'Back inside,' shouted Martinez, just as the side door of the Black Hawk opened up and two shooters jumped out. They started raining covering fire towards the house as another six or seven people spilled out of the helicopter. Martinez followed the others, into the relative safety of the house.

'*What's happening?*' screamed Raul. Martinez looked in disgust at his nephew, who was unable to keep control of himself, and spoke instead to Cruz.

'Hide,' he said. 'They are coming for me, not you.' He waved his arm around. 'If they get me, all this is yours. The business, the men . . . everything. Do not disappoint me.'

Cruz turned to the guard. 'Give me your gun,' he said.

The guard looked shocked that Cruz had spoken to him like that.

'*Give it to me.*'

The man handed over the M16. It was fitted with a silencer to suppress the noise, and Cruz held it firmly. Even Raul looked taken aback by the determination in the face of Martinez's son.

'*I* will not disappoint you, Father,' Cruz said.

The chopper touched down. Two members of the unit jumped from the body of the aircraft and started laying down covering fire. The air stank of cordite.

'Stick close to me,' Gabs told Zak. They exited along with the rest of the unit.

Zak, Raf, Gabs and the four commandos approached the house using a leapfrog formation: two of them holding back to give cover while the others advanced ten metres, then covered the other two while they caught up. It took about a minute to reach the house like this. When they did, Zak and Gabs led the way into the atrium, followed by the others.

It was empty. There was no noise apart from the chirruping of the birds in their cage, and the distant rotary blades of the chopper out in the grounds. Raf took charge. He pointed at Gabs and two of the commandos, then at the stairs. Gabs mouthed the words 'follow me' at Zak, and the four of them moved swiftly up to the first floor.

One of the commandos took the lead, his assault rifle pressed tightly in to his shoulder. Gabs was carrying a Colt automatic pistol and went next, with Zak beside her. The second commando followed.

The upstairs corridors were deserted, but Zak's heart was in his mouth every time they turned a corner. They passed the door to Zak's room. The two commandos burst in, guns at the ready; but it was empty. The same went for the room beyond it – the one Zak had entered via the roof the day before.

The third room they tried was Cruz's. Here they struck gold.

Martinez – or a version of him – was cowering behind the bed.

'Get up,' hissed one of the commandos in Spanish.

'Please,' begged the lookalike. 'Do not shoot . . .'

'Is that him?' Gabs asked.

Zak stared at the man. It was almost impossible to tell, but . . . 'I don't think so,' he said.

'Get him downstairs,' Gabs told the commando.

'Roger that.'

The rest of them continued their sweep of the first floor.

They found the second body double – if that's what he was – behind the door of an ornate bathroom. His face twitched in terror and he put his hands up the moment he saw them. The remaining commando took him down to the ground floor, which left Gabs and Zak to continue the sweep.

'Stay close,' she breathed as they continued down the corridor.

They moved silently, checking two more rooms, one on the left and one on the right, before coming to a turn in the corridor.

A quick nod and they turned the corner.

Zak had only taken a couple of paces when he heard two shots from behind – suppressed shots from a silencer, as quiet as someone knocking on a door. The overhead lights in the corridor shattered, like broken ice and Zak felt something cold and hard pressed against the back of his neck, between the helmet and the body armour.

A voice.

It was Cruz.

'Drop your gun,' he said. 'Otherwise I'll kill Harry.'

Zak could see the shape of Gabs's body in the gloom up ahead. She spun round, her weapon pointing out in front of her.

'*Drop it*,' Cruz hissed.

A dangerous look crossed Gabs's face, but she lowered her weapon and laid it on the floor.

'Put your hands on your head, both of you,' Cruz

instructed. 'Now turn around. We're going back to the atrium and you're going to tell these intruders to leave my father's house. Unless you want me to kill Harry, that is.'

'Cruz,' Zak said. '*You're* not in danger. You can come with us . . .'

'Shut up, Harry. You've made enough trouble for yourself today. You're not going anywhere.'

'We've closed down the compound, Cruz. You can't win this.'

'Aren't you the one that told me I should stick up for myself?'

'Cruz, I can help you—'

'*Shut up!*'

They walked in a line: Gabs first, then Zak, then Cruz, who kept his weapon dug firmly into Zak's neck. Thirty seconds later, they passed his room, which meant they were nearly at the top of the stairs. He had to do something – and fast.

He checked ahead. Gabs was walking in front of him and slightly to the left. If he moved, Cruz would be aiming just to her right . . .

It was a sudden movement. It had to be if he was to keep the element of surprise. Zak jerked his head to the left. For a millisecond, Cruz's weapon was pointing not into his neck, but over his shoulder. Zak dug his right heel into Cruz's shin. The gangly boy gasped in pain and the sound made Gabs spin round. In the confusion, Cruz fired a single shot. It slammed into Gabs's chest and she span round from the impact and fell down onto her face.

'*Gabs! No!*'

Zak turned round. Cruz was re-setting his gun, lowering it so he could take aim. Zak clenched his fist, swung his arm and punched Cruz in the side of the face. The Mexican boy staggered against the wall, but he still had his gun. Zak did a high kick, whacking his right foot against Cruz's wrist. The assault rifle clattered to the floor. Zak grabbed his pistol from his belt and held it up to Cruz.

Blood dripped from Cruz's nose and his eyes burned with hate. 'I thought you were my friend,' he hissed.

'Last time I checked,' Zak replied, 'friends don't try to kill each other.' He glanced down at Gabs's motionless body. Tears of anger came to his eyes. '*She* was my friend,' he said. He twitched the gun in the direction of the stairs. 'Move,' he instructed. 'If you say a word, you'll be next.'

The tables were turned. Zak forced Cruz down the corridor. He tried not to think of what had just happened to Gabs. She wouldn't want him to. She'd just tell him to keep his mind on the job.

Not easy. Not easy at all.

As they approached the landing overlooking the atrium, they stopped.

'Get on the floor,' Zak whispered. Cruz lay down on his front while Zak peered down to see what was going on.

Raf was in the atrium. Four of Martinez's guards were face down on the floor, their hands cuffed behind their backs. Raul was cowering in a corner, trembling like a frightened animal – so much for *his* bravado. Six men were lined out in front of Raf: six identical versions of Cesar Martinez Toledo. Only one of them was the real drug lord. He couldn't see any of the commandos.

He knew he needed to identify the real Martinez, and he had a plan to do it. But he had to wait for the right moment, so he stepped back and hid himself from view.

Raf spoke into his comms unit. '*Come in, Gabs. We've rounded up the body doubles. We need Agent 21.*' He was careful not to say Zak's real name.

'Do you copy, Gabs? Do you *copy*?'

Radio silence.

He cursed. What was happening up there? *What was happening?*

Raf turned to the line of body doubles. One of these was the real Cesar Martinez Toledo. But only one. He couldn't believe how identical they were – down to the exact fatness of the face and the tiny mole on the left-hand cheek. They were all in night attire and, frankly, they all looked terrified. Raf raised his gun and pointed it at each one in turn, looking into their eyes, hoping to see something. Some kind of clue.

There was nothing.

A voice came over his comms. It was one of the commandos he had stationed outside the house in case any of the perimeter guards got brave. '*Mexican police chopper overhead. We need to extract.*'

'Roger that.' He swore under his breath. They'd spent too long in the compound already. He needed Gabs and Zak. *Where were they?*

He couldn't wait for them. The sand was running out of the egg timer. No doubt the Mexican police were here to help Martinez and if they caught this deniable unit, there'd be hell to pay. He needed to identify Martinez for himself. Raf stared at the lookalikes. 'You're scared,' he said quickly in Spanish. 'You think that the real Martinez will hurt you or your families if you betray him now. Well, think again. We're not leaving here until the real Martinez is in custody. He can't threaten you any more. You're safe.'

Nothing from the lookalikes except a blank look.

Raf didn't give up. He walked up and down the line of body doubles, examining their faces carefully. 'You all want Martinez behind bars just as much as I do. You *know* he's a monster. You *know* he's a murderer. Now's your chance to see to it that he pays for his crimes.'

Still nothing. The body doubles stared straight ahead, acting like he wasn't even there.

Fine, thought Raf. The promises hadn't worked. The appeal hadn't worked. That meant it was time to start on the threats . . .

'You know he's a monster. You know he's a murderer. Now's your chance to see to it that he pays for his crimes.'

From his hiding place on the top floor, Zak could hear every word. He could also sense Cruz's anger. Raf was right – Martinez *was* a monster and a murderer. Zak knew that better than anyone. But to Cruz, he was just a father.

Raf's voice reached them. 'OK,' he announced. 'Here's the deal. The fake Martinezes take a step backwards on the count of three. Otherwise, I kill the lot of you before we leave.'

Cruz hissed, so Zak bent down and put the gun to his head. 'I mean it, Cruz. Just one word . . .'

'One . . .' Raf shouted.

Zak's mind turned over. He knew the kind of fear the body doubles had for Martinez. He knew they wouldn't betray him, even now.

'Two . . .'

When Raf counted to three, he'd have played all his cards. The real Martinez would be feeling confident, but that might make him more vulnerable . . .

'Three . . .'

A pause.

'*Damn it, Gabs!*' Raf's voice was full of frustration. '*Where are you?*'

Now was the time to move. Zak grabbed Cruz by his shirt collar and quickly pulled him to his feet. He dragged him the three or four metres to the top of the staircase and pushed him so he staggered down the steps. Raf turned to look at him. '*What are you doing?*' he bellowed, but Zak ignored him.

Zak trotted down the steps, aiming his gun at Cruz. 'Say bye-bye to your son!' he shouted.

There was no doubting the real Martinez. He was three from the left and the moment he saw his son in danger, he stepped forward. With a sudden, sharp movement, he whacked Raf on the shoulder. The guardian angel crumpled, dropping his gun, which Martinez picked up and – with obvious skill – aimed directly at Zak.

He fired. A burst of fire, and a single round caught Zak on the side of his right arm. A flash of red, and his gun went spinning. Zak collapsed onto the stairs, blood gushing from his arm, wincing with the sudden, sharp pain.

Martinez was shouting. 'You dare to threaten my son? *You dare to threaten my son?*' All the body doubles scrambled and so did Raul, leaving Martinez alone at the bottom of the stairs with Raf unconscious at his feet and Cruz escaping towards him.

He turned back to Zak. 'And now, Agent 21, whoever you are, you will pay the price for your arrogance! You will pay the price for crossing Cesar Martinez Toledo!'

Martinez fixed Zak with his mad eyes.

He dug the butt of the assault rifle into his shoulder, ready to fire.

But the sound that filled the atrium was not the burst of automatic fire. It was a dead, wooden noise – a single shot from a suppressed weapon, and it came from the first floor. The round hit Martinez in the chest and threw him onto his back.

Zak looked up. There was Gabs. She had Cruz's M16 in her hands and her blue eyes blazed fiercely.

'*Father!*' Cruz's ran towards Martinez's fallen body. He knelt down beside him and put two fingers to his jugular.

Silence in the room.

Blood oozed into Martinez's shirt; red foam seeped from his mouth. It was a horrible sight, and yet Zak couldn't help feeling a wild flash of triumph that the man who had ordered the death of his parents had paid the price for his crime. Was there even a twinge of regret that the gun which had killed Martinez had not been in his own hand? He put that thought in check. There were too many other things to think about right now . . .

Cruz dropped his head. 'You killed my father,' he shouted. '*You killed my father!*'

He stretched out his hand, reaching for the rifle Martinez had let fall. 'Don't even think about it, Cruz,' Gabs shouted. 'I didn't want to kill your father but I was prepared to, and I'm prepared to kill you too.'

Cruz shrank back.

Seconds later, Gabs was beside Zak. She checked his wound. 'Can you walk?' she asked.

'I think so. Blimey, Gabs, I thought you were dead.'

'Body armour, sweetie. But do me a favour and save the emotional reunion for later, huh.'

Zak nodded. 'The Mexican police are overhead. Martinez has them in his pocket . . .'

'We need to get out of here. Cruz, put your hands behind your head and lie on the floor.'

Martinez's son did what he was told as Zak and Gabs ran down into the atrium. Zak clutched his bad arm with his good hand, but he couldn't stop the blood pumping through his fingers.

'We need to get Raf to the chopper,' Gabs shouted. 'Can you help me carry him?'

Zak nodded. 'Just give me one second,' he said. He walked over to Cruz, leaving a little trail of blood as he went. He stood above him. 'I would never have shot you, you know.' For some reason it seemed important to say it.

Cruz turned his head. 'You should have,' he said, his voice filled with tears and hate.

'I lost a father too, Cruz. I know how you're feeling.'

'You will *never* know how I'm feeling. You should kill me now because *you* are responsible for my father's death, Harry Gold. And I swear that as long as I am alive, I won't rest until I have hunted you down and killed you myself.'

Zak looked down at him. 'Save yourself the trouble,' he said. 'You'll never find me.'

'Believe that if you want to,' replied Cruz. And then he spat at Zak's feet.

'We've got to get out of here,' Gabs shouted. She was bending down beside Raf and lifting one of his arms over her shoulders. 'Help me.'

Zak nodded. He grabbed Martinez's assault rifle to stop Cruz from using it. Ignoring the pain in his bleeding wound, he slung Raf's other arm over his shoulder. Between them, they lifted him to his feet and dragged him towards the exit. Zak only looked back once. Cruz was still lying on the floor, his hands on his head and his dead father right beside him.

He put Cruz from his mind. They had to concentrate on getting to the chopper. The moment they stepped outside, however, it was clear this was going to be a problem.

The four commandos were in front of the house, kneeling in the firing position. The Black Hawk was still waiting for them by the main gate. But between them and their aircraft was the Mexican police helicopter. It hovered twenty metres in the air, lighting them up with its spotlight. Zak could just see police snipers leaning out of the doors and above the thunder of the rotary blades, a voice rang out in Spanish from some kind of loudspeaker: 'DROP YOUR WEAPONS. IF YOU DO NOT DROP YOUR WEAPONS, WE WILL OPEN FIRE . . .'

'What are we going to do?' screamed Zak. His wound was shrieking at him now, and he was feeling weaker and weaker. 'They're police – we can't fire on them!'

Gabs's eyes were wild and she desperately looked around. 'We need another exit!'

'There isn't one.'

Gabs shouted into her comms system. 'We need immediate exfiltration. *Now!*'

That one instruction was all it took. The Black Hawk immediately took flight. It raised above the level of the perimeter wall and swooped around the larger helicopter before turning to face it.

The choppers hovered in mid-air, nose to nose.

A moment of standoff. 'DROP YOUR WEAPONS. IF YOU DO NOT DROP YOUR WEAPONS, WE WILL OPEN FIRE . . .'

The Black Hawk answered with its Miniguns, operated by the two commandos they had left with the aircraft. They let out a burst of fire – not directly at the police chopper, but just below it. Bright orange tracer fire curved like tiny meteors towards the ground and an immense, mechanical chugging filled the air. The pilot of the police chopper clearly understood the threat: the Miniguns had missed them on purpose; next time they wouldn't be so lucky. It swerved away, out of the Black Hawk's line of fire.

The special forces chopper didn't mess around. It lowered itself to the ground in front of the house.

A shout from one of the commandos. '*Go! Go! Go!*'

Zak and Gabs hauled Raf down the front steps. The four commandos made a corridor for them as they sprinted to the Black Hawk. Zak was feeling faint from blood loss, but as they reached the chopper he knew he had to find a final reserve of strength to get the unconscious Raf up into the bird. He heaved and his knees threatened to buckle; but they got Raf in.

Zak forced himself up into the Black Hawk, smothered by nausea and weakness. As the four commandos jumped in, Gabs was removing her jacket and tying the arm of it around Zak's wound to stem the bleeding.

They left the ground, suddenly and sharply. Zak felt the world spinning. '*Stay with me,*' Gabs shouted. '*Stay with me!*' But he knew he was about to lose consciousness, and his head lolled. He looked out of the side of the Black Hawk. Down below, there was a figure, thin and gangly, standing at the front of the house.

Even in his state of near delirium, Zak could tell it was Cruz. His supposed friend was looking up, watching the Black Hawk as it disappeared into the night sky. Watching it take Zak away from the scene where Cruz's father lay dead.

It was the last thing Agent 21 saw before he passed out, high in the night sky of central Mexico, as the Black Hawk and his guardian angels ferried him to safety.

EPILOGUE

Two days later

Zak Darke awoke to the smell of cherry tobacco.

He was in a stark bright room. No windows and no furniture. Just a bed and a drip stand, with a bag of saline solution feeding through a tube into the back of his hand. The wound on his arm was tightly bandaged. His vision was blurred, and as he looked round it took a moment to realize that he wasn't alone. There were three other figures standing in the room.

'Nice of you to join us, sweetie,' Gabs's voice said. 'We thought you were going to sleep for a week.' She walked round to the side of the bed and put a hand tenderly on his shoulder.

'Where am I?' he asked in a croaky voice.

'London. We airlifted you out two nights ago. You're a lucky boy – there aren't many people who get a C-17 Globemaster chartered just for them, you know.'

'Where's Raf?' Zak asked. 'Is he OK?'

'I'm fine, Zak.' Zak's vision was clearing now and he saw Raf's distinctive, flat-nosed features. 'But next time you want to pull a trick like that, you might like to give me a couple of seconds warning.' Maybe Zak was still a bit concussed, but he could have sworn that Raf was *almost* smiling.

Which left the third figure. He was standing at the end of the bed and he had a thin black cigarette between his fingers.

'I thought you weren't supposed to smoke in hospital,' Zak said.

Michael inclined his head. 'I believe you're right, Zak. But this isn't quite an ordinary hospital.'

'What's that supposed to mean?'

'Let's just say you're not being cared for by the NHS.' Michael looked at Gabs and Raf. 'Gabriella, Raphael, I'm sure you're as glad as I am to see Zak awake, but perhaps you would excuse us. Zak and I have a few things to discuss.'

Gabs rolled her eyes. 'All these secrets,' she said. 'What's a girl to think?' But she and Raf quickly left the room.

'That's quite a hole you had in your arm,' Michael said.

'M16s have a habit of doing that.'

'Quite. You'll be glad to know the doctors have been

318

able to save the limb. Raphael and Gabriella told me what happened in Martinez's compound. It was a good idea of yours – to get Martinez to show himself by threatening Cruz. You might have discussed it with them first, though.'

'As far as I can remember,' Zak said, thinking back to the events of that night, 'we didn't have much time to chat.' There was a silence as Zak lay back in his bed and briefly closed his eyes. 'You knew all along, didn't you?' he said. 'About Martinez and my parents, I mean.'

'Of course.'

'Then why didn't you tell me?'

Michael took a suck on his cigarette. 'If you had known the truth, do you really think you'd have been able to look Martinez in the eye and pretend to be Harry Gold?'

Zak thought about that. 'I suppose not.'

'By a happy coincidence, that's what *I* supposed too.'

Another silence as something occurred to Zak. 'You didn't really want Martinez because he's a drug lord, did you?'

Michael's eyes gleamed with approval. 'Not really, Zak. Not really.'

'Then why did you want him?'

The older man started to pace the room. 'It all

started a year ago in a hotel in Lagos. You don't need me to tell you what happened then. There were a number of British citizens killed in that attack. Thirteen in all, of which your parents were two. We knew Martinez was responsible, but we couldn't prove it. Naturally we couldn't let the murder of these thirteen people go unpunished, but we needed a pretext under which to detain Martinez. That was why the evidence you gathered was so important. Even with Martinez dead, though, the evidence is still useful. We'll be passing it on to the Mexican authorities. I'm sure that little processing plant in the jungle will be wiped out in the next few weeks.'

'Was Gabs supposed to kill him?' Zak asked.

Michael looked mildly surprised. 'Of course not,' he said. 'She only shot him to protect *you*. I have the impression, Zak, that young Gabriella would do almost anything to keep you safe. In that, she and Raphael are not unalike. No, our plan was very much to take Martinez alive, even though there are plenty who will not mourn his death.'

Zak remembered Martinez's body, dead on the floor, with Cruz kneeling beside it. 'And some who will,' he said. He felt himself frown.

'What is it?' Michael asked.

'I don't know,' Zak replied. 'I guess it's just ... When my parents died, I knew it wasn't food poisoning like they said. Sometimes I wondered if they were killed, and I dreamed about going after the person who did it. And now . . .' His voice trailed away.

'And now,' Michael continued, 'it doesn't feel the way you thought it would.'

Zak shook his head.

'Revenge never does. People think it will solve everything, but life is more complicated than that.' He gave Zak a serious look. 'I had hoped to make it easier for you,' he said.

'What do you mean?'

'I had hoped to be able to tell you the truth once your evidence had put Martinez behind bars. My plan was to give you the opportunity to avenge your parents by bringing Martinez to justice. You have the makings of a remarkably good operator, Zak. As time passes, you will become better and better. I would not have been able to stop you from going after your parents' murderer yourself, and you are a little young to have blood on your hands, don't you think?'

Zak thought about the surge of triumph he had felt at the sight of Martinez's dead body, and he nodded.

'I think I told you once before that too much knowledge can sometimes be a dangerous thing. I hope you understand that now. Perhaps you feel angry with me for the way things have turned out, but I will not apologize for trying to keep you safe. In the future, Zak, you'll have to get used to not knowing the whole story.' He looked away for a moment. 'Assuming,' he added, 'that there *is* a future for Agent 21.'

A long pause.

'Well, is there?' Michael asked.

Zak closed his eyes. He thought about the last six months. About Raf and Gabs and the training. About the Martinez operation. About how much his life had changed in the past few months . . .

And then he spoke. 'Yeah,' he replied. 'I guess there is.'

Michael smiled. 'I hoped you'd say that,' he said. 'Now if you'll excuse me, I have a few matters to attend to.' He made his way towards the door, but stopped at the last minute and turned round. 'Oh, and well done, Zak,' he said. 'You did better than even I could have expected.'

Michael winked at him, then left the room, closing the door quietly behind him.

Six thousand miles away, a young man sat behind his father's desk. He was thin and gangly, but in the last two days he had developed a look of steel.

On the other side of the desk stood a man with one eye, wearing a green Mexico football shirt. He didn't look like he wanted to take orders from this person; he also looked like he didn't have a choice.

'How much did my father pay you, Adan?' asked Cruz Martinez.

Calaca told him.

'From today, you earn double.'

Calaca looked surprised. 'That is very generous, señor,' he said.

'Generosity has nothing to do with it,' Cruz replied. 'I am buying your loyalty. If I suspect you are short-changing me, I will ask for more than my money back. You will serve me as you served my father. Is that understood?'

'Yes, señor.'

'The other cartels, do they know of his death?'

'By now, señor, all of Mexico knows it. Your position is dangerous. The other cartels will move in on your business very quickly – more quickly, even, than the authorities will destroy the processing plant your father took the boy to.'

Cruz considered that for a moment. 'Every government official we are bribing, and every police officer, they too are to have their payments doubled.'

'Yes, señor. But you will have to do more than that. You will have to show that you have the stomach to stand up to your enemies, and to crush them when necessary.'

Cruz shook his head slowly. 'You still have Raul in custody?'

'As you instructed, señor.'

'Good. Take him away and kill him. Leave his body on the doorstep of a police station. Let it be known that he had a problem with me taking over the family business. That will show that I'm not to be trifled with.'

An unpleasant sneer crossed Calaca's face, as though he very much approved of the suggestion.'

'Yes, señor.'

He turned to leave.

'One more thing before you go, Adan.'

Calaca turned and Cruz gave him a flat, dead stare. 'Harry Gold. Agent 21. Whatever you want to call him. Find out *who* he is. Find out *where* he is. Find out who he *works* for. Then find him. And when you have found him, bring him to me.'

'Dead or alive, señor?'

Cruz raised an eyebrow. 'Alive, Adan. Very much alive. Because when I have Agent 21 in front of me, I will require the pleasure of killing him myself. Is that understood?'

'Yes, Señor Cruz. It is understood.'

And with that, Adan Ramirez walked out of the room, closing the door behind him and leaving his new boss alone with his thoughts.

AGENT
21

Zak uses the stars to help him navigate. Check out how helpfu

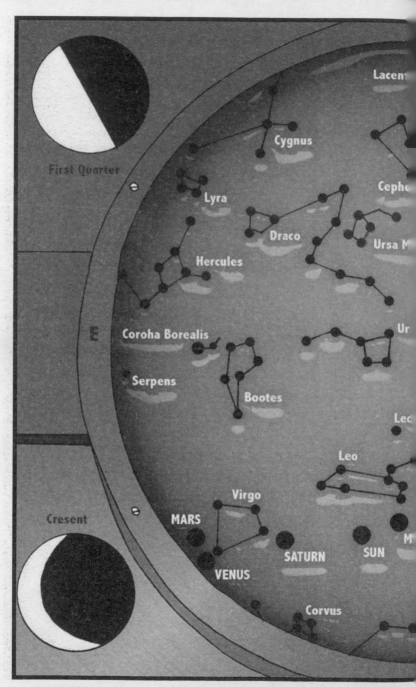

our night sky can be . . .

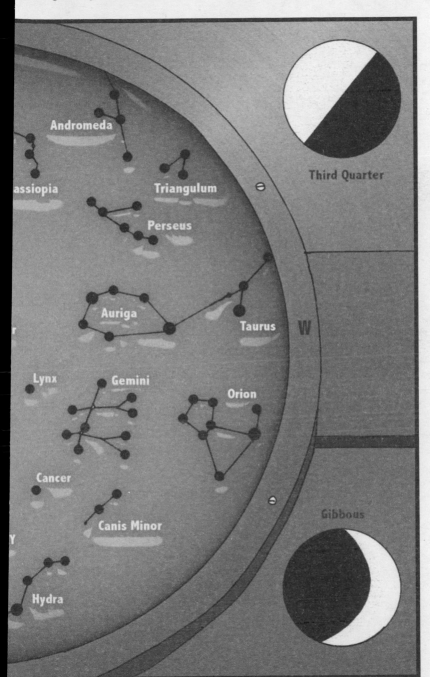

Andromeda

assiopia

Triangulum

Perseus

Third Quarter

Auriga

Taurus

W

Lynx

Gemini

Orion

Cancer

Canis Minor

Gibbous

Hydra

AGENT 21 is still active.

Zak Darke's mission is not over.

Look out for him in the action-packed book two,
coming soon . . .

Read on for a look at Chris Ryan's famous,
real-life tale of courage and survival

THE ONE THAT GOT AWAY

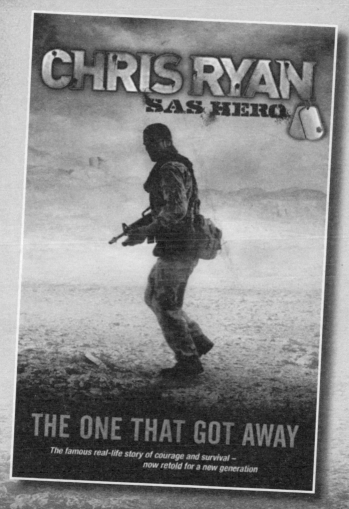

CHRIS RYAN
SAS HERO

THE ONE THAT GOT AWAY

The famous real-life story of courage and survival –
now retold for a new generation

CHAPTER 1
STAND BY . . . STAND BY . . . GO!

Our target was a disused mental hospital.

Five terrorists were inside, holding nine hostages captive. After a three-day siege, matters were moving swiftly to a head.

As commander of the SAS eight-man sniper team of 'B' Squadron, I was in charge of seven other men. We were positioned with our rifles at observation points in outhouses, trees and on the ground. Two men were watching each face of the hospital and sending back running commentaries over their throat-mike radios to the command centre. This had been set up in a separate building 200 metres from the front door. Each face of the hospital had been given a special code so that everyone knew which bit they were talking about.

From the command centre a police negotiator was talking to the chief terrorist. The terrorist was demanding safe conduct to Heathrow airport for himself and his colleagues; otherwise he would shoot one of the hostages. Meanwhile, the military officer commanding the SP (Special Projects, or counter-terrorist) team was working out how to attack the building if the negotiations failed.

Suddenly a shot cracked out from within the hospital. A hostage had been executed. The terrorists called for a stretcher party to take the body away. The front door opened briefly, and a limp figure was bundled out. A four-man team ran over to collect it. Then the chief terrorist threatened to kill another hostage in half an hour if his demands were not met.

The moment had come for the police to hand over to the military. The police chief signed a written order passing command to the OC (Officer Commanding) of 'B' Squadron, the senior SAS officer present. The OC then gave the three eight-man assault teams their orders. The moment he had finished, the men moved to their entry points.

Now it was just a question of waiting for my snipers to get as many terrorists in their sights as possible. Listening to our commentaries on the radio, the OC suddenly called out the order we'd all been waiting for:

'I have control. STAND BY . . . STAND BY . . . GO!'

For the past two days the grounds of the old hospital had been eerily silent. Now the whole place erupted into action. Two vehicles screamed up to the building and a swarm of black-clad assaulters jumped out. Explosive charges blew in the windows. Within seconds, a Chinook helicopter was poised above the roof and more black figures were fast-roping out of it, abseiling down to the windows or entering through the skylights. Stun grenades blasted off; smoke poured out. The radio carried a babble of shots, shouts, explosions and orders.

In a matter of minutes the building had been cleared, the five terrorists killed and the remaining eight hostages rescued. The assault commander reported that he had control, and command was formally handed back to the police.

* * *

On this occasion, this had all been just an exercise – but as always, the assault had been realistic in every detail, and had been excellent training. Just another day for the Regiment, as members of the SAS refer to themselves. And exactly the kind of task we could at any time be called upon to perform, efficiently and explosively. Practice was essential.

'Well done, everybody,' the OC told us. 'That was pretty good.'

We packed our kit into the vehicles and set out for SAS headquarters in Hereford. But on the way events took an unexpected turn.

It was 2 August 1990, and on the news we heard that Saddam Hussein, the tyrannical leader of Iraq, had just invaded Kuwait, a small country on his southern border.

'So what?' said one of the guys scornfully. 'Saddam's an idiot.'

'Don't be too sure of it,' said someone else. 'It'll make big trouble, and we'll probably find ourselves out there.'

He was right. Saddam's invasion of Kuwait was the opening salvo of the 1990–1991 Gulf War. I don't think any of us realized just how this news would change our lives.

* * *

For the next two months, nobody knew what was going to happen. The leaders of different governments around the world got together to discuss the situation and the UN Security Council called for Iraq to withdraw from Kuwait – and gave them a deadline. When the Iraqis did not leave Kuwait, a war was inevitable. In total thirty-four countries joined together in a coalition to oppose Saddam Hussein. These countries included not only the USA and Great Britain but also Arab countries in the Middle East region, like Egypt and Syria.

'A' and 'D' Squadron went out to the Gulf for build-up training; but me and my mates in 'B' Squadron were told we wouldn't be going, as it was our turn to take over what are known in the SAS as team tasks – assignments for which small teams of men are needed in various parts of the world.

The SAS is made up of four squadrons – A, B, D and G. Each squadron is made up of four troops – Air Troop, Mountain Troop, Boat Troop and Mobility Troop. There should be sixteen men in each troop, but because it is so difficult to get into the SAS, there are often as few as eight.

Rumours started to fly. Some people said we might become sky-marshals on civilian flights to the Middle East. It would mean pretending to be normal passengers, but in fact carrying weapons to deal with any terrorist who might attempt a hijack. The idea seemed quite likely – on the SP team we'd done lots of assaults on and inside aircraft, so we knew what to do.

But then, a week before Christmas, we were dragged into the briefing room at Hereford and told that half of 'B' Squadron was going to deploy to the Middle East after all.

That meant me.

When I heard the news, I went home and said to Janet, my wife: 'Listen, we're heading out.' Normally, as so many missions are top secret, SAS guys say nothing to their wives and families about what they're doing, but in this case it was obvious where we were going. After Saddam's invasion of Kuwait, there had been so much coverage on television and in the newspapers, our destination could only have been the Gulf.

Christmas was not a relaxed time. The Regiment was stood-to throughout the holiday period, and we were busy getting our 'green' kit ready. In the SAS, 'green' refers to normal military operations, as opposed to 'black' work, like that on the SP team, for which you wear black gear from head to foot. I'd been in black roles for at least three years, so now I brought my webbing and bergen home to paint them in desert camouflage colours. We were having an extension built onto our house, and a builder called John was digging the footings. Seeing me at work outside, he came up and asked what I was doing.

'Just painting my webbing.'

'Those colours are a bit light, aren't they?'

'Well,' I said carefully, 'you'd be surprised. It works quite well.' In fact, he was right: I had the colours too light and sandy, as I was to find out to my cost.

Packing our kit took some time. All our weapons

were bundled together and went separately, rolled up in canvas sleeves. When I asked the squadron quartermaster (SQMS) if he'd included pistols, he said, 'Yeah, twenty of them.' I was glad about that, because pistols were essential back-up weapons. We would need them if our own weapons failed or if we were caught in a confined space like a vehicle, or an observation post. Most of us would be carrying either M16 203s – a combination of a 5.56 calibre automatic rifle in the top barrel and a grenade launcher below – or Minimi machine guns. Both are over a metre long and awkward to handle or conceal.

As I was sorting my personal equipment, I asked the SQMS if I could take some cold-weather mountaineering gear.

'Nah,' he replied. 'You're going to the desert! It won't be cold there.' Little did he know what the winter in Iraq would be like. I kept thinking that we might end up at high altitudes, in the mountains of northern Iraq on the Turkish border, where snow might be lying. It was as if I had some premonition. But I did nothing about it, and most of us didn't take any cold-weather gear at all.

At last we heard that we were to fly out.

   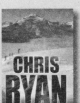 

FOR ADULT READERS

COLLECT THE
FULL CLIP OF BESTSELLING
CHRIS RYAN
NOVELS

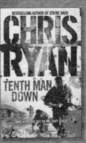

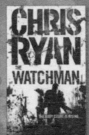

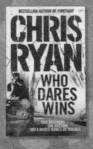